SPECIAL MESSAGE TO READERS

This book is published under the auspices of
THE ULVERSCROFT FOUNDATION
(registered charity No. 264873 UK)

Established in 1972 to provide funds for research, diagnosis and treatment of eye diseases. Examples of contributions made are: —

A new Children's Assessment Unit at Moorfield's Hospital, London.

•

Twin operating theatres at the Western Ophthalmic Hospital, London.

•

A Chair of Ophthalmology at the University of Leicester.

•

The establishment of a Royal Australian College of Ophthalmologists "Fellowship".

You can help further the work of the Foundation by making a donation or leaving a legacy. Every contribution, no matter how small, is received with gratitude. Please write for details to:

THE ULVERSCROFT FOUNDATION,
The Green, Bradgate Road, Anstey,
Leicester LE7 7FU, England.
Telephone: (0116) 236 4325

In Australia write to:
THE ULVERSCROFT FOUNDATION,
c/o The Royal Australian College of Ophthalmologists,
27, Commonwealth Street, Sydney,
N.S.W. 2010.

Love is
a time of enchantment:
in it all days are fair and all fields
green. Youth is blest by it,
old age made benign:
the eyes of love see
roses blooming in December,
and sunshine through rain. Verily
is the time of true-love
a time of enchantment — and
Oh! how eager is woman
to be bewitched!

THE LOVERS

Richard, King of England, fifteen years of age, was to marry Anne, Princess of Bohemia. She came to wed a stranger with joy in her heart — she had seen his portrait and had fallen in love. The royal uncles, John of Gaunt, Edmund of Langley and Thomas of Woodstock, watched with growing unease as the wedding day approached. They approved of the bride most heartily, but the handsome youth, with an almost girlish beauty, was perhaps not all that he seemed.

*Books by Philippa Wiat
in the Ulverscroft Large Print Series:*

WEAR A GREEN KIRTLE
THE CLOISTER AND THE FLAME
THE HAMMER AND THE SWORD

PHILIPPA WIAT

THE LOVERS

Complete and Unabridged

ROCKINGHAM COUNTY PUBLIC LIBRARY
OUTREACH   EDEN
MADISON   REIDSVILLE
MAYODAN   STONEVILLE

ULVERSCROFT
Leicester

First published in Great Britain in 1993 by
Robert Hale Limited
London

First Large Print Edition
published October 1994
by arrangement with
Robert Hale Limited
London

The right of Philippa Wiat to be identified as
the author of this work has been asserted by
her in accordance with the
Copyright, Designs and Patents Act, 1988

Copyright © 1993 by Philippa Wiat
All rights reserved

British Library CIP Data

Wiat, Philippa
 The lovers.—Large print ed.—
Ulverscroft large print series: romance
I. Title
823.914 [F]

ISBN 0-7089-3177-4

Published by
F. A. Thorpe (Publishing) Ltd.
Anstey, Leicestershire

Set by Words & Graphics Ltd.
Anstey, Leicestershire
Printed and bound in Great Britain by
T. J. Press (Padstow) Ltd., Padstow, Cornwall

This book is printed on acid-free paper

Part One

The Arrival

1

THE lovers lay side by side on the great bed, their passion spent. A rumpled silken coverlet and garments tossed aside to fall at random upon chairs or sheepskin rugs, suggested frenzied lovemaking. Long parti-coloured hose had landed atop the bedhead — masking the fine carved coat-of-arms and hanging now with erotic symbolism just above the lovers' heads.

"I have something to tell you," one said unhappily, breaking the silence and waking the other with a start. "Yet in truth I am loath to do so, lest the knowing cause you displeasure."

The other looked rueful. "You are with child perchance?" he asked in mock alarm.

"There is little fear of that — though, by my troth, it might resolve a problem or two!"

"You are serious, are you not?"

"About the revelation? Never more so."

"Tell me, I pray you — but beat not about the bush! There are better things to do than mull over your fears and fancies."

"By my faith, you are uncommonly churlish tonight!"

"Speak and be done with it."

"A marriage has been arranged for me — *they* wish me to marry."

"*They* can go to hell!"

"And probably will — but still in the mean season they wish me to marry."

"Then simply say them nay," said the other laconically. "Refuse them utterly."

"I have told them nay but they will not hearken — they have set their heads if not their hearts on an advantageous match for me."

"Saying nay is not your forte, I fear. You say nay to me sometimes — only sometimes — but do I desist? Never. I too refuse to hearken — seeing your 'nay' as a natural perverseness. In this case, you should stand firm — let the rascals know that you have no intention of complying."

"One day I must marry."

"One day, with a bit of ingenuity, is

like the morrow — it never comes!"

"Oh, they will marry me off sooner or later — I doubt it not! Could you bear it were I to agree? Once wed, I would as we both are aware have certain duties to perform — onerous duties which would be anathema to me."

"Bear it? I would bare anything, my pretty one, to please you!"

"Why, my lord, cannot you be serious — just for once? Why . . . "

"God knows I am always serious — at times of crisis. Could I bare it, you ask — well, we both look pretty bare at this moment. As regards your performing, as you say, certain duties — well, with a little practice . . . "

"Unhand me, sir!" exclaimed the other then, shrugging off the caressing hand. "And have the goodness to shelve not the question."

"Wed whom you please — and be damned to them!"

"Whom I please, you say? Certes, my lover, we both know for truth that such cannot be. Such is out of the question, alas, alas!"

"Hearken to me — and hearken well!

Wed in accordance with *their* wishes — assuming that the one elected is not too displeasing to you — and perform as many *certain duties* as are necessary. But always you will remain mine, body and soul. You know it and I know it, God help us both!"

"Hear me, my lover. You mean more to me than anyone else in the world, and always will. But at this moment, I wish only to contemplate — Nay, Robby, unhand me! Not now, I say, not now . . ."

"You lie there, naked as the day you were born — if not more so — "

"More so?"

" — assuring me of your undying devotion, your body giving credence to the assurance — "

"Give heed to me. The arrangements are already under way. Burley has gone to Prague to sue for an alliance with a certain member of the Bohemian royal family. The matter is all but settled — signed and sealed, it is all over bar the shouting!"

"You really do express yourself colourfully at times," chuckled the other. "You lie there rampant —"

"Rampant?"

"With everything rampant that could possibly be so, my innocent! You speak of marrying some unseen and doubtless obnoxious foreigner — as if it were of some consequence to us. Put the matter from your mind, is my advice. You are here with your own Robby — naught else matters . . ."

"Nay — unhand me, my lord . . ."

"Never. You are mine, my lover — and mine, by my troth, you shall remain! The foreign royals can stew in their own juice!"

"Unhand me, I say. I . . ."

"Be silent or I'll take a whip to ye! After such provocation . . ."

"Have a care, my lord. Lay so much as a finger on me in wrath and I shall have them put you in irons!"

"So much as a finger, you say? By sweet St George! Your Robby would dare a good deal more than that — see! Hey presto, a whole handful of fingers! Now, what is my pretty one going to do about that? Yea, methought as much . . ."

"Alas, my lord, why do I put up with

7

you — you tease me cruelly at times!"

"And you enjoy every moment of it."

"I love you, Robby — God forgive me! I shall always love you best in all the world — but I fear for the future and what lies ahead."

"Here in my arms, are you still fearful?"

"Nay, your embrace acts as a palliative. For a while, I forget the world and my duty and obligations — but later, when I lie alone and give thought to our union, I feel as one who has sold his soul to the Devil!"

"Hush now — let me caress you and make you forget all the bad things. We belong to each other. We love each other — till death do us part!"

"Speak not so! You tempt fate with such words. Robby, my dear lord, what would I do without you! Nay, you are paining me — unhand me, I beg you!"

"Be still — or Robby must needs remind you again as to who is master!"

2

THE princess Anne's journey to England was perilous in the extreme. Fifteen years of age and the daughter of Charles the Fourth, Holy Roman Emperor and King of Bohemia, she had been eager to meet the young king with whom she believed herself already in love.

She had set out happily enough from her homeland, attended by the Duke of Saxony and his duchess, her aunt, and an impressive retinue of knights and damsels. Travelling overland by way of Brabant to Brussels, Anne was received there most graciously by Duke Wenceslaus, her kinsman. But her joy at the duke's welcome was lessened when she learned next morning that she must remain at Brussels for some weeks.

"But I am expected in England very shortly," she said in dismay to her aunt. "Such a delay is out of the question, my lady."

"We are informed that it would be unwise for you to proceed further at present," her aunt said firmly. "The English will already be aware of the difficulty, I doubt not."

Anne looked aggrieved. Was aggrieved. "My lady, I have waited many months to make this journey to England — to wed my affianced lord," she said.

"Better a late bride, child — " her aunt said cheerfully, ignoring Anne's accusing gaze, " — than *the* late bride!"

"Are you suggesting I might be in danger, my lady — " Anne asked uneasily " — that were I to embark forthwith for England, I might forfeit my life?"

She was close to tears. For two years she had nurtured a dream — of a handsome prince and a fairytale wedding. The journey across the sea might well be hazardous — she was aware of that. Was not the sea which separated England from the Continent renowned for its sudden squalls? Shipwreck was after all commonplace. But how else than by sea could she reach her bridegroom?

"Out there on the wild seas, niece — " said her aunt, waving her hand vaguely towards what she took to be the English Channel " — there are twelve large vessels filled with fierce Normans. They hug the coast, we are told, standing guard as it were betwixt Calais and Holland!"

"But what are these fierce Normans to me, my lady?" asked Anne on a puzzled note. "They are naught but fishermen, I dare say — and, as such, no reason for my postponing my journey."

"We are informed that the Normans are awaiting the coming of the King of England's bride-to-be — since the King of France much mislikes Richard of England's marriage alliance," the duchess explained. "These seamen are untrustworthy rogues, niece. They seize and pillage all who fall into their hands, without regard to rank or person!"

Anne paled. "But why should this be, my lady? What matters my marriage alliance to the King of France?"

"Ah, dear child!" sighed the duchess. "You in your innocence know naught as yet of the ways of princes! We ladies, I fear, are but pawns in their hands — and must needs accept the inevitable!"

"I have waited many moons for this

meeting with my husband-to-be," sighed Anne, close to tears. "First it was a rising of English peasants which kept me from England — and now, it seems, Norman pirates are to keep me from my affianced lord."

"Alas the impatience of youth!" said the duchess ruefully. "The duke my husband will do all in his power to expedite your departure. Just a few weeks — a month at the most — and then I doubt not you will be on your way."

"A month, you say?" Anne asked aghast. It was worse than she had imagined. "A whole month?"

The duchess smiled wryly. "Is it so terrible to contemplate biding here with your kinsfolk for a few weeks, child? A month soon passes — but a marriage, remember, is for ever."

"Pray forgive me, my lady," Anne said contritely. "You are so good to me and I am an ungrateful wretch. But I have long awaited this meeting with Richard of England — he has written many letters to me, assuring me of his devotion. I just know we shall be happy!"

I wonder! thought the duchess. We

have heard tales of Richard of England and his unnatural tastes and fancies — if a quarter of them be true, then my impatient niece's confidence could well be unfounded, alas! Yet one cannot help but be touched by her innocence and her youthful enthusiasm for a match with one she has never seen. There was a new warmth in her voice when she spoke.

"Please God it will be so, child," she said fervently. "The King of England, I doubt not, will be enchanted with you. A word of advice though — a maiden should not appear too eager for the nuptials. Some small reluctance in a bride can work wonders, niece."

"But since I am not a reluctant bride, would not such pretence be dishonest?" Anne asked innocently. "Besides, His Grace has ofttimes told me in his letters of his impatience for the bridal."

"Dear child!" smiled the duchess. "How young and innocent you are! As to your departure, we must all of us practise patience. Rest and compose yourself meanwhile — all will be well, please God."

★ ★ ★

In the event, it was almost five weeks before Anne was able to continue her journey.

Wenceslaus, Duke of Brabant, had meanwhile sent envoys to Charles, King of France — Anne's cousin — remonstrating with him and telling him that the two young people were so set on the match that it might be an act of folly to continue to thwart their intentions. Charles responded by commanding the Norman ships to return to port, declaring that he did so, not out of deference to the King of England, but solely out of regard for his kinswoman, the princess Anne.

The reasons for Charles's change of heart were of little consequence to Anne. She prayed fervently that no more obstacles would impede her journey to England.

Escorted by one hundred spears, she finally left Brussels and proceeded to Bruges and a further delay of three days. Thence to Gravelines where William de Montacute, Earl of Salisbury, was awaiting her arrival with an escort of five hundred spears and a like number of archers.

After a tearful leave-taking of her aunt, Anne proceeded to Calais — her husband-to-be's domain. Here there was no delay, Salisbury being as anxious as his royal charge to see the journey completed without further incident.

"The king my master has commanded me to bring you to him with all speed, my lady," he told her with a smile. "We understand that you have suffered some delay during the journey from your homeland — methinks you must be weary of travel."

A man of some fifty summers, Salisbury had served as constable in Edward the Third's army and had won distinction at the Battle of Poitiers. Highly regarded, he had in the previous year led the king's troops with some success against rebellious peasants in the West Country. A gentleman who smiled easily, he had been selected by the king for this special duty.

Anne took to him at once.

"I cannot deny it is so, my lord," she replied with a winning smile. "I yearn to reach journey's end."

"We shall dally here at Calais only until the wind is favourable, my lady," Salisbury told her. "The Channel can be turbulent at times and one must needs treat it with respect!"

In the event, they embarked the following morning, the night's storm having abated somewhat and the wind being then in their favour. Anne was smiling joyfully as, soon after daybreak, she and her entourage set sail in three ships for England.

But the sea, like brides and lovers, can be mighty temperamental. One third of the crossing had been accomplished when the weather changed. A strong wind blew up and a few minutes later the ships were struggling in the teeth of a gale.

The vessels were flung to and fro like flotsam; at the mercy of giant waves which at one moment were tossing them high into the air and the next plunging them down into the deep.

Anne thought her last moment had come. Unaccustomed to sailing, she resolved there and then that if she were spared she would never again cross the seas — not even to visit her beloved homeland.

The heaving of the ship and the howling of the gale made speech impossible. Anne was grateful for Salisbury's strong supporting arm, without which she would probably have been swept overboard. The ship plunged again and again, as if into the jaws of hell . . .

She had waited many weeks to go to England and meet the young king for whom already she had a high regard. The journey from Prague had seemed endless, beset by obstacles she could not have envisaged — and now here she was, almost within sight of her goal, balanced betwixt life and death on a plunging ship which seemed no match for the relentless sea.

Is it truly God's will that I marry Richard? she wondered wretchedly. To herself, she always gave her affianced lord his Christian name. Could it be that God is opposed to the match? came the next question. Does He in His wisdom know that no good will come of it — that I am not a suitable bride for Richard of England? God then is unkind, she thought — very unkind! He allowed me to fall in love with Richard, to leave my beloved family and journey overland these many weeks. Only now, when I am midway across the Channel, does He show His disapproval by sending a violent storm to destroy me.

"All is well, my lady — be not a-feared!" shouted Salisbury, one strong arm supporting her and the other gripping the ship's rail as he endeavoured to make himself heard above the storm. "'Tis naught but a squall — we are almost there!"

Even as he uttered the reassuring words, as if in mockery, a towering wave broke amidships. The vessel rolled violently — and as the wave retreated, it took with it a seaman and one of Anne's ladies.

"Elizabeth!" Anne screamed in horror. "Elizabeth! God have pity!"

"One of the other vessels will pick her up, I dare say," Salisbury said to console her, his mind wholly on protecting his charge. "Hold tightly to yonder rope and we shall try to keep you steady. Be not alarmed, my lady — all will be well!"

"Not for Elizabeth," Anne said tearfully. "Not for poor dear Elizabeth!"

Salisbury made to answer her but another wave nearly swept them both off their feet; and the need to reply was thankfully lost in the commotion. And what in truth could he have said? Elizabeth, part of Anne's retinue, could not have survived more than a few moments in that tempestuous sea. Salisbury knew it and in her heart Anne knew it also.

The remainder of the journey was like a nightmare, with the wails and prayers of Anne's terrified ladies accompanying each fresh onslaught of the elements. The seamen did their utmost to maintain the ships and protect their passengers, and Anne was grateful for the strong arms which kept her from being swept overboard. She none the less came close to fainting at one point — and would have done so, had not a great fountain of seawater slapped her hard in the face, like an admonitory hand. She spluttered, fought for breath and somehow survived . . .

At last the storm subsided a little and the ship, battered but in one piece, made

Dover. Rowing boats were launched and men, joined together by ropes, waded out to carry the female passengers to the shore.

As Anne and her surviving ladies set foot on English soil, still the ground beneath their feet seemed to sway alarmingly and they staggered and fell about as if intoxicated.

Salisbury, still at Anne's side, looked concernedly at her. "Are you all right, my lady? I confess the storm was unlike any other winter storm I have seen — it was quite remarkable."

"A commotion it was, my lord," called out one of the sailors on the shore. "So violent and troubled was the sea, I've never afore seen the like. And there's more to come by the looks of it!"

Salisbury nodded. "Yea, it has not done with us yet, I fear. The ships . . ."

He got no further. His words ceased abruptly and he gazed out to sea in sheer disbelief.

"Christ save us!" exclaimed one of the seamen, staring out to sea and crossing himself. "It's got the old ship!"

And so it had.

In the words of the chronicler, Froissart, who had himself been waiting on the shore to greet the arrival of the future queen, "Scarcely had the Bohemian princess set her foot on the shore, when a sudden convulsion of the sea took place, unaccompanied with wind and unlike any winter storm; but the water was so violently shaken and troubled, and put in such furious commotion, that the ship in which the young queen's person was conveyed was very terribly rent in pieces before her very face, and the rest of the vessels that rode in company were tossed so, that it astonished all beholders."

All eyes had turned to the ships, drawn by the sounds of splintering wood and groaning rigging — dreadful sounds that, once heard, are never forgotten. As those on the shore watched in fascinated horror, there was vague talk of rescue. In truth, nothing could be done for those still aboard the first ship — it had all happened so quickly. Even as those on shore watched, they saw two of the crew throw themselves over the side of the fast-disappearing vessel, to be instantly crushed by falling rigging.

As the leading ship sank, so near to shore and yet so inaccessible, it took with it most of its crew and a number of Anne's servants who had been supervising the removal of the baggage. Caught off guard, none had stood a chance.

Anne, watching helplessly and assailed by a nightmare which seemed to have accompanied her all the way from her homeland, fell into a swoon...

★ ★ ★

Anne soon recovered and was at once conveyed in a horse-drawn litter to Dover Castle where preparations had been made for the accommodation of herself and her retinue.

"The ships, my lord Salisbury?" she enquired as memory returned. "What of the ships — and all the poor sailors?"

"There has so far been but one survivor from the leading ship, my lady," he told her. "The other ships are damaged but intact and as yet, God be thanked, no fatalities have been reported."

"Methinks I should not have come here, my lord," Anne said, trying to restrain her tears. "England welcomes me not — it shows me a cold face!"

"Such is not the case, my lady," insisted Salisbury, anxious to reassure her but, in the wake of such a calamity, secretly sharing her doubts. It had been a bad start, to say the least. He sought for words of encouragement. "Has not England claimed you from the sea — taken you in defiance of the elements?"

Anne smiled — a small smile, it was, but a beginning. "Yea, my lord, it may be so. Methinks I have no liking for the sea — it has shown me a harsh mien. Those Norman pirates must surely have cast a spell upon the waters, to prevent my marrying the King of England!"

"Bravo, lady princess!" smiled Salisbury, riding alongside the litter. "That is exactly it. One day, when you are wed, you might speak to King Richard of your hazardous journey — telling him how you defied the storms, the ocean and the Normans to reach his domain."

Anne gave thought to that. A short while ago she had felt rejected — a stranger in an inhospitable land. Salisbury apparently saw it differently. She liked Salisbury and already trusted his judgement.

"England has claimed me — is that your meaning, my lord?" she asked uncertainly.

"It has indeed, lady princess," he told her with a smile. "I know England — and, believe me, already it has taken you to its heart!"

Anne liked that. It gave her a warm feeling — a sense of coming home after a long absence. Yea, the earl was right. All would yet be well. Very soon now she would come face to face with him she had fallen in love with several moons ago.

She recalled the portrait of her husband-to-be and how it was that which had won her consent to the marriage — it was that with which she had fallen in love. She could see it still in her mind's eye.

Primislaus, Duke of Saxony, her kinsman, had returned from England with the portrait. Desirous of persuading her to give her consent to the proposed marriage, he had presented it to her with many a flourish.

Opposed to the match until then, Anne

had despite her misgivings, gazed at the portrait in wonderment, her eyes shining — saying nothing.

The portrait had been painted chiefly in varying shades of gold, with splashes of red, brown, black and terracotta. The golden-haired king was seated upon a throne, his gold crown on his head and the orb and sceptre one in each hand. The portrait, as Anne had seen it then, was that of a golden-haired angel.

Had she been required to give a title to the portrait, she would have called it ISOLATION, she had told herself. Robed in splendour, surrounded by all the trappings of sovereignty, the youth had none the less appeared remote from the world about him.

Against all her expectations, Anne had there and then fallen in love with the figure in the portrait. Thenceforth she had looked eagerly to the day when the sitter would come alive and she would wed the golden-haired king.

Now, mulling this over and reassured by Salisbury's words, her spirits rose. She was here in England. Very soon she would be with the king and all would be well. The recent past, with its trials and sorrows, was behind her. A rosy future lay ahead . . .

"England has claimed me, you say, my lord," she said then to Salisbury — and he heard tears as well as joy in her voice. "Methinks I shall never leave England. I shall remain here all my days."

3

THOMAS OF WOODSTOCK, Duke of Gloucester, was the seventh and youngest son of Edward the Third, King Richard's grandfather. An eminent warrior and strategist, he had three years earlier prevented a French landing at Dover; and in the year prior to Anne of Bohemia's arrival in England, at the time of the peasants' revolt, he had dispersed a sizable rebel army in Essex — the latter having endeared him, if temporarily, to the king his nephew.

A nobleman of integrity and much charm, he possessed great strength and was of commanding stature. Dark-haired like his paternal grandmother, Isabella of France, he none the less had the features and brilliant blue eyes of his Plantagenet forebears.

It said much for the young king's opinion of him that Thomas of Woodstock had been entrusted with escorting

Richard's bride-to-be from Canterbury to Westminster — the last lap of her journey from Prague. In his twenty-seventh year at this time, the duke was his nephew's senior by a mere twelve years.

Anne had remained at Dover for two days, thus giving herself and her retinue time to recover from their hazardous journey. There was much distress at the loss of Elizabeth who had been one of Anne's closest companions — the more so since she had simply disappeared without trace.

On the third day, Anne set out for Canterbury, where she spent the night and made ready for the last stage of her journey.

Thomas of Woodstock received Anne with great courtesy — putting her at her ease, enquiring solicitously about her protracted journey, and assuring her of the English people's joy at her arrival. A gallant, chivalric figure, he rode beside her, heading a long and colourful cavalcade.

"Very soon now, lady princess, we shall be in sight of Blackheath — " he told Anne as they drew nearer the

City. " — thence, if the day be clear, you will have your first glimpse of the City of London."

They conversed in French. Despite Edward the Third's attempts to make the English language more widely spoken, French was still the first language of the Norman-descended nobility — and though Anne's first language was German, French was a close second.

"This black heath, my lord — " she asked curiously " — why is it black?"

"I know not — " replied Thomas, meeting her gaze and liking what he saw " — unless it be that last year, during the commotion time, it being the gathering place of Wat the Tyler and his rebels, it was black with men!"

"I liked not the rebels," Anne confided with a sidelong glance at her future uncle-in-law. "I liked them not at all."

Thomas watched her, seeming to give thought to her words. In truth, it gave him an opportunity of studying her face. He found her enchanting and knew stirrings of quite un-unclelike interest. Already the chronicler Froissart, journeying in their train, had dubbed her "the beauteous queen!" The complimentary description had been well said, thought Thomas, and well received by those around him.

Her eyes, large, wide-set and vividly blue, were her chief beauty, together with a fair and faultless complexion. Her mouth was perhaps a little too wide for conventional beauty, but her figure, tall and shapely and enhanced by her grace of movement, was in Thomas's opinion superb.

"Then that is a bond between us, my lady," he smiled. "I also did not like them — is not that a coincidence? Why, it makes you one of the family already!"

"But, you see, my lord, I had my own special reason for not liking them," Anne ventured, not looking at him.

"Indeed? Might one enquire as to the reason, my lady? Or is it a maidenly secret?"

She blushed at that — and yea, it is a secret, Thomas thought. I hope for all our sakes that it is something to do with my kingly nephew!

"But for your peasants' revolt, sir, I might have been permitted to come sooner to England," she explained quietly. "Then would I have had an opportunity of learning the ways and manners of my affianced lord's subjects ere we wed."

If this fair damsel cannot wean my nephew from his foppish friends and unnatural practices, then God help him, none can! thought Thomas.

"The omission in respect of His Grace's subjects is shortly to be remedied, my lady," he said at length, disturbed by his own thoughts. "Blackheath will soon be within hailing distance — a very different Blackheath, I trow, from that of a few months ago!"

"That could well be so, my lord," Anne said with a notable lack of enthusiasm.

Thomas glanced at her and smiled. "Meanwhile, lady princess, since dusk is almost upon us, we shall, with Your Grace's permission, pitch our tents here for the night, take our repast — and make a fresh start upon the morrow."

Anne smiled. "You must surely be a mind-reader, my lord," she said happily.

And so the tents — those colourful circular pavilions much used on such journeys — were set up and the whole company passed a restful night. The morrow was, after all, another day . . .

★ ★ ★

As Blackheath hove into sight it was at once apparent that it was still a gathering-place — but for others than rebels. The whole heath was alive with colour and noise — with the lively chatter of Londoners who had come there to get a first glimpse of their future queen.

Cheer upon cheer filled the air as Anne and her escort were sighted. The royal cavalcade was quickly surrounded by a happy laughing throng which good-naturedly jostled for the most advantageous view.

At a signal from Thomas, knights and men-at-arms closed in protectively around the princess, and he called a halt during which those in the forefront of the gathering, and particularly the children, were permitted to present small gifts to her — posies of wild flowers, ribbons and tiny cakes made of marchpane. Anne, surprised by the spontaneous welcome, was delighted with it all and accepted the gifts most graciously.

"The citizens of London have of their own will come here to greet you, my lady," Thomas told her, himself entering into the spirit of the occasion. "They are here to welcome you and to escort you the rest of the way to the king."

"To the king?" asked Anne vaguely as they rode on. It was as if in the excitement she had for a moment overlooked her reason for being there. "Indeed, my lord — to the king."

"His Grace awaits you at the Guildhall, my lady," Thomas said quietly.

He was puzzled by her sudden seriousness. Gone was the happy princess who had smiled so delightfully and acknowledged with such grace the gifts of her future husband's subjects. Had not her apparent enthusiasm for the match been genuine? he asked himself. Had she been coerced for political reasons into consenting to the alliance? He had heard mixed reports of her reception of the proposed marriage contract. Is she aware of the true nature of him she is to wed? he asked himself then — and the question and its implications troubled him.

"Is the Guildhall a royal palace?" Anne was enquiring.

Thomas, disturbed by his thoughts and feeling as if the sunshine had of a sudden gone from the morning, collected himself.

"Nay, my lady," he told her. "The Guildhall is used for assemblies of the citizens, it being the seat of municipal government. The citizens of London regard it as very much their own — and a suitable place therefore for the king to make the acquaintance of his bride-to-be."

"Truth to tell, my lord, already I feel that I know my lord the king," Anne told him — but Thomas thought he heard doubt in her voice all the same. "We have exchanged many letters and are both eager for the match."

Thomas glanced at her again. He found her ingenuous, even naïve — and her gentle manner suggested an innocence that was wholly enchanting, if not provocative.

God grant the lass is not in for a disappointment! he thought. Richard is a lucky fellow — a very lucky fellow.

One hopes that he will recognise his good fortune and mend his ways. *I feel that I know my lord the king*, my lady says innocently. Alas, alas — and again alas! I doubt she has been informed of my pretty nephew's peccadilloes — though I'd wager that, young though he be, his unnatural preferences are already common knowledge throughout the courts of Europe. The King of France, it is said, has laid bets amounting to a small fortune that Richard of England will one day meet a similar fate to that of his great-grandsire . . .

"May God grant you every happiness!" he said with sincerity, a reply seemingly called for. "May your marriage be congenial — and fruitful."

Anne blushed and turned away, patting her horse's neck to hide her confusion. Her own horse-drawn litter was following the cavalcade, having accompanied her all the way from Prague and was available for her use at any time. But despite the rigours of riding side-saddle for many, many miles, she rarely used it. Piled high with cushions and of sumptuous appearance, the litter, being unsprung, was a bone-shaker indeed.

She liked the king's uncle and asked herself whether there was a close resemblance between him and his nephew. She had heard that he was a champion of the joust and a warrior of repute — one who, it was whispered, would make a fine king . . .

Richard is young, very young, Thomas himself was thinking. Perchance with this enchanting lass beside him, he will turn a new leaf and conform thereafter to normal standards of behaviour . . .

They had reached the further side of the heath by this time and Mayor Walworth and other dignitaries, all splendidly arrayed in civic robes, stood ready to greet their future queen.

Thomas assisted Anne to dismount and then she and her ladies were escorted to a gaily coloured pavilion, erected specially for their use. Here, Anne and her ladies donned fresh clothes and took refreshment.

When Anne reappeared, cheer after cheer rent the air — and her radiant smile was mirrored by hundreds of others.

She was dressed now in a blue

cotehardie with a white border, worn over an apple-green undergown that fitted to the hips and was encircled by a jewelled hip-girdle; her sleeves, long and tight-fitting, having both buttons and tippets. Her long, flowing mantle was of dark-green silk and worn open to display a lining of white ermine.

Every eye was upon her as, after smilingly acknowledging the cheers of the onlookers, she was escorted to her grey palfrey.

"They have taken you to their hearts, my lady," Thomas said in a low voice as he assisted her to mount. "The citizens of London approve of you — all is well. What London approves today, it is said, the rest of England will approve on the morrow!"

"You are kind, sir," Anne said quietly, as he mounted up and gave the order for the cavalcade to move off.

Thomas of Woodstock is gallant and very handsome, Anne thought to herself — though not as handsome as the king himself I feel sure! His manner is a trifle cold at times, and I sense him watching me and wonder what he is thinking. Could it be that he questions my worthiness to become the king his nephew's bride?

I wonder what my lady is thinking, Thomas was saying to himself. The citizens have indeed taken her to their hearts. They approve of her, as I said — and the rest of the country will surely follow. But what of my foppish nephew? He acquitted himself well enough at Smithfield, facing single-handed that great body of rebels — but now, complacent and pleasure-loving to a degree, he is fast losing interest in statecraft, preferring to pass his time with his friends, God help us all!

As — with Thomas and Anne and their retinues, plumed gentlemen and bejewelled ladies, leading the way — the colourful procession slowly moved off, the mayor and City dignitaries, some on horseback, others on foot, fell in behind. A joyful, happy occasion with much laughter, it suggested nothing as much as a great carnival. This is our new queen, the citizens seemed to be saying to the world at large. This is our queen, who has journeyed many miles, crossed many lands and storm-tossed seas, to come to England and marry our king — and give him an heir to reign after him. She is gracious and comely and smiles like an angel — and she is ours, our very own.

As the grand procession entered the City, crowds pressed in from every side. A group of minstrels, seven in number, played with enthusiasm, the sounds filling the air and rivalling those of the onlookers. The minstrels, wearing hats decorated with foil, had been hired by the Goldsmiths' Company at a cost of sixty shillings — with a further two shillings for refreshments. The civic dignitaries were very finely clad in honour of the occasion and, as with the minstrels, refreshments were supplied to them by the Goldsmiths' Company.

When Thomas pointed out the Guildhall to Anne, she made no reply and he wondered at first if she had understood.

"The Guildhall, my lady," he said again, raising his voice against the cacophony of sound around them. "It is but a short distance ahead. Already the king will be there, I doubt not, waiting to greet his bride."

He saw her pale and wondered at it. Had her expressions of joy and longing been merely feigned — or a brave attempt to hide her fears? I would, he thought, that she were here to marry another — almost anyone but Richard. How, as things stand, could such a union bring happiness? Happiness? he asked himself cynically. Royal brides should not look for happiness, it is said — wealth, power, position, all of these, but not happiness! They should look solely to duty and obedience — to God and their royal lord.

He thought then of his own marriage — to Eleanor, daughter of Humphrey de Bohun, Earl of Hereford, Essex and Northampton. Formerly Earl of Cambridge, he had been granted as part of the marriage settlement the earldom of Essex in right of his wife. But had the alliance brought him and his lady true happiness? Not as far as he could see . . .

4

"SO this is journey's end," Anne said as if to herself — and there was that in her voice which prompted Thomas of Woodstock to look questioningly at her. "Now, at last, I am to meet Richard of England."

As the cavalcade drew to a halt, the cheers of the populace increased rather than lessened and Thomas hastened to assist his charge to dismount.

Two of Anne's ladies came forward to discreetly smooth and arrange her apparel, and coax a few wayward curls into place under her white veil. Having surveyed her critically, they nodded their satisfaction and resumed their places in the procession.

"I am ready, my lord," Anne said quietly to Thomas, glancing towards the Guildhall. "Is the king truly there?"

"He is indeed," came the sturdy reply. "See there, my lady — His Grace is waiting and watching from the top of the steps. Ah, now he is descending the steps, ready to greet you!"

Anne went forward, her retinue following and Thomas at her side — moving towards the single figure which was standing motionless now at the foot of the great steps.

As they drew nearer, the retinue came to a halt, leaving Anne and her escort to proceed alone. Thus had it been arranged. Those moments when the young couple would meet for the first time, touch hands and exchange courtesies, would be memorable, private moments for them both. Thomas of Woodstock, curious but finding this the most onerous duty of all, must needs remain.

As Anne crossed the now-empty cobbled forecourt, she was conscious that a sudden hush had fallen upon the great concourse of people behind her. It was as if this meeting, long looked-for by herself, was of no less importance to the king's subjects. The almost total silence and the empty forecourt were a little unnerving to one who had spent the past ten weeks in the close company of many.

She faltered and would have fallen but

for Thomas's steadying hand. She looked up at him — and he saw the glint of tears in her eyes.

"I can go no further," she said softly, and he only just caught the words. "I am here in a foreign land, amongst strangers whose very language is alien to me — and I yearn for my homeland."

She looked confused and defenceless — a child still. Thomas's heart went out to her in those moments — and was to remain hers for a long time to come ... He made to reassure her but it was hard to speak the words — words which might at this late stage propel her into an unhappy alliance.

Even as he hesitated, torn between his concern for her and his duty, the matter was taken out of his hands.

The king, seeing Anne stumble and attributing her apparent hesitancy to that, was already hastening towards her — in one of those spontaneous gestures which, as at Smithfield during the peasants' revolt, delighted his subjects.

Magnificently apparelled — the fifteen-year-old king's love of rich and opulent dress was already a byword — he advanced with outstretched hands.

"Welcome to England, lady princess," he said with a boyish smile, taking her hands to raise her from her curtsy. "My subjects, as you have doubtless seen, are in transports of joy at the arrival of their future queen — and I, my lady, fully share their joy."

"Your Grace is kind," Anne replied with a smile — though still beset by a sense of unreality. It was as if, she thought, the meeting, so joyfully awaited, were part of a dream. Shall I wake presently, and find myself still in my own chamber at Prague! "The journey from my homeland was overlong, alas! Methought it would never end."

"And from all accounts, my lady, it very nearly ended too soon — in disaster," Richard said quietly. "The ocean, I am told, had a sudden convulsion upon your arrival, the ships being tossed so as astonished the beholders. God be thanked for your safe arrival!"

The populace, kept at a distance by men with halberds, was still hushed, eager to overhear what was being said. Those in the forefront caught the king's last words and repeated them to those in the rear, this prompting a unisonal cry of "God be thanked for her safe arrival!"

The young king laughed at that and cheerfully acknowledged the acclamations which followed — and then, turning graciously to Anne, indicated that they should return to the steps of the Guildhall, that she might better be seen by his subjects.

"A pageant is to take place at the upper end of Cheapside — this having been arranged by the citizens themselves to greet your arrival," he told Anne, raising his voice in order to be heard above the cheering. "We shall be served there with refreshments. Should you be willing, my lady, we shall ride in procession to Cheapside, it being but a short distance."

Anne assented, feeling that she had little choice — but telling herself that she had lately had more than enough of horseback riding.

As the company proceeded to Cheapside, through narrow streets thronged with cheering people, Anne saw a tall building ahead which closely resembled a castle.

Following the direction of her gaze, Richard smiled.

"The castle is not all it seems, my lady," he told her.

"It is very beautiful — " she said " — though I confess I have not before seen so small a castle."

"'Tis erected only on special occasions," came Richard's reply — and then, seeing her surprise, he added, "In truth, it is but a replica of a castle — having a tower at either end but little else."

"Each tower is surrounded by people, laughing cheerful people," remarked Anne. "What could it be, my lord, that claims their attention?"

Richard looked at Thomas, who was riding on Anne's other side, and both men smiled.

"Shall we let my lady princess into the secret, my lord of Woodstock?" Richard enquired cheerfully. "Or shall we guard our state secret, lest my lady reveals it to her kinsman, Charles of France?"

"Tell her, my lord, is my advice," Thomas replied, resting his gaze briefly on Anne. "As your *future* queen, it is methinks her right!"

Richard, registering the other's gaze on Anne and his inflexion on the word 'future', was taken aback. So, he thought, mine uncle is enamoured of the lady! Well, that is no bad thing, since she is shortly to be mine. A little competition in the family is to be welcomed — a new ingredient can, as is well known, lend piquancy to the sauce! But my lord's *double-entendre* is vexing in the extreme — Thomas of Woodstock, in common with his brothers, will have to be watched! *Future* queen, indeed!

But none of this showed in his manner towards Anne.

"The towers on yonder castle are perfectly proportioned — thus the castle appears in the distance larger than it is," he told her pleasantly. "On two sides of each tower, there is a fountain — a fountain that runs with wine."

"That is truly an innovation," smiled Anne. "No wonder the people crowd around it with such enthusiasm."

"It was first installed by King Edward, my grandfather of happy memory," Richard explained. "There is, as you will shortly see, a stone balcony at the front of the castle — it was from there that my grandfather and his company viewed the tournaments in Cheapside."

"That is most interesting, my lord," Anne said with a smile. "Is it from that same balcony that we shall watch the pageant?"

"It is indeed, my lady — but first, if you be willing, we ourselves will partake of wine at one of the fountains," Richard said and without waiting for her reply, dismounting, he himself helped her dismount. A large concentration of citizens had already gathered near the castle, both to watch the pageant and quench their thirst at the fountains. "If naught else, it will please the people that we refresh ourselves at the same fount as themselves. What says my lady?"

"Is it truly wine, my lord?" Anne asked doubtfully. "In my homeland, we do not drink wine before . . . "

"Before someone else has tasted it?" asked Richard, his eyes twinkling. "You are right, my lady. And since my lordly uncle is yet with us . . . "

He turned to Thomas who had remained silent during this exchange.

" . . . we will grant him the honour of being chief wine-taster!"

Richard suspects that I am enamoured of the lady Anne, Thomas thought to himself. I shall have to watch my step — for her sake as much as for my own.

"And should it taste like bilge-water, sire, think you I would admit as much?" he asked carelessly.

"Yea, you would admit it — " came the reply " — since my lady princess will, in honour of the occasion, partake before her affianced lord!"

Thomas was taken aback and tried unsuccessfully to hide the fact. I have indeed given myself away, he thought. My nephew, I doubt not, is a dog in a manger — but such a one, when he be the king, can give a fatal bite.

Richard was gleeful — but did not show it. So, *mon oncle*, he said to himself, you are indeed enamoured of my bride-to-be! Well, well — and you with a lady fair already!

Thomas smiled ruefully and, when an attendant filled a silver cup from the fountain and presented it to him with a bow, he tasted it consideringly.

"Well, sire, it *is* wine — and a good wine at that," came the verdict. Thomas took another sip. "Yea, it has my wholehearted approval — it is indeed fit for a princess!"

Richard next led Anne into the mock castle which was already packed with people. They seated themselves on the stone balcony which offered an excellent view of the surrounding area — whilst at the same time giving those *in* the surrounding area an excellent view of their queen-to-be, as was the king's unspoken intention.

Richard and his bride-to-be sat side by side, in the midst of a group of noblemen and courtiers, all of whom — with the exception of Thomas of Woodstock who had somehow merged into the background — were strangers to her. Shy and a trifle overwhelmed, Anne told herself she would never remember all the new faces — or the names of those who had been presented to her by Richard. Only one caught her attention and held it — a young man, darkhaired and unusually handsome, whom the king addressed frequently and referred to as de Vere . . .

An entertainment followed, with music and dancing, and tumblers a-plenty out there in Cheapside — and then a mock joust which caused much merriment. There followed an interval when refreshments were served, and two shapely damsels, each wearing a rose of a different hue, climbed up some outside steps to the stone balcony. Each holding a gilded plate containing gold leaf, the damsels gently blew the gold leaf into the faces of the king and his bride-to-be.

As tiny pieces of gold leaf glinted on the skin, hair and clothing of Richard and Anne, achieving a surprisingly elegant effect, there were roars of laughing approval from the onlookers.

Anne gave silent thanks that none of the particles had gone into her eyes or made her sneeze, while Richard stood up and shook himself like a dog which, as pieces of gold leaf floated down from the balcony, caused further merriment among the onlookers.

Thomas of Woodstock, who had seen it all before, groaned inwardly. Why does my kingly nephew delight in making a spectacle of himself? he wondered. He becomes more foppish with each passing day and I doubt not that it has much to do with the Earl of Oxford. I can see de Vere now, out of the corner of my eye. He is gazing neither at the entertainments nor the lady Anne, but at Richard — as if he fears a rival!

The pageant was for the most part over, although the crowds in Cheapside had now increased rather than diminished. As the royal cavalcade passed by on its journey to Westminster Palace, the populace, good-natured but over-enthusiastic, swelled forward as if to overwhelm the procession. This prompted cries of "Stand back! Stand back!" from the men with staves and bills who patrolled the streets on state occasions.

Richard had enjoyed it all — the pageantry, the adulation, the noise and excitement, were all grist to his mill. Above all, he loved the finery and the full panoply of kingship which such occasions merited. The wafting of the gold leaf had not been new to him — as was the next and quite unexpected happening . . .

The damsels who had earlier delivered the gold leaf, dressed now as Greek goddesses, stepped of a sudden into the path of Richard's and Anne's horses — and threw counterfeit gold coins in front of the horses' hoofs.

Only Richard's quick-thinking in seizing the reins of Anne's horse as well as his own, prevented her horse from rearing and throwing her off — and the damsels themselves from serious injury.

Thomas meanwhile, riding behind Richard and Anne, had leapt from his horse to detain and furiously admonish the two young women, before handing them over to the patrol.

Part Two

The Bride

5

THE year of 1382 was only fourteen days old when Richard Plantagenet, King of England, and Anne of Bohemia were married at St Stephen's, the newly-built royal chapel of the palace of Westminster.

The royal couple were fifteen years of age, she being the elder by eight months. Richard had been declared no longer a minor but it would be a further seven years before he was declared king *de facto*.

Magnificent banquets followed the Nuptial Mass; and tournaments were held at Cheapside to mark the occasion. The celebrations continued for almost a week, the bedding ceremony being deferred in accordance with custom until the royal couple had reached Windsor.

At Windsor, together with Joan, Princess of Wales, Richard's mother and her married daughter, the Duchess of Bretagne, the newly-weds were to remain until the twenty-first of January when the royal family and the court would return to London for Anne's coronation.

★ ★ ★

During the journey to Windsor, Richard and Anne rode at the head of a procession of courtiers, servants and administrators who of necessity accompanied all such undertakings.

The lady Joan and her married daughter travelled in a litter because Joan, though in good spirits, had suffered ill-health following her molestation at Blackheath during the peasants' revolt, together with the ransacking and partial destruction of her palace at Kennington.[1]

The newly-weds spoke little on the journey, each glad of a respite from the public celebrations and feasting of the preceding days. They were leaving London for the peace and tranquillity of rural Berkshire and the

---

[1] See *The Hammer and the Sword* by Philippa Wiat

comparative seclusion Windsor offered for the completion of their marriage.

Anne's infatuation with Richard, awakened by the portrait and fed by youthful romanticism, had in no way lessened with their meeting.

Tall and elegant, possessed of the golden-haired good looks which had blessed many a youthful Plantagenet, Richard's behaviour towards her was courteous, gallant and at all times pleasing.

They had so far met, needless to say, only in the company of more senior members of the royal family or those officially appointed for the king's protection and tutelage. Shy and apprehensive like many a bride before her, Anne had none the less longed for the celebrations to end, that she might be alone with her new husband — and, in due course, truly his wife.

Joan had shown Anne much kindness, sympathising with her in her total and probably lasting separation from home and family. A woman greatly loved and respected, both by her family and her son's subjects, Joan had welcomed Anne as a daughter and assured her of her support.

"The bedding ceremony will be quiet — " she told Anne, " — not the public show which beset many of our past monarchs. Only the priest and an official representative of each party is required to be present — in this case, the Bohemian ambassador and Thomas, Duke of Gloucester."

Anne's heart missed a beat. Why, she thought, does that last piece of information make me uneasy? Thomas of Woodstock has shown me much kindness and is a master of circumspection. 'Twas he escorted me on my first journey in England and presented me to the king. Why then does my lady's well-meant information trouble me?

Joan registered her uneasiness, her sudden pallor, and thought she understood. The lass is nervous, she said to herself — and no wonder.

"After the blessing, the priest and both representatives will make their departure," she said reassuringly. "And so, my lady, there is naught to fear — no toasts, no public spectacle!"

Conscious of a sense of relief at this piece of information, Anne was none the less aware of a slight uneasiness in Joan's manner. Could it be that speaking of so delicate a matter, though necessary, is distasteful to her? she wondered. But nay, the lady Joan is a woman of the world, a descendant of kings. Is not she the granddaughter of King Edward the First — as well as the widow of a prince and the mother of a king! Many men, it is said, have loved her — not least the late king her kinsman — and yet, married three times, she remained faithful to each of her husbands.

Her present uneasiness then is for myself — or her son. Does she perchance fear I shall not be a good wife — that I shall be neglectful of my duty? Does she imagine that I shall shy from the marriage-bed? She need have no concern there. I fell in love with a golden-haired sitter in a portrait. Now, the sitter having taken on reality, my regard for him is manifold.

"Madam — " she said with the courtesy due to the king's mother — a woman with whom she already had a bond of sympathy and understanding " — pray be assured that I shall be a good and dutiful wife to the king your son."

"I am aware of that, my lady," Joan said with a reassuring smile. "Never, from the moment we met, have I had doubt. Nay, child, my uneasiness stems from a different source. There are some, you see . . . "

She paused, hesitated — and seemed to change tack.

"The king is young for such high office — " she said then, " — and thus is easily influenced. God grant that now, with yourself beside him, he will cleave to his bride and cast off other influences!"

"Madam, I fail to understand — "

Joan placed a gentle hand on her arm.

"Dear child!" she said warmly. "I am speaking foolishly — pray forgive me! I wish you long life and happiness — God grant it will be so!"

6

THE priest, flanked by two acolytes, the official witnesses — Thomas of Woodstock and the Bohemian ambassador — facing him from the opposite side of the bed, intoned the bedding prayers and sprinkled holy water, first on the marriage-bed and then on bride and groom.

Anne, a trifle nervous and wishing the ceremony over, recalled of a sudden Joan's words on the previous day. Joan had seemed troubled, anxious, beset by doubt. But doubt, not of Anne's worthiness to be her son's bride, it seemed — but of his worthiness to be her husband. Nay, that cannot be, Anne thought to herself. I must surely have misunderstood. My lord is the last of the lady Joan's offspring; the only surviving child of her marriage with Edward, the Black Prince — he who became a legend in his own lifetime. Her doubts were naught but a mother's reaction to losing a well-loved son.

The double doors of the nuptial chamber were opened at that point silently and by unseen hands, and the witnesses, their faces impassive, their duty done, went from the chamber, the priests and acolytes following . . .

The bedding ceremony was over and Anne's wandering thoughts returned abruptly to the present.

The nuptial chamber with its magnificent hangings, its great bed with the royal coat-of-arms carved on the oak bedhead, seemed of a sudden empty and over quiet.

Richard kissed her perfunctorily on the cheek. Anne turned to look at him, meeting his gaze. He looked uncertain, hesitant, unsure of his next move — like the youth of fifteen he was. The panoply of state, the adulation of the multitude, the deference shown to him by his ministers and courtiers — even by his tutors — had hitherto given him an air of maturity and assurance which belied his years.

That he was handsome, a golden-haired youth of tall stature and easy grace, there was no doubt. But under the tightly-tucked bedcovers and the coverlet of white fur, he was naked as the day he was born.

Richard loved finery — and his taste for fine raiment and opulence, for robes made of rich materials bedecked with gold chains and jewels, was growing apace. *Manners maketh man* William of Wykeham, the chancellor, was wont to say — but Richard was privately of the opinion that it was manners *and* clothing that produced the right effect!

Now, on his wedding night, he wore no raiment, no clothing — not even a plain linen shirt. He felt naked, was naked . . .

"We are truly wed — " Anne said nervously, breaking the uneasy silence, " — truly man and wife."

"We are indeed," acknowledged the king with an involuntary sigh and a notable lack of enthusiasm. "We are so."

Anne managed to conceal her disappointment.

This was the queen's bedchamber — the king's bedchamber being at the opposite end of the royal apartments. Thus, when necessity arose or affairs of state intervened — or simply out of preference — each might lead their own separate life. But this was their wedding night. This was not the time for dwelling on that . . .

Accustomed to a large family structure — aunts and uncles, cousins and in-laws, as well as an unusual number of half-brothers and half-sisters, all of whom were uninhibited in displaying their emotions within the family circle — Anne was surprised to say the least at the coldness of her bridegroom's kiss.

Kiss? In reality it had been more a peck on the cheek — a cold, obligatory gesture. Telling herself that out of courtesy he was waiting for her to make the next move, Anne leaned over and kissed him firmly on the mouth — the tucked-in bedclothes untucking themselves in the process and revealing the newly-weds in all their nakedness.

Richard was conscious of her breasts pressing against his chest, and resisted the urge to push her away. She was a forward hussy, he told himself — not at all as he had expected. But, God help him, they were man and wife and she had a right, he supposed, to expect some kind of action from him!

He sat up on one elbow and, carefully avoiding any physical contact, spoke quietly.

"Perchance we should give ourselves time, my lady," he said. "After the rigours of the journey from your homeland and the pomp and ceremonial of the past days, you must surely be a little fatigued."

"Fatigued?" asked Anne, gazing at him in astonishment. "Fatigued, my lord?"

Fatigued? she asked herself. Why, I enjoyed every moment of the journey to Windsor, showing an avid interest in the towns and villages through which we passed. On reaching Windsor, I followed the example of Joan and her daughter and rested prior to this evening's celebratory banquet. After the banquet, as was expected, my lord and I left the banqueting hall early, bound for a bedding as all the world knew — running the gauntlet, also expected, of exaggerated cheers and ribald comments from the assembled company.

Fatigued? Nay, she was not that. She was alone at last with the youth she loved — had loved ever since she had first seen his portrait. She had dreamed about him these many months past, by night and by day — and here she was, the wedding and bedding a *fait accompli*, lying naked and willing beside her new-wedded lord.

"Fatigued?" she asked again — troubled by his silence. "Nay, I am not so, my lord. I recall all those letters that passed between us, assuring each other of lifelong devotion — of our yearning to be united in wedlock. Now we are so united — and nay, Your Grace's bride is not fatigued."

Richard told himself there was no escape, that he must show willing, make some kind of effort to reassure her. He leaned over her.

"I do love you," he said — and he meant it.

In his own way he meant it. She looked enchanting, was gentle and kind, and his subjects had taken her to their hearts. He loved her in his own meaning of the word. She was his bride, his lady, the one with whom over many months he had exchanged love-letters. He loved her with affection, would cherish her with devotion, speak well of her at all times and to everyone, and hear no word against her. He would protect her always — with his life if necessary!

In every way possible he would love her — save the one.

"I love you — with all my heart and soul," he said then.

His lady took this as a declaration of intent — a preliminary announcement, a warning — even permission to come aboard.

She lay back on the pillows and drew him into her arms. He followed her lead without demur, kissing her lips — but tenderly, without passion.

"My sweet lord, I am yours," she whispered. "We are man and wife — pray let us complete our marriage as is expected of us. They will look on the morrow, you know, inspect the bed linen, make a report . . . ."

"I know," he said unhappily. "I know. But why tonight? Why not morrownight — or the one after that?"

"Because it is what we wish," she said simply. "To complete our marriage — that none might put it aside."

He moved away a little, the better to look at her. Anne registered his expression but was at a loss to interpret it — or so she told herself.

She wanted him with all her being — she wanted him to caress and make love to her, to do as he would with her. Mating was still a mystery to her. Oh, she knew the facts, the basic unromantic facts — as explained by her governess, as whispered about by her half-sisters. But words and facts were not mating. Words, facts and whispered confidences were the enemies of mating — of copulation. Mating, her body told her, had everything to do with yearning and sensation, and a special kind of love . . .

She took one of his hands and pressed it to her breast. Her pulses quickened and she was conscious of a new appetence — but then, in the manner of one stung by a bee he withdrew his hand.

He was fearful of hurting her, Anne told herself then. He loved her but was a little unsure of himself — though he had not seemed so before.

"Love me, my lord," she pleaded, close to tears. What was wrong? Was her nakedness displeasing to him? "I love you with all my heart and wish only to please you — oh how greatly I desire to please you! Tell me how I might do so."

"You do please me," he said with sincerity. "You please me greatly — are not you mine own? Are not you my chosen bride? I love you for your beauty and gentleness — and I thank God for having given you to me."

"I understand you not, my lord," she said, as he still kept his distance from her. "If it is as you say . . ."

"I love you, my lady, and shall always love you as I love no other — " He paused, seeking for the right words, weighing them up before he continued. " — but love is not lust."

She watched him for a few moments in silence, considering what he had said.

"I know not your meaning, my lord," she admitted at length.

"I lust not after you," he told her quietly. "It is as simple as that. Love and lust, though close kin to each other, do not always go hand in hand. One might lust without loving — and vice versa."

Frustrated and as it seemed to her rebuffed, Anne started to weep.

"I know naught of lust," she protested through her tears — failing in her innocence to ask the obvious question or to draw the right conclusion. "I know only of love."

Richard climbed from the bed and drew on a nightrobe of purple velvet sewn with jewels and embroidered with gold thread — covering his nakedness with a sense of overriding relief.

"Queen of my heart," he said then, gazing down lovingly at her, his eyes bright with emotion. "Always will you be queen of my heart — none shall gainsay it without I call them rogue!"

"Leave me not so soon, my lord," Anne pleaded. "Our marriage is not as yet — "

"Complete?" he asked with a wry smile, seeing her hesitation. "Has not been perfected, as the saying is? As far as Richard of England is concerned, it is already the most perfect marriage in the world — we shall share much happiness, I promise you."

"But . . ." Anne hesitated and glanced at the pristine white sheets. "But on the morrow . . ."

"We shall just have to keep the court busy-bodies guessing, shall we not? On the morrow, my lady, all will be well," Richard said coolly — if ambiguously. "You, I doubt not, will have regained your composure — and I shall on morrownight, with your permission, again visit your chamber. How say you?"

Anne nodded, unable to speak — and in truth having nothing to say. She was confused, puzzled. *Why does my lord say that all will be well on the morrow?* she wondered. *If on morrownight, why not tonight? I lust not after you, was his saying — love and lust do not always go hand in hand. What was his meaning?*

"And so good night, fair lady," Richard said lightly, bending down to kiss her cheek. "Remember you are mine, all mine — never mind the rest of it! I love you and shall love you always, come what might. Never have doubt of it. Never forget it — whatsoever the future might hold."

But Anne had turned away from him and was burying her tear-stained face in the pillow. Her muffled sobs followed him as he made for the door . . .

7

THE morrownight came and went without the king paying a visit to his lady's chamber — as did the three succeeding nights.

He was attentive and courteous whenever their paths met. He spoke with her frequently, complimented her often and could in no way be faulted in his concern and apparent regard for her.

But Anne was upset and not a little alarmed when he failed for the fourth night running to put in an appearance. *Are his protestations of regard merely a pretence?* she asked herself more than once. *Has he given his heart to another — and, wishing to spare my feelings, behaves as if naught were amiss?*

She was only too well aware that, until their marriage was consummated, it was not fully a marriage. *Does my lord wish to wed some other?* she wondered, *and see non-consummation as a means of eventually doing so?*

If so, she thought, why did he consent to the match in the first place? Could it be that pressure was brought to bear by his uncles, they being then his guardians?

Doubt and self-doubt went round and round in her mind. She had none to whom she wished to, or could, confide her anxiety. He to whom she would under normal circumstances have spoken her mind, was distancing himself from her.

* * *

On the fifth night, Richard did eventually put in an appearance — having advised Anne earlier of his intention.

Anne retired early to her chamber and, in *déshabillé*, having dismissed her servants for the night, she seated herself before the log-fire and began diligently to work at some embroidery to while away the time.

The expected hour of ten passed without a sight of her lord — and eleven also. Half an hour later, telling herself he had changed his mind, Anne extinguished most of the candles and climbed into bed.

She fell asleep almost at once, only to be troubled by strange dreams and fantasies. She saw a young child standing beside her bed, silently watching her — a child clad only in a thin shift and whom she judged in the half-light to be about two years of age. Having dark-brown curls and eyes of a brilliant blue, sturdily built, the little one reminded her of someone — though she could not think who.

As she met the child's gaze, it held out its arms to her in mute appeal. She reached out for it but, even as she did so, the child fell down beside the bed and disappeared from view . . .

"My dear! My dear!" she cried out, peering over the edge of the bed. "Where are you? I saw you fall but, alas, I cannot find you!"

The child, naked now and its face wreathed in smiles, appeared of a sudden on the further side of the bed — a boy child, it looked younger this time, scarcely more than a baby.

"*Maman!*" it cried, trying unsuccessfully to climb in beside her. "*Maman*, do not you want me? See, I am here, waiting for you to take me in your arms!"

But again as Anne reached out, frantically this time, the child vanished — and Anne, yearning to hold the child and fearing it might be harmed, began to weep.

"Where are you, my precious — where are you?" she cried distractedly. "Where are you hiding? *Maman* is here, waiting for you — of course she wants you!"

She awoke then, to find herself out of bed, grovelling on the floor, and with tears streaming down her face.

"Where are you?" she cried, her eyes raking the half-lit chamber. "Where are you, my precious? I know you oh so well — and yet, God have pity, I cannot place you!"

As reality returned and she thought she recognized the dream for what it was, Anne could feel tears running down her cheeks and soaking the front of her nightgown. She put a hand to her face to wipe away the tears — but nay, they too had been figments of her imagination.

She climbed slowly back into bed, distressed by the dream, feeling doubly bereft — but not in truth knowing why. What does it mean? she asked herself. Who is the child who imagines I am his mother? Who is he, that little lost boy?

It was a few minutes past midnight when, telling herself she must put the visitation from her mind, Anne composed herself for sleep. But the vision of the supplicating child, the little lost boy, was still very much with her and was to remain so for a long time . . .

She was almost asleep when her chamber door opened noisily to admit a shuffling, close-wrapped figure. As the figure moved stealthily towards the bed, Anne gave a little scream — only to press a hand to her mouth as recognition dawned.

"So it is you, my lord," she said, feeling a mite foolish.

"It is I," cheerily came the answer. "Better late than never, one might say!"

He swayed towards her — this allied to his slurred speech and dishevelled appearance convincing Anne that he was well and truly intoxicated. She said nothing, having nothing to say.

"I want you," he said abruptly,

throwing aside his robe and climbing not without difficulty on to the bed.

"Indeed, my lord?"

"Why else would I be here, madam! Are not you my wedded wife?"

"Not as yet, my lord — not fully," Anne replied pointedly. In truth she was more than a little fearful — the dream had unnerved her and now, it seemed, she must contend with a leering drunken youth. "We are, if Your Grace recalls, wedded but not bedded, alas!"

"Alas, she says!" He laughed as if at some great jest. "Then 'tis well your lord and husband is here to remedy the matter."

"I fear you are a trifle inebriated, my lord," Anne said coldly — trying not too successfully to keep the note of disapproval from her voice. "Methinks Your Grace is in need of sleep."

"Later. Later." He waved a heavily-beringed hand vaguely in the direction of the door, the rings contrasting bizarrely with his nakedness. "He gave me a lecture, you see — duty before pleasure, he said. Richy had been a bad boy, he said — but once he had done his duty, he could look for a reward!"

Having not the least idea what he was talking about, Anne watched him in puzzlement. He seemed of a sudden much younger than herself — 'tis as if, she thought wearily, he is a mere child and I am an old woman.

"Of whom do you speak, my lord?" she asked.

"Ah-ha!" he said mysteriously, putting a finger to his lips. "That is your lord's secret — his great great secret. You must not speak of it — 'tis against the rules."

"My lord, you have taken too much strong liquor, I fear," Anne said again. "Should not you return to your apartments and rest till morning!"

"Is not this my lady's chamber?" asked the king, gazing around him as if in some doubt. "But where is my lady — she to whom I am betrothed?"

"Betrothed?" asked Anne aghast, but since that too met with no response, she added, "Your lady is here beside you, my lord."

He continued to gaze around the room, apparently looking for Anne — and then he lay back on the bed. "Nay, you are mistaken, madam — my lady is not here, alas, alas!"

Anne was troubled. He seemed ill, quite unlike himself — she wondered if she should have someone summon the court physician.

"My lord, you seem unwell," she said anxiously. "Would you have me send for the physician?"

There was no reply and, concerned, she looked more closely at him in the half-light. Already he had fallen asleep.

She lay sleepless beside him for several hours before she too fell asleep — to awake to find daylight seeping in through the shutters and Richard gazing down at her.

"Pray forgive me, my lady," he said contritely, and Anne registered with surprise that he now seemed quite himself. He was showing no after-effects of intoxication. "I should have stayed away. Did I say aught to you?"

She hesitated but then nodded.

"*He* had given you a lecture, you said," she told him.

"He? Who in Christ's name is he?"

"Methought you would know the answer to that, my lord," Anne told him. "Someone, you said, had been a bad boy — but that once he had done his duty, he could look for a reward!"

"I know not the who nor the why," came the light-hearted reply — but Anne sensed his uneasiness. "Pray put the matter from your mind, my lady — all is now well."

"Well, my lord?" Anne asked quietly. "Might I remind you, sire, that you have kept from my chamber these four nights past!"

He met her gaze thoughtfully — as if he were debating the wisdom of his next words.

"Anne, help me, I pray you," he said then. She registered his anxiety and was reminded forcibly of the lost child. But the child's hair was dark! she thought inconsequentially. "Help me, my lady. You see . . . There is the matter of the succession."

"Help you, my lord?" Anne asked lightly. "How so?"

There is indeed the matter of the succession, she thought ruefully. Could it be that I am but a means of my lord getting himself an heir? Is it a child that he wants, rather than myself? Even as she gave life to the thought, the dream child, the little lost one, leapt again into her mind . . .

But Richard's next words and the sincerity in his brown-gold eyes overcame her doubts.

"I love you with all my heart and soul," he said. "But I cannot explain how it is with me and I doubt you would be able to understand. Only love me, I pray you — and teach me how to make love to you."

She watched him for a few moments in silence. There was indeed much she did not understand. She loved him and he loved her — of that she no longer had doubt. Someone had spoken to him of his duty, he had said — of a reward for doing his duty. As to who the someone was she had no idea. The chancellor perchance? Her lord's former tutor maybe — or one of his uncles? Memories of the chivalric Thomas of Woodstock leapt into her mind at that point, but she dismissed them hastily . . .

She drew her lord close, kissing and caressing him. He needed her, though for the present apparently not in the way she wished. He needed her love, her understanding, her support — and she must respond to his need. The rest must wait.

Her own needs, as yet not as clearly defined as his, must wait.

8

THE story of Richard of Bordeaux, King of England, is that of a prince who came to kingship too early and too suddenly; of one unprepared for the burden of statecraft, of rebellion and dissent and their attendant ills.

Richard's culture was French. He had been born and reared at the Provençal court — that favourite stamping-ground of troubadours who sang mainly of chivalry and courtly love. His first language therefore was French, his second Latin — with English coming a very poor and much despised third.

His was a glorious dynasty. His father and his grandfather had been the greatest heroes of their time. His grandfather had ascended the throne as Edward the Third at the age of fifteen; had married early and sired a large and distinguished family, and had reigned for over fifty years. Richard's father, the Black Prince, had won his spurs when only sixteen at the battle of Crécy — his exploits and heroism on the battlefield, both there and later at Poitiers, earning him a special place in the hearts of the English people.

But the Black Prince and his elder son — Richard's brother — had both died prematurely during the reign of the third Edward. The latter had on his death-bed passed over his three remaining sons — John of Gaunt, Edmund of Langley and Thomas of Woodstock — naming his grandson, Richard of Bordeaux, as his successor in accordance with the dynastic law.

The peasants' revolt had blighted the year prior to Richard's marriage. The great conflagration — popularly known as *the hurling time* — had come perilously close to destroying both monarchy and government. It had seen the sack of the Tower of London, murder and arson in the City streets and the brutal assassination of the chief ministers of the Crown.

But Richard, in the opinion of many, had saved the day. Then a youth of fourteen, he had gone forth alone to address the rebels at Smithfield and to listen sympathetically to their grievances. Thus had he won the hearts of the commonalty. As they saw it, he had saved the day to no less a degree than had his father on Crécy field.

Following that courageous encounter at Smithfield, Richard's confidence in his own powers of leadership had increased tenfold. As he saw it, he had earned the confidence and support of his subjects and they would henceforth follow him, come what might. To the alarm of his more warlike uncles, he thereafter refused to heed their advice and that of his ministers, ignoring their counsel and greater experience, and gathering around himself a circle of dissolute young men, the leader of which was the twenty-one year old Robert de Vere, Earl of Oxford.

As the months went by and the rumours became widespread, the more elderly of Richard's subjects recalled the scandalous behaviour of his great-grandfather, Edward the Second. They spoke disapprovingly of the second Edward's homosexual relationship with Piers de Gaveston and his neglect of his beautiful if wilful young bride, Isabella of France. They recalled the erring monarch's downfall, the execution of his favourites, Piers de Gaveston and Hugh le Despenser, and the brutal murder of the king himself at Berkeley Castle . . .

But this king is only a lad, they said to themselves — one who showed the heart of a lion at Smithfield! Now, with the advent of his young bride, he will surely forsake his false friends and their evil influence — and remember his duty. The new bride, they said to themselves and each other, the smiling princess from Bohemia, will soon wean him from his dalliance with Robert de Vere and his ilk.

* * *

"Ain't they lovely, Lettice!" exclaimed the young cockney woman to her companion, as they stood in Old Jewry along with the rest of the onlookers, watching the passing of the royal cavalcade. "Both of 'em golden-haired and wearing them rich clothes — they look to be rivalling the sun!"

"Lord love us, they could be a couple

from fairyland!" enthused the other.

"Fairyland indeed! Why, if what I've heard be true, King Richard and 'is pal, de Vere, are from fairyland all right. Pity the poor queen, say I!"

"I don't know what you're on about, Kate. I can't see naught wrong with Robby de Vere. He's handsome and looks very grand — to see 'im, you'd think as 'ow *he* was the king! All them jewels and furbelows . . . "

"Furbelows? What be they when they're at home?"

"Look, Kate, the queen's smiling at us — ain't she just lovely!"

"Not pretty, some say — well, I dunno about that. She smiles like she really means it, and her eyes are blue as periwinkles!"

"Periwinkles is white."

"Not the ones I've seen."

"She's got a lovely figure, Kate — wish I 'ad dukkys as big as them!"

"Must you speak so, Lettice? Dukkys indeed — why, if you — "

"I'd like the queen's complexion too, Kate. Pale as a lily, it be — and smooth as silk."

"Have you ever felt silk, Lettice?"

"You don't need to feel it to know what it's like, silly! Oh well, smooth as butter then — does that suit Your Ladyship?"

"Butter is all greasy — the queen's complexion ain't at all like that!"

"She is German, of course."

"Bohemian."

"It's all the same — they've all got big dukkys and pale complexions. And I've heard it said — though I must keep me voice down — that most of 'em have got — "

"Wenceslaus."

"Wenceslaus? What d'yer mean, Kate?"

"He was King of Bohemia, was Wenceslaus — as well as being the queen's great-grandfather."

"Never 'eard of 'im. And why did you say it like that — as if you'd lost a penny and found sixpence!"

"The carol we sings at Christmas — that's about King Wenceslaus."

"Oh that!"

"Don't you remember it, Lettice? Why, I recall you singing it last Christmas — all out of tune, you were!"

91

"No law against being out o' tune, is there? Besides, if I didn't remember the carol, I would be out of tune, wouldn't I? Stands to reason, don't it?"

"It goes like this, Lettice:

> *In 'is master's steps he trod,*
> *Where the snow lay dinted.*
> *Heat was in the very sod . . .* '"

"Cripes! — remember where you are, Kate! Everyone's looking at you —"

"Shush, Lettice! The procession will soon be out of sight and we don't want to miss anything, do we? Look — see here! The king's leaning over and saying something to the queen in a low voice — and she's really laughing."

"Laughing at you singing out of tune, I expect!"

"Love's young dream, ain't they, Lettice!"

"I'm not so sure, Kate. I expect he was telling 'er as how he was giving up that there Robby de Vere — and it made her laugh!"

"Really, Lettice, you're so — so —"

"Yes, I know — but I can't help it!"

" — unromantic! That's the word. Why, they look so happy, it does your heart good to see 'em! They're in love, I tell you — any moment now they'll be announcing she's going to 'ave a babby."

"Give 'em a chance, Kate — they've only been wed five days!"

"What's that got to do with it? You 'ad your first five days *afore* you was wed!"

"It's different with the likes of them, Kate — but I knows what I knows. Queen Anne will give birth on the dot of nine months — you'll see."

"Let's hope it looks like the king, then!"

"Like the king? Well, it might, I suppose — and again it might not. It might look like its ma after all."

"That wasn't me meaning — as well ye know! You see, Lettice, they do say as 'ow the king's uncle, Tom of Woodstock, 'as taken a fancy to the queen!"

"Shush, Kate — remember where you be! Why, everyone's looking at us — and anyway I don't believe a word of it. There's one thing certain though — the babe'll not look like Robby de Vere!"

9

DURING the two years that followed the royal marriage and the attainment *de jure* of Richard's majority, he found his uncles and parliament united in their reluctance to relinquish their power. Without reference to either therefore, he had appointed Michael de la Pole as chancellor.

A fiery encounter with John of Gaunt, Duke of Lancaster, inevitably followed this provocation. The eldest and most influential of the uncles, many believed that John of Gaunt should have been king. Richard, encouraged by Robert de Vere, next devised a plan whereby — on the basis of divide and conquer — he might separate Edmund of Langley and Thomas of Woodstock from their elder brother.

This plan worked to the extent that John of Gaunt — furious at his nephew's double-dealing and having declared in favour of his youngest brother, Thomas of Woodstock — resolved to undertake a long-deferred expedition to Spain. Following the death of Blanche, his first wife, John of Gaunt had married by proxy Constance of Castile and assumed the title of King of Castile. He now wished the marriage completed.

Thomas of Woodstock, as magnate, was to prove in the event a more troublesome thorn in Richard's side than had the newly acclaimed King of Castile.

Speculation and rumour as to Richard's ability to rule, were meanwhile growing apace throughout the land. It seemed to many of those around the young king that during the three years since the peasants' revolt, he had degenerated alarmingly from his former virtues. He had given himself over to the pursuit of pleasure; revelling in finery and extravagant display, and indulging in bouts of unrestrained debauchery.

However, while Richard's popularity had been declining, Anne's had increased — and was to go on increasing. She too took pleasure in finery — perhaps initially out of a desire to please her husband. At the Garter festival, she wore to great effect a robe of violet cloth, lined with fur, its hood lined with scarlet. A train of high-born ladies attended her, each wearing a robe similar in style and colours to that of the queen.

Anne's arrival was greeted with enthusiasm by the bystanders, who clapped and cheered and generally made known their approval. But Anne had a warmth, a generosity of spirit, that won many hearts — and not least those of her lord's subjects.

Richard looked foppish to a degree, his attire overshadowing the dignified and pleasing apparel of his queen. His coat alone, adorned with precious stones, was said to have cost some thirty thousand marks.

But it was his footwear that caught the attention of the onlookers and prompted cries of astonishment. Introduced by Robert de Vere, shoes with exaggeratedly-pointed toes had recently become the fashion in court circles, the younger courtiers vying with each other to achieve an ever-longer point.

Richard on this occasion, however, had put all the others in the shade. He was wearing not shoes, but pattens — soles attached under the foot to the hose — the points extending a full sixteen inches beyond the toe. Stuffed with tow — in the absence of toes — each point was held in place by a gold chain attached to a jewelled garter just below the knee.

Exclamations of approval and disapproval greeted Richard on his arrival for the ceremony. That he outshone both his queen and his nobles, there was no question — but Richard was quite unabashed. Was not he starting a new fashion in footwear!

"Would my subjects prefer to see their sovereign in plain attire!" he asked rhetorically in English of Thomas of Woodstock who openly disapproved. "Think you, *mon oncle,* that they wish to see one garbed as a peasant!"

Since the revolt, the word 'peasant' had somehow taken on new meaning — notably in the de Vere set. It now suggested a rough unruly fellow — an outlaw. Thomas of Woodstock, misliking the reference and piqued by the mannered *mon oncle* from one a mere twelve years his junior, none the less concealed his chagrin. Richard, whilst as has been said preferring and speaking chiefly in French, had an infuriating habit of using English when he wished to score a point — or so it seemed to his long-suffering uncles.

"Doubtless, my lord, your subjects will in time become accustomed to such vulgar display," said Thomas then. "At present, God be thanked, they show indulgence. He is young, they say — but time will take care of that!"

Furious at these observations but unwilling at that time to force an open confrontation with the duke, Richard swallowed his anger.

"If *mon oncle* likes it not, then he must blame the queen," he was later overheard to say amusedly to de Vere. "The pattens were Her Grace's idea."

"Ah, that would no doubt put a different complexion on the matter!" declared de Vere with an affected sigh. "Whatsoever the queen approves, Thomas of Woodstock approves also!"

"And that is as it should be!" declared Richard whole-heartedly — and to his hearer's annoyance. "Whatsoever the queen approves, Richard of England approves also!"

"Thomas of Woodstock, Duke of Gloucester, holds the queen in high regard," remarked de Vere, well aware that in using that nobleman's full title, he was reminding his hearer of his increased power, thus seeking, by no means for the first time, to drive a wedge between Richard and his kinsman — and indirectly the queen. "I have heard it whispered — though needless to say not in Your Grace's presence and quite without foundation I am sure — that your esteemed uncle is enamoured of the queen!"

"What a rascal you are!" laughed Richard, not taking him seriously. "One day I might take you seriously — and that very same day would see Robert de Vere locked up in the Tower!"

De Vere laughed with him.

"Jesting apart, sire, how came you by the pattens?" he asked lightly. "Were they indeed Her Grace's idea?"

"Nay, not entirely," Richard told him. "My lady brought the idea from her homeland. 'Tis a style much favoured in Cracow, she tells me."

"Indeed?" De Vere looked rueful. "Then one must assume that the Bohemian male has given up walking!"

"A little practice, my friend — and hey presto!" lightly remarked Richard. "Truth to tell, I spent the greater part of a day mastering the art of wearing them — with some success methinks."

"Your Grace's modesty becomes you!" facetiously replied de Vere. "It is an example to us all!"

"I must away now to inform the queen of my decision."

"Your decision, sire?"

"Henceforth, I shall say to her, pattens of that type shall be referred to as *crackowes*!"

★ ★ ★

That Richard's love for Anne was deep and genuine, could not be doubted. But it was not the love of a man for a woman, a husband for a wife — a lover for the beloved. It was love of her as a person, one who was kind, gentle and beautiful, who shared his love of finery and ostentation — one who was his, solely his.

To Richard, Anne was a younger version of his mother — a woman to be loved and cherished, revered and protected, given all the honour due to a consort and a pleasing and virtuous bride. That he might lose Anne — whether to death or in her heart to another — was unthinkable.

The marriage had remained unconsummated. Richard had at no time fully discussed the matter with Anne — nor indeed with anyone else. There was plenty of time, he told himself. They were both young — perchance their extreme youth at the time of their alliance was the reason for his inability to complete the union.

Inability? Was that in truth it? he asked himself at moments of self-doubt. But nay, not exactly. In fact he knew neither the urge nor the wish to complete the marriage, to take from her, as he told himself, that which so delighted him — namely her innocence and purity, her completeness in her virginity. Sometimes, giving thought to the matter, he equated

Anne with the Mother of God: both were, as Richard saw it, gentle, loving, serene and giving — always giving — for ever pure, whole, undefiled.

Giving? Yea, she attended him lovingly and sympathetically, as a mother her son — as his own mother in his early years had attended him. She returned caress for caress, fondled, kissed and spoke words of love to him. She held him to her breasts, as a mother her suckling — and he took them with an enthusiasm that gave no quarter to the fact that, until the marriage was consummated, her breasts would remain as empty as her womb.

He knew joy and peace when she held him thus — and a great love and reverence for her. It was as if she were indeed the Blessed Virgin — a creature of benignity, one for ever loving and kind. His senses became inflamed at such times with a kind of desire — but the urge for satisfaction was spiritual rather than physical.

Afterwards, Anne would turn away from him, her tears falling, though never a word of reproach crossed her lips . . .

There was plenty of time, Richard told himself after such encounters. He was but in his nineteenth summer — why hurry! There was, after all, no urgency — if he waited another year, or even five, he could well have sired a brood of offspring ere he had attained his thirty-fifth birthday.

10

RICHARD having now passed his nineteenth birthday, Robert de Vere, recently created Marquis of Dublin, was urging him to throw off entirely the guardianship of his three uncles. During the next session of parliament at Salisbury in April, Richard saw his opportunity when the Earl of Arundel complained of misgovernment.

"Misgovernment!" he exclaimed furiously and with a notable lack of finesse. "If there be misgovernment, my lord, tell us pray who should be held culpable."

"Why, Your Grace, who but the sovereign of this realm is head of government!" responded Arundel pointedly. "That being the case, whilst there might be some excuse for — "

Richard caught de Vere's eye — and his temper, already inflamed by the latter's taunts about John of Gaunt's so-called interference, suddenly flared.

"Body of Christ!" he interjected. "You

go too far! As you are doubtless aware..."

John of Gaunt, seeing signs of an impending storm, was already on his feet; and Arundel, seeing this and having as he believed made his point, sat down.

"Sire, my lord of Arundel was but pointing out that Your Grace, though sovereign only *de jure*..." interposed John of Gaunt, seeking to pour oil on troubled waters.

He got no further.

" — has mismanaged the government of the realm," put in Richard. He turned to Arundel. "I suggest, my lord, that you make your complaint in the proper quarter."

"I pray you have a care, my lord!" John of Gaunt's words were calmly spoken — but there was a steely glint in his eyes that some there had seen before.

"My lords, once I am *truly* sovereign of the realm, and not before — " Richard said angrily — and with a nod in the direction of John of Gaunt " — I shall accept full responsibility for any sins and omissions."

"Sins, sire?" enquired Arundel with

raised eyebrows — and an unmistakable snigger came from the back of the chamber. "With respect, it is not Your Grace's sins we are discussing — "

"Go to the devil, old man!" interposed Richard, his temper getting the better of him. "Go to the devil and take my lord of Lancaster with you!"

And so saying, he strode from the chamber, de Vere following.

★ ★ ★

A Carmelite friar named John Latimer celebrated Mass one morning in Robert de Vere's apartments in the recently built King's House, which stood opposite the west door of Salisbury Cathedral. Afterwards, the friar requested an audience with the king.

Ushered into Richard's audience chamber, he appeared hesitant and ill-at-ease.

"Your Grace, my name is John Latimer," he said. "I have information to impart — information I deem to be of importance. Bound by the seal of confession, I cannot reveal the source of this information, as Your Grace will understand — but since my sovereign's life could well depend on having knowledge of this same information, I am duty bound to tell what I know."

Richard nodded — telling himself wryly that it looked like a case of much cry and little wool! Impatient to begin his day, he hoped the fellow would get a move on.

"Conflicting loyalties, eh!" he said cheerily. "Speak on, sir friar, if you will."

The friar lowered his voice. "The Duke of Lancaster — him they call John of Gaunt — is plotting to kill Your Grace. So shocked was I when I learned of this, that this morning I begged my lord of Oxford's chaplain to allow me to take his place."

Richard, taken aback by the alarming revelation, gazed at the friar in dismay. Was it a practical joke? he asked himself. De Vere perchance? If so, he thought grimly, I shall have his hide for this!

"Are you certain of what you say?" he enquired — and there was an unmistakable edge to his voice. "Could it be overheard gossip?"

The friar slowly shook his head. "Nay, sire — I wish it were so, that one might disregard it. He who revealed the facts to me was plagued by a great anxiety — he feared for Your Grace's life, you understand, but knew not what to do about it without forfeiting his own! I told him to go in peace — assuring him that I would acquaint Your Grace with the information without reference to its source."

* * *

Richard had at first been doubtful as to the veracity of the friar's information. De Vere, however, when it was recounted to him, saw it as a golden opportunity for driving a wedge between Richard and John of Gaunt.

"My lord, I fear you are in mortal danger," he said sorrowfully, giving no hint as to his true reaction. "You must openly accuse your uncle, or indeed uncles — I doubt not they are one and all party to the plot!"

"You are suggesting that I have John of Gaunt charged with treason?" Richard was white-faced — even to him, the idea was ludicrous and he still doubted the truth of the friar's revelation. "Or, worse still, all three of my uncles? Christ save us, the king my grandfather would turn in his grave!"

"Better he should turn in his grave, than that you, my sweet lord, should lie prematurely in yours!" came the smooth response.

"Then you believe the friar's tale?" Richard was still harbouring a suspicion that de Vere might have contrived the whole thing — even that the friar was not truly a friar. He had, after all, not seen him before. "I confess the fellow, if not his tale, made me more than a little uneasy."

"You must put the matter before the Privy Council — " de Vere said urgently " — and without delay."

"Must, you say?" Richard's voice was cold. "Since when do you say 'must' to your king, my lord?"

De Vere disregarded the correction.

"Richy, I beg you as I love you, to summon parliament and place the matter before their lordships," he said fervently.

"I fear that what the friar said was the truth — and that Your Grace is in grave danger."

"I shall do as you suggest," Richard agreed, suddenly convinced — and affected by the emotion in his lover's eyes. "I shall insist that my lord of Lancaster be condemned as a traitor without further enquiry."

★ ★ ★

John of Gaunt, the most powerful man in England at that time, was forty-five years of age. Highly respected by his peers, he was much loved by his immediate family. His first wife had taken the plague and in the words of the chronicler, Jean Froissart, had "died fair and young, being then in her twenty-second year. Gay and glad she was, fresh and sportive, sweet, simple and of humble semblance, the fair lady whom men called Blanche."

John of Gaunt had in fact arrived in England following the Spanish war, to learn of the death of Queen Philippa his mother, Lionel his brother — and

Blanche, the mother of his eldest son, Henry of Bolingbroke.

But withal, John of Gaunt had never won the hearts of the commonalty — as had his younger brother, Thomas of Woodstock. Perhaps because of his natural reserve, the English people saw him as cold and calculating.

Recently returned from Castile, he was an impressive figure, tall and sun-tanned. He turned not a hair as the charge was read out in parliament — if he were alarmed, he certainly did not show it. He appeared surprised but not more so than the others in the chamber.

"My lords," he said mildly, "I confess myself astonished by the accusation, as I doubt not are Your Lordships."

There were cries of assent to this, and some smiled sympathetically at him — it was clear where their loyalties lay.

"Methinks it is your duty, my lords, to send me for trial, the charge being so heinous," he continued. "I shall gladly submit myself to the judgement of Your Lordships."

"The charge is frivolous, I doubt not," remarked Arundel, standing up and glaring belligerently at the king. "I for one believe not a word of it. I therefore suggest, my lords, that — the majority here I dare say sharing my sentiments — His Grace allows the charge to rest for the time being."

"Allows the charge to rest, say you, my lord?" demanded de Vere, getting lithely to his feet and looking daggers at Arundel. "Would you have them kill your king, sir — whilst we wait around doing naught?"

Northampton, a close supporter of John of Gaunt, rose to his feet at that.

"My lords, if I might make a suggestion," he said smoothly — as if the charge were a mere matter of drunkenness in the cathedral precincts. "I submit that the friar, John Latimer, be committed to Salisbury gaol — and there held whilst the charge is comprehensively investigated."

"My lords, the friar as far as we know has committed no crime," Richard pointed out — he had a curious feeling that by one means or another he was being manipulated. Someone was playing a game — a dangerous cruel game — and someone else, whose identity was a mystery to him, would eventually be called upon to pay up, with his life! "He, John Latimer, is not the subject of our charge. It is not he should be apprehended — but the one who is plotting to take our life!"

"Only the friar — a hedge-priest I understand him to be — can enlighten us as to the fiend's name," pointed out Arundel.

"Your lordship has the right of it," agreed John of Gaunt — the least impassioned of the speakers. He turned to Richard. "Believe me, nephew, I am as eager as Your Grace to discover the source of this wild allegation. I therefore ask you to bear with me in the matter."

Richard nodded, having in truth little choice — but unhappily aware of de Vere's scornful gaze.

★ ★ ★

John Latimer, the friar, failed to reach Salisbury gaol.

Since he was merely being taken for questioning — as to what form the questioning was meant to take, was debatable — he was accompanied by only two men-at-arms. The party was about half a mile from the gaol when it was intercepted by a band of nobles. Masked to conceal their identity, the newcomers were headed by John Holland, the king's half-brother — he wearing no mask since he was confident of the king's protection.

John Holland, Duke of Exeter, and his elder brother, Sir Thomas Holland, Earl of Kent, were the Princess Joan's sons by her first marriage. Many years older than the king — John was thirty-three at the time of the Carmelite friar affair — the brothers Holland had idolized Richard from the moment of his birth. The Black Prince, the infant's father, being absent for much of the time on military campaigns, his half-brothers together with their mother had spoiled him greatly, indulging his every whim and instilling in him a sense of his own importance and infallibility.

Thomas and John Holland — seventeen and fifteen years of age at the time of Richard's birth — had shown him always a deep and protective love. Richard could do no wrong in the eyes of his mother and half-brothers, with the result that he had inherited next to nothing of his father's and grandfather's strength of character, but much of his mother's levity and readiness to see only perfection in those she loved.

Richard, in his turn, dearly loved his mother and half-brothers — each was entirely without blemish as far as he was concerned. It was the sight of his mother's distress when, during the peasants' revolt the Tower of London had been under siege, which had prompted Richard against the advice of his ministers to give the order for the gates to be opened to the mob. Thus had he committed both his chancellor and treasurer to a brutal death and put himself and his government at the mercy of vengeful outlaws.

What part had the Holland brothers played in that? For once, they had not seen fit to rush willy-nilly to the aid of their mother and half-brother. Arriving in the City with only a small escort, they had found themselves at the rear of a vast mob of rebellious peasants who, howling for blood, were threatening to storm the great fortress. Realizing that the chances of their gaining entrance to the Tower at such a time were nil, and that a show of partisanship toward the beleaguered royalist guards inside the gates, would doubtless cost them their lives, the brothers had looked questioningly at each other. Then, shrugging, they had wheeled their horses and, their men following, ridden fast from the City — to live, as they told themselves and each other, to fight another day ...

* * *

Four years had passed since that day of carnage. Now, this particular Holland was all for confrontation — not with a vengeful peasant mob, but with a mild, helpless and dutiful Carmelite friar.

John Holland, clearly in charge, curtly dismissed the friar's escort — saying that he was acting under government orders. The guards, rough unlettered men, taking the newcomers to be noblemen of some importance, feared reprisals if they objected to being summarily relieved of their prisoner. They handed him over, despite his protests — having sworn as was demanded of them that they would speak of the matter to none.

The friar, alarmed at the change of plan, fearing the worst, continued to voice his objections until, a little further down the road that led to the prison, the party turned off in another direction. Recognizing then that he was in great danger, he made no further protest, meekly accompanying his new captors down a narrow track for a further half mile. At that point, an apparently derelict barn came into view and the friar was pulled none too gently from his horse and dragged protesting into the dark and deserted building.

"What do you require of me?" he asked nervously of John Holland, who seemed to be the leader. "I am but a poor friar, sir — a hedge-priest who goes about the countryside preaching and saying Mass."

"And speaking out of turn methinks," remarked John Holland. "A priest who speaks out of turn and respects not the secrets of the confessional, deserves to die — would not you agree, sir?"

"I would indeed," said the friar guardedly, trying to control his trembling limbs. A man well past his prime, he felt his heart pounding alarmingly and offered up a silent prayer. "Such a one would be an abomination, my lord — but never in all my born days have I suffered the misfortune of meeting such a wretch."

"Then what of the tale you told the king?" demanded John Holland.

The friar gave a start — and sought for words. "The king, my lord? I know not what you mean."

"Know you who I am?" demanded John Holland.

"Nay, sir," came the answer — but the friar, having had little practise, was not a good liar. He had recognized John Holland, knew him to be the king's half-brother and was aware of his reputation for brutality — who knew such things better than a priest? "That is to say, I cannot recall having seen you before."

"Again I ask you — what of the tale

you told the king?" demanded John Holland unpleasantly.

"I named no names — and a secret without a name is like unto a ship without a rudder! I was asked to speak out — by one in the king's service."

"His name?" asked John Holland — and he could feel his associates pressing closer to hear what was being said. "His name, sirrah?"

"As I said, I am not at liberty to reveal his name," replied the friar. "Indeed, I see not what his name has to do with the case."

"That is so," came the unexpected response. "And we are here to ensure that you do not reveal his name — or that of any of his companions."

The friar looked frightened — was frightened. His captors, with the exception of Holland, wore kerchiefs over the lower part of their faces — to conceal their identity, he supposed. But he was certain he knew the identity of one of the others — by his voice. Why is *he* here? he asked himself. Why, when 'twas he bade me inform the king . . . He thought he knew the answer to that — but it brought him no joy. Why would John Holland be acting with him? he asked himself then. He is surely not on the side of that reprobate!

"There is no plot against the king's life — is there?" John Holland was asking him. "The plot was an invention — your invention!"

"I was informed that there was a plot — why else would I have gone to the king?"

"I know not." John Holland spoke slowly, thoughtfully, as if debating the question. "I know only one thing for certain, friar — that never again will you cry warning!"

"I swear it was as I said," protested the friar, alarmed by the way the men were gathering more closely around him — as if for some kind of spectacle. "I was asked to warn the king — and was given a bribe to do so."

"Indeed?" John Holland seemed surprised by the admission.

"I should not have taken it. I realized that at the time, you understand, but I saw it as a means of feeding some of the hungry peasants."

John Holland looked at one of the others — he whose voice the friar had recognized.

"Think you we can trust him?" he enquired briskly.

"If we silence him not, another will — *after* they have dragged the truth from him," came the chilling reply. "Better settle the matter now, my lord."

"Then say your prayers, friar!" said John Holland with an unpleasant grin. "Best get the matter done."

"As God is my witness, I have committed no crime," insisted the friar. "I was asked to pass on a message. I did so. God knows there is no more to it than that, sir."

"God knows, you say — but what of he who gave you the message for the king, sirrah?"

"He is standing there beside you, my lord," the friar replied. "The tall one in the dark cloak."

"But his face is concealed by a kerchief, friar," chortled John Holland. "You'll have to do better than that!"

"In the confessional, you understand, there is only a voice," came the reply.

"Kerchief or not, my lord — I would know his voice anywhere!"

John Holland looked at his companions, shrugged ostentatiously and then turned again to the friar.

"Alas, friar — you have just signed your own death warrant!" he said coldly, summoning his henchmen.

Two brutish-looking men came forward, each holding a dagger. They seized the victim and threw him on to a pile of evil-smelling sacking.

"I beg you have mercy!" cried the friar, his face livid with terror. "Have pity, kind sir!"

"A pity it is!" said John Holland with an exaggerated sigh. "But there, death comes to all of us in the end!"

"I have done harm to no man," insisted the friar. "You, sir, are making a terrible mistake."

"Go to it," John Holland carelessly ordered his henchmen. "Get the matter over and done with."

"Nay, wait!" ordered the voice the friar recognized — and the background figure stepped forth into the lamplight. "I shall be the one to silence him — if one wishes a job done properly, one must do it oneself!"

Dagger in hand, he bent over the terrified prisoner who was now in the grip of the two stalwarts.

"Hold his mouth open," he ordered. "Nay wider than that!"

A half-scream followed by a gurgle fell on the ears of the watching men — and the mysterious figure with the knife triumphantly held up his hand. Between finger and thumb he was brandishing a tongue — a tongue dripping with blood.

"He will keep his word now sure enough," he said carelessly. "Now, what next? No point in disfiguring him too much — if he's not recognized later on, he'll not be a warning to others who give thought to playing fast and loose with the king's friends!"

The victim struggled and gurgled helplessly, placing his hands over his loins by way of protection as again the knife descended.

"He's done for now," remarked John Holland some time later, having turned not a hair during the display of savagery. He turned to his henchmen. "Wait till the coast is clear and then put the body across your saddle and take it to the prison. Place it, suitably arranged, just outside the door — the rascal was on his way there, after all!"

"But for a small diversion — " chuckled the man whose voice the friar had recognized " — the fellow would have been there half an hour since. Pity he missed his supper!"

"Supper?" asked John Holland with a grin. "I know not about that — but the friar has certainly had his just deserts!"

There was some laughter at this — but there was more than one man there who, powerless to intervene, had watched the torture of Friar John Latimer with pity and revulsion. Giving a fellow a good hiding for speaking out of turn was one thing, but torturing him to death — and dead the friar most certainly was — that was another matter. Now they too must hold their tongues — for if they did not, they knew what to expect. A weak king, a weak government, bred a lawless society — each of them knew that.

And so it would go on, and on, unless or until . . .

11

THE affair of the Carmelite friar and his supposed revelation that John of Gaunt was plotting to murder the king, was never satisfactorily resolved. Rumours abounded, many people believing that the friar had been a scapegoat for some in high places — and others that John of Gaunt had been directly involved. But the most popular theory was that Robert de Vere and his associates were the true culprits.

Whatever the truth and the obscure motives behind it, the repercussions were rapid and only too obvious. Not least of these was the hasty dissolution of parliament — and, hot on the heels of that, the first serious confrontation between Thomas of Woodstock and the king his nephew.

The charge made by Richard against John of Gaunt had been dropped, if temporarily — but it was a foregone conclusion that Richard, encouraged by de Vere, would make a further attempt to incriminate him.

As if by way of warning, a close friend of John of Gaunt, John of Northampton, who had during the year following the peasants' revolt been elected Mayor of London, was sent for trial before the king's council on charges of causing riot and public disorder in the City. Judged guilty, the mayor was sent to prison at Tintagel Castle.

John of Gaunt, seeing this as a more subtle attack on himself, swallowed his fury and decided not to intervene — for the time being. He would sit tight, he told himself, and await events. If the attack on John of Northampton had, as he suspected, been a barb to pierce his own armour, others would surely follow. Then, and only then, would he take steps to protect himself and his friends, seeing to it that his enemies were hoist by their own petard . . .

But if he could wait, Thomas of Woodstock could not. Concerned for his brother's safety, he resolved without his knowledge to call a halt to the harassment or know the reason why.

"I intend to beard the lion," he told his other brother, Edmund of Langley. "Our nephew must be given warning — and in no uncertain terms."

"Have a care, my brother," warned Edmund of Langley. A warrior of repute, he was none the less the most cautious of the three brothers. Suspecting, like John of Gaunt, that they were up against forces whose power must be seen before it could be controlled — or if necessary destroyed — he was wary of decisive action at that stage. "It might be wise to follow our brother's example."

"John has much at stake, and judges it wise at present to play the game by the rules," came the reply. "Perchance I have less at stake — or perchance my ambitions are more diffuse than his. But I judge the time ripe for action — I will no longer stand by, wringing my hands like a helpless maiden, whilst our nephew consorts openly with a sodomite and makes our noble family a laughing-stock. Think you the late king our father would have stood by and done nothing? Nay, *par Dieu*!"

His last words apparently convinced Edmund of Langley, for the latter's voice when he spoke was calm, accepting.

"You have made your decision — so be it!" he said. "How and when will you make your attempt to bring Richard to heel?"

"As to the *how*, I shall leave you in the dark, brother," came the cool reply. "The *when* will be tonight."

There was a few moments' silence — and Thomas watched with a mixture of chagrin and amusement the changing expressions on his brother's face. Dear Edmund, he thought — so without guile arc you, that I can read you like a book!

"Tonight, you say?" Edmund asked at length.

"Tonight."

"Is such wise, my brother? John and I are well aware of your regard for the lady, but to use such a means of evening the score . . ."

"Wise?" enquired Thomas. "Wisdom, it seems to me, has naught to do with the case."

"I find it hard to believe that you

would act so," persisted Edmund of Langley. "In dishonouring the king thus, you would dishonour yourself also."

"Alas, my brother!" interposed Thomas in mock reproof — but unable to keep the twinkle from his eyes. "Think you I would use such a means of punishing the king?"

Edmund smiled ruefully. "The situation in regard to the royal marriage being what it undoubtedly is, it might not be such a bad thing!"

"Richard dotes on the lady," Thomas said shortly — no longer amused. "Strange as it might seem, he dotes on the lady Anne."

"Love has many faces, it is said — but Richard, I fear, lacks the one essential for getting himself, and England, an heir!" observed Edmund. "We must hope and pray that time will alter the case."

Thomas shrugged. The subject was not to his liking — he preferred not to dwell on it.

"Maybe. Maybe," he said dismissively. "But as to the plan, my brother, I pray you trust me."

12

A MAGNIFICENT tapestry in the king's chamber covered almost the entire length of the wall facing the royal bed. It depicted a forest scene with, centrally, a naked and blatantly well-endowed John the Baptist lying on a bed of moss. Smiling but apparently asleep and dreaming, the latter was supported caressingly by five nubile maidens, with small breasts and large wings, apparently representing angels. Salome and King Herod were there, one at each end of the arras — she, with large breasts and no wings, holding up the dreamer's blood-dripping head, and Herod looking on, rubbing his hands, huge-eyed and gloating.

Richard and de Vere were wont, in their less intense moments, to jest and invent stories about the figures in the tapestry. They bestowed on the nubile maidens names which were not in the least flattering, discussed John the Baptist's anatomy in terms wholly flattering — and made lewd suggestions as to what the sleeping figure was dreaming.

On the night in question — that which followed Thomas of Woodstock's conversation with Edmund his brother — Richard was lying naked and lethargic upon the bed, his gaze directed, not at the tapestry, but at de Vere who was putting on an opulent silk robe preparatory to leaving.

"Robby — " Richard said suddenly, as if he had been giving thought to the question " — do you truly believe that the duke my uncle is plotting to kill me?"

"I fear so," de Vere replied carelessly. Surprised by the suddenness of the question, he was determined not to show it. "And methinks I know the reason."

"He covets the throne, do you mean? I sometimes ponder as to why my kingly grandfather elected myself as king, instead of his eldest surviving son."

"Maybe you do — and I dare say half England ponders with you," de Vere said absently — pausing for effect with one arm in and the other out of his robe. "But be assured that Gaunt's wishing to be rid of you has little or nothing to do with your grandfather and your being king, Richy — but everything to do with my being your lover!"

"Gaunt disapproves, do you mean?"

"Well, yea, there is that. Your being his nephew and king, he might disapprove, I suppose, in a minor sort of way." De Vere's tone was dismissive. "But the true honest-to-God reason for his wishing you dead, is that he covets your lover."

"He covets my lover, you say?" asked Richard incredulously. "Yourself, do you mean?"

"What a question, Richy!" sighed de Vere. "How many lovers have you, that you should ask such a question?"

"But . . . "

"Answer me truly, my lord — keep me not in suspense. Reveal all — and I swear to God I'll have slit the throat of every one of the rogues ere morning!"

But Richard had not been listening. He was still digesting de Vere's revelation with some incredulity.

"You are saying that John of Gaunt,

Duke of Lancaster — " Richard spoke as if there were a number of Johns of Gaunt and he suspected that de Vere had got the wrong one " — that he, like myself, is . . . "

"Yea," put in de Vere, words apparently having failed his companion. "Whither think you I am bound now, by God's grace — and in such indecent haste!"

"Methought . . . " It was at this point that Richard registered de Vere's expression. "Robby, you old reprobate — you are trying to provoke me!"

De Vere smiled wickedly and, his robe still open and revealing more than it concealed, gazed down mockingly at the bed and its naked occupant.

Thus they were when the disturbance came.

The John the Baptist tapestry, thrown violently awry by the opening of the heavy door it concealed — the which was kept always locked and the key held against emergency by Richard's master of the bedchamber — had collapsed on to the floor. The now-huddled needlepoint figures suggested a drunken orgy — only King Herod remaining unmoved, still rubbing his hands, huge-eyed and gloating. Two large spiders, disturbed and seemingly in a panic, scuttled, legs bent for speed, down the empty wall — one pausing for breath on a portion of John the Baptist's anatomy, a fact which, recounted with embellishments, was to entertain the de Vere set for several nights to come.

The half-fallen tapestry was somehow reminiscent of a curtain on a stage, such as was used for the court's Twelfth Night celebrations — with the star of the show a handsome smiling prince, satin-cloaked and bejewelled, his hand on his sword-hilt.

But this prince was not smiling and his hand was not merely resting on his sword-hilt, but had partially drawn the sword from its scabbard in a gesture more threatening than celebratory. This handsome prince meant business.

Both Richard and de Vere looked up in alarm, and the latter's right hand went spontaneously for his sword — before he recalled that he being in a state of undress, it was lying on a table a dozen or more feet away.

"So!" cried Thomas of Woodstock, the one word somehow suggesting both fury and challenge.

"My lord . . . " started to say Richard, but then he fell silent — leaving it open to debate whether he was addressing his uncle or invoking the Almighty.

"My lord of Woodstock — " said de Vere with a bow " — the king your nephew was saying just now how pleasant it would be to have you join us!"

Thomas glared at him. "Cover yourself, sir — the sight of your nakedness offends me. Cover yourself and then leave us — I would speak with the king alone."

De Vere obediently tied his robe but was uncertain whether, for Richard's protection, he should remain. Woodstock looks mighty vexed, he thought, and his method of gaining an audience is unorthodox to say the least. But already the latter had turned his glare upon Richard.

"Cover yourself, my lord," Thomas ordered the king. "God help you — indeed all of us — if you do not mend your ways. You disgust me, sire."

He heard de Vere leave the chamber

but guessed rightly that he was not far away.

Richard registered with no small alarm that Thomas had made no attempt fully to sheath his sword. He was on the point of calling for de Vere's return, when his uncle's voice stayed him.

"Summon that son of Sodom, and I shall slay you here and now," Thomas said furiously — and Richard was in no doubt that he meant it. "I came hither merely to give you warning but, finding you thus flaunting your depravity, I can scarce contain my wrath!"

"Might I remind your lordship that to brandish a naked weapon in the presence of one's sovereign is a crime punishable by death!" Richard spoke with a bravado he was far from feeling.

"Might I remind you, nephew, that I am not *brandishing* a naked weapon — in truth, I was as I recall the only one not doing so when I entered this chamber! However, to convince you that I am in earnest and that I care not an iota for your boyish plaints and threats, I *shall* draw my sword and we shall see."

As he suited the action to the word,

Richard blanched and made to move to the further side of the bed.

"Move not!" Thomas ordered. "Your Grace shall hear me out."

"I am listening, my lord," Richard said meekly enough. "Speak your mind and be done with it!"

"Take good heed of what I am about to say — I shall not again give you warning," declared Thomas — and so saying, he raised his sword and held the point less than an inch from the white-faced youth's chest. "I, Thomas of Woodstock, knight of this realm, shall slay any man, my lord the king and his sycophants not excepted, who attempts henceforth to impute treason to my brother of Lancaster!"

"I hear you, my lord — " Richard said earnestly " — and so be it. We have had our differences, John of Gaunt and I — but never have I seriously considered him a traitor."

"Glad am I to hear it," Thomas said coldly. "I shall away now, nephew — by the path I came."

"Glad am I to hear it, my lord," Richard parodied, smiling ruefully. "I fear

I shall never more look with equanimity on yonder tapestry!"

Thomas of Woodstock smiled, and the smile was as sunshine after rain.

"King Herod, I see, is standing firm," he said. "His reign was punctuated by feuds among his ten wives and their sons — I doubt Your Grace will achieve such notoriety!"

"I have but the one wife, my lord — and she means more to me than all the world!" Richard said — and Thomas heard with a mixture of feelings the warmth in his voice. "I sometimes think she is my one true friend."

"Beware your other friends, my lord — they are more dangerous to you by far than your foes!" Thomas, assailed by what he himself recognized as unreasonable jealousy, tried to speak dispassionately. "I once knew a Carmelite friar who could have vouched for that!"

"Are you friend or foe, *mon oncle*?" Richard was recovering his equilibrium — though the reference to the murdered friar troubled him.

"I love my brothers dearly," came the evasive reply — and Richard registered that the other had not answered the seemingly light-hearted question. "I love them and would, if the need arose, willingly give my life for them — pray remember that, sire."

13

NEXT came the Scottish campaign. This was seen throughout the land as a testing time of the king's ability as a warrior and leader, as well as of his courage and endurance.

Richard and Anne were separated for the first time by the campaign but, as events would show, happenings at home were to cause more dissension and debate in the realm than this particular extension of the war with Scotland.

The Scots had for some time been raiding the northern counties of England with impunity. Intelligence being received that they were planning with France a joint invasion of England by both sea and land, parliament decided to raise an army for the defence of the kingdom.

Charles, King of France, urged Robert, King of Scotland, to commence hostilities in the north — but the latter refused, preferring to wait until he received cognizance of a French landing in the south. He requested, however, a body of cavalry and to this Charles responded by sending John de Vienne, Admiral of France, with fifteen hundred men.

Richard resolved to march against the Scots in person and assembled with a large body of troops at Newcastle — a fleet of transports carrying provisions bringing up the rear.

He entered Scotland, advancing as far as Edinburgh and burning and pillaging as he went, only to learn that, even as he had been advancing on the east, thirty thousand Scottish and French troops had invaded England on the west. On the advice of his more experienced officers, he therefore changed direction, leading his men westward in order to intercept the enemy on its return.

The Scottish and French troops had meanwhile devastated the counties of Lancashire, Westmorland and Cumberland — afterwards returning with an immense booty to Scotland two days ahead of the English troops.

Richard by this time had wearied of the campaign. The long marches, the unpalatable food, the noise, the grime — even the panoply of war was alien to him. He yearned to return to court; to Anne and the company of his friends.

A few days later, having missed the chance of a lively encounter with the enemy and incurred much expense to no purpose, Richard returned with his disgruntled troops to England.

But progress with a sizable army is of necessity slow and it was during this time that there occurred the most remarkable and far-reaching incident of the campaign . . .

★ ★ ★

There was in the queen's household a Bohemian knight named Sir Meles, one highly regarded throughout the court for his courage and chivalry. He was Anne's own special knight, one who carried the queen's colours at joust and tournament and was responsible at all times for her personal safety. Anne customarily referred to or addressed him as 'my knight'.

Sir Meles had been part of Anne's life

for longer than anyone else at court. Before her father, the emperor Charles the Fourth had died, just prior to her departure for England, he had spoken to her of her forthcoming marriage and presented to her a valuable and unique gift.

"Sir Meles shall henceforth be your own knight, my daughter," the emperor had said — as the young man was ushered into the chamber where he was lying, mortally ill. "He has served me well and faithfully these twelve years past — a brave and valiant knight, skilful in fight, he is loyal and trustworthy to a degree. I shall better sleep the long sleep, child, knowing that Sir Meles will be your protector!"

Anne's smile was radiant as she had looked, first at Sir Meles, and then again at her father. She had been four years of age when the young knight, new then in the emperor's service, had taught her to ride a horse. His skill and patience, as well as his penchant for making her laugh, had won him a special place in her heart. 'My knight' she had called him then and the appellation had stuck — 'my knight' he was destined to remain.

Sir Meles, now thirty-five years of age and having a fine physique and dark good looks that set many a maiden's heart aflame, had remained in Prague until after the solemn obsequies which had marked the first anniversary of his royal master's death. Then he, too, had set sail for England — and the service of its new queen. He had been welcomed at the English court with much joy and some tears by Anne and her Bohemian entourage. Initially his lack of English had caused some difficulty — but his jousting skills, Anne's patronage, and his readiness to laugh at himself, had quickly made him a popular and colourful member of the court.

To Anne, Sir Meles was a link with the past, with her homeland and family, with those loved ones she had left behind for ever; one with whom she frequently conversed in her native language.

Richard had approved whole-heartedly of the new arrival, regarding him and referring to him as the queen's champion. Since it pleased Anne to have Sir Meles at court, it pleased him also. Such was ever Richard's philosophy in respect of his lady.

* * *

During the Scottish campaign, perhaps on account of her separation from Richard and the sense of loneliness it engendered, Anne kept much to her own apartments. She and Richard wrote regularly to each other during the months of separation. The exchange of letters, reminiscent of their correspondence prior to their marriage, brought joy and satisfaction to them both.

The practicality of such an exchange of letters was not without its dangers and complications, however. Travelling for many miles alone through enemy territory, or even through the ravaged counties of northern England, was out of the question and it was customary to have as escort a body of archers. Any lone English horseman was more than likely to be in no time at all a dead horseman — or, if captured, to be tortured in an attempt to force him to reveal the actual location of the English army.

It was to Sir Meles that Anne entrusted the task of courier. Accompanied by a body of archers, the knight rode to wherever the army happened to be at the time and, having delivered his royal mistress's letter to the king, returned in due course to court, bearing Richard's letter to the queen.

On one of these missions Sir Meles was returning with his escort from the north with a letter for Anne when, taking a rough but much-used path through woods, he came upon some horsemen he at once recognized by their livery, as of John Holland's household. Some were still mounted but others were sprawled across the narrow path, laughing noisily and seeming the worse for drink.

"Make way! Make way!" cried the officer in charge of the archers, signalling to his men to halt. "Make way for Richard of England's messenger."

The men on the ground looked up, stared balefully at the newcomers — and remained where they were.

"The king's messenger?" asked one, the leader, whom Sir Meles recognized as Alain de Glanville, a favourite squire of John Holland. The man turned boldly to Sir Meles who had the distinct impression that the meeting had been contrived. "Your name, sir?"

"Sir Meles, knight to the queen of England," came the reply. "And now, sir, if you please . . ."

"Sir Meles?" De Glanville turned with a grin to his companions. "Heard of him, have we not, lads? Why, we have here the queen's fancy man!"

"I fear you are the worse for drink, sir," remarked Sir Meles, keeping his temper with an effort and convinced by then that he had fallen into some sort of trap. The meeting was no coincidence — that was becoming more apparent with each passing moment. "I shall therefore for the time being ignore the insult to the Queen's Grace. Pray clear a passage — I am on the king's business."

"Christ save us!" De Glanville's ribald laughter echoed eerily through the woods. "Did ye hear that, my friends? The queen's fancy man claims to be on the king's business."

"What business be that?" asked one

of his henchmen, scratching his head consideringly. "I know not what — "

"You know not what, you say?" interposed de Glanville. "Then shall I tell ye. Since the king cannot as they say manage his own business and beget us an heir, who better than a Bohemian knight to do his work for him! I dare say — "

He got no further. Whatever it was that de Glanville dared say — he had already dared too much!

Sir Meles — with a speed that defeated the eye and gave credence to the legend that he was a peerless chevalier — drew his sword and plunged it with a minimum of movement and deadly accuracy through the slanderer's heart.

De Glanville died instantly and, as Sir Meles withdrew his blood-dripping blade, he fell sideways, crashing like a sack of turnips to the ground.

The dead man's companions gaped in dismay at their fallen leader but said nothing. Then they fell back, giving silent passage to the knight and his archers. Only one of their number recovered his speech in time to call after the fast-disappearing Sir Meles.

"My master, the Earl of Huntingdon, will have your guts for this, you Bohemian bastard!" he shouted hoarsely. "Why, he loved that one like a son — so you can take that message to your lady-love!"

Sir Meles rode on, careless of the threat and content that the slander had been avenged. He offered up a silent prayer that when John Holland learned of the matter and the slur on his half-brother and the queen, he would regard the punishment as well merited and the matter over and done with. Otherwise — and it was this that concerned the knight — it could well be that the queen would learn of the slander and be deeply distressed. Such an eventuality must be prevented at all costs.

But Sir Meles, it seemed, had been reared to a different code of knightly conduct from that of John Holland. To the former, the chivalric code was everything — sacrosanct, it governed one's life. Courtesy and considerate behaviour, especially towards women, were paramount. Those who flouted the code were anathema — and must be treated accordingly.

★ ★ ★

Nothing was heard or said of the incident for more than a week. Having delivered the king's letter to the queen, Sir Meles remained at Westminster for about eight days and then, furnished with another letter from the queen to her royal lord, he again made ready for departure.

Intelligence having informed him that the king and his army were making for York, he was on the point of again mustering an escort, when he was approached by Lord Ralph Stafford.

Now, Lord Stafford was a knight amongst knights; a young man of impeccable manners and courtesy, one greatly revered by the men who served under him. The only son of the Earl of Stafford, he had been brought up in the royal household, where his chivalric demeanour and his generosity to those less fortunate than himself had won him a place in the affections of all.

"Whither are you bound, my friend?"

he enquired of Sir Meles in the courtyard, where the latter was plainly making ready for a long journey. "Might I be of any service?"

"I am bound for wheresoever the king happens to be by the time I arrive!" smiled Sir Meles. "Roughly speaking for the north, my lord."

"Then, sir, might I suggest that we go a-searching for His Grace together? I am similarly bound for the north and I would count it an honour to have your company on the journey. Two heads are, as they say, better than one!"

"You are truly gracious, sir," said Sir Meles with a courtly bow. "I accept your offer most thankfully."

"Then, sir, if it please you to be ready for departure within — " Stafford paused consideringly " — say one hour, we shall set forth with my archers, you and I together."

Thus it came about. Two chivalrous knights of the royal household — the one Bohemian, the other English. A courteous invitation, a gracious acceptance — a happy arrangement. And the knights, as in all good fairytales, rode off into the sunset — or did they? This is, after all, not a fairytale, alas, alas!

The repercussions of this happy setting forth were to cause the death of at least two persons, bring about the exile of one, break the heart of another, and have dangerous consequences for the monarchy itself . . .

★ ★ ★

The weather was fine but not too warm, the muddy highways that criss-crossed England had hardened to a reasonable texture, and the two men — with a fine body of archers wearing the Stafford livery, and pack-horses laden with provisions, great-cloaks and changes of clothing — covered the first hundred miles without incident.

Cheerful and relaxed in each other's company, they talked of many things, laughed and jested — sometimes riding for many miles in companionable silence. They made good time and were approaching York when they espied, across the moors, a group of horsemen riding in their direction.

"Whom have we here!" said Stafford, in a the-more-the-merrier tone of voice. "Whosoever he be, the fellow is in a mighty hurry. Why, God bless him, 'tis John Holland!"

As Stafford raised his banner to indicate his identity to the leading horseman, Sir Meles remained silent. He too had recognized the horseman; and had registered with some uneasiness that he was advancing towards them at a furious pace whilst making no response to Stafford's friendly gesture.

"The fellow is certainly in a hurry," observed Stafford with interest, as John Holland and his men bore down on them. "Never does aught by halves, does my lord Holland — he'll be here one moment and gone the next. Perchance he brings us news of a glorious victory in the Borders!"

As John Holland drew rein only a short distance away, Stafford signalled to his men to halt.

"God's blessing on ye!" Stafford called pleasantly to the newcomer. "Are you the bearer of good tidings, my lord? Would one be correct in assuming that the commotion time is over — that the Scots have capitulated and Charles of France is now the king's prisoner!"

Sir Meles smiled at this piece of nonsense but his eyes were wary — and his right hand, as if of its own volition, moved convulsively towards his sword hilt. Already he had guessed what had brought John Holland there — and, having no wish to involve his gallant companion in a possibly violent encounter, he wished for the first time that he was journeying alone with his own body of archers.

"I have no quarrel with you, sir," John Holland told Stafford — but his expression was grim and his voice harsh. "'Tis yonder Bohemian knight for whom I seek."

"Meles at your service, my lord!" responded that gentleman genially — telling himself there was no point in meeting trouble half-way. "In what manner might I be of service to Your Lordship?"

"You, sir, are a murderer and a despot!" cried John Holland, beside himself with fury. "You slew in cold blood Alain de Glanville, my faithful squire."

Having no idea as to what it was all about but seeking to pour oil on troubled waters, Stafford spoke good-humouredly.

"My lord, I doubt not you are mistaken in your assertion and that it is not Sir Meles, the queen's knight, but another against whom you should voice your grievance." Stafford's tone was nothing if not conciliatory. "We were about to draw rein and take some refreshment — it would please me therefore to have Your Lordship join us. I have some fine burgundy wine with which to please your palate and — "

"Whither are you bound, sir?" interposed John Holland, ignoring the proffered hospitality.

"To the king, my lord — on the queen's business," replied Stafford — swallowing his chagrin at the other's hectoring manner.

"And the nature of that business?" demanded John Holland.

"Is none of yours," replied Stafford shortly. "Now, my lord — "

"Speaking for myself, my lord — "

interposed Sir Meles, determined that, should there be a confrontation as now looked likely, Stafford should not be involved " — I am entrusted with letters from the queen to the king."

"Then, sir knight, you had better hand them over whilst they are still in one piece. I shall deliver them to His Grace as soon as I have informed him of your demise!"

Stafford laughed heartily. "A good one, that — a fine jest. 'Tis well that I know you, my lord, or I might have taken you seriously! Now, as to the wine . . . "

"Pray desist, sir, from interfering," John Holland said unpleasantly. "I have no quarrel with you but only with this wretch here — with he who slew my faithful squire."

"I slew your squire, my lord, because he made treasonable utterances regarding the queen, whose knight and servant I am," Sir Meles said steadily. "I confess I have no regrets in the matter — as my lady's knightly protector, it behoves me to punish any who cast a slur upon Her Grace."

What happened next took place so

rapidly that the onlookers, Stafford's archers and John Holland's men-at-arms, watched in bewilderment.

Even as John Holland pressed spurs to his horse, he was simultaneously unsheathing his sword. Hell-bent on reaching Sir Meles and, as he saw it, avenging his dead squire, he rode furiously at the knight.

Stafford who, despite his outward calm, had been closely watching the encounter between the two men, immediately rapped out an order to his archers. As the archers smartly stepped forward to surround and protect Sir Meles, Stafford ostentatiously sheathed his sword before wheeling his horse and riding in between the two adversaries.

Thus, unarmed and conciliatory, his right arm raised in a staying gesture, he again made to address John Holland.

Sir Meles meanwhile, preferring to fight his own battles but having no choice on this occasion, aware that as a foreign knight any complaint made against him must be left to the king's jurisdiction, found himself and his mount ringed by grim-faced, raring to go archers.

"Out of my way, sir!" John Holland ordered Stafford, beside himself with fury as he realized that Sir Meles was to all intents and purposes beyond his reach. "The Bohemian is mine!"

"Desist, my lord!" cried Stafford. "Such conduct is unworthy of you!"

"Release the murderer to me, that I might mete out justice," insisted John Holland. "Protect him not, my lord — he is a scallywag of the first order and a seducer, I doubt not!"

"Watch your words, Holland," said Stafford with a calm he was far from feeling. "Sir Meles is under my protection — and that is where he shall remain, please God!"

"Enough!" raged Holland. "Since I am refused the one who did the deed — then, so be it, I'll take another! You, Stafford, shall pay the price of your interference!"

And so saying — even as Stafford reached swiftly for his sword — John Holland, livid with fury, raised his two-handed sword and smote Stafford a mighty blow that decapitated him.

As the dead knight crashed, headless,

to the ground, his archers gaped in shock and disbelief.

Then a unisonal roar of dismay and grief went up from the now leaderless men — a sound that seemed to pursue John Holland as, wheeling his horse, his men following, he rode swiftly from the scene . . .

14

THE Earl of Stafford, grief-stricken at the murder of his only son, at once petitioned the king for justice.

John Holland had meanwhile fled for sanctuary to the shrine of St John of Beverley. Richard, appalled by the circumstances of the incident but predictably dismayed by the need to commit his half-brother for trial, prevaricated. Public outrage, however, eventually prompted him to avow that, as soon as John Holland ventured from sanctuary, an act of exemplary justice would be performed on the murderer.

* * *

It seemed to Richard on his return from Scotland that the private wars and skirmishes within his kingdom, the enmities, jealousies and murders, put in the shade the war with his hereditary enemies, the Scots. The incursion into Scotland had been his first real test of leadership, his first taste of war — but, in the event, it had been little more than a skirmish or two, a series of punitive exercises intended to warn the Scots against further incursions into England. The expedition had been costly in monetary terms — but not in lives.

Richard returned to Westminster, eager to be reunited with those he loved and to resume a way of life which was more congenial to him by far than warfare.

Anne, as always, received him warmly. But after their initial greetings, Richard noticed her *distraite* manner. She seemed to be troubled by some inner conflict — as if there were something that must be said but about which she would if she could remain for ever silent.

"Is aught amiss, my lady?" he asked concernedly, as soon as they were alone. "Are you unwell — or in some way troubled?"

Anne registered his anxiety for her and, despite her sorrow, was gratified. My lord loves me, she thought — he truly loves me. Perchance now, after our separation, all will be well. Perchance very shortly . . ."

"I am in blooming health, my lord," she told him with the merest glimmer of a smile. "Nay, if you see concern in my gaze — an unwillingness to convey unwelcome news so soon after your return — be assured it has naught to do with she who is your devoted lady."

Something has happened to Robby de Vere, Richard told himself in alarm. Some ill-fortune has befallen he who is my beloved friend and companion. Robby is dead . . .

"The Earl of Oxford?" he asked — the sudden constriction in his throat giving away his alarm. "Is he — ?"

"Nay, my lord, the earl is well enough," Anne interposed, thrusting down her sense of resentment at his concern — a resentment she had spoken of to none and would, she had told herself, take with her to her grave.

"And what of the lady Joan?" enquired Richard. "Is she, pray, the cause of your anxiety?"

Anne hesitated, loath to speak of the matter so soon after his homecoming.

"Your lady mother is expecting you, my lord," she told him then. "She is in some distress and awaits you in her apartments here at Westminster — the matter is, she says, of the utmost urgency."

"Then news has reached her of my half-brother's crime," Richard said unhappily. "I must speak with her ere he leaves sanctuary."

"I understand that, on learning of your Grace's return to the capital, confident I dare say that you would deal leniently with him, the earl your half-brother left sanctuary and fled to the princess your mother's palace at Kennington."

"How in God's name could he be so heartless!" cried Richard. "In acting so, he has placed our mother in the position of harbouring a murderer — she neither would nor could refuse him refuge!"

"It did not come to that, my lord," Anne said quietly. "Even as Sir John entered the palace precincts, he was recognized and arrested — and lies now a prisoner in the Tower. Your lady mother is, needless to say, distraught."

Richard's heart sank. John, he thought, was ever an artful rogue! I love him dearly — was not he always my fond protector! Loving and loyal to a degree, he could none the less show jealousy of any who came between me and mine. I call to mind his open resentment of Robby de Vere. This time, I fear he has gone too far — public feeling is against him and, though I shall do my best to extricate him from his predicament, 'twill be no easy task. I had hoped to speak to my mother of this; explain the situation and the difficulties, and prepare her for the worst.

"And what of yourself, my lady?" Richard asked, watching Anne's expression consideringly. "Was not it Sir Meles, your knight, that Lord Stafford was protecting when he was slain?"

Anne averted her gaze but already Richard had seen her tears.

"It was indeed, my lord," she said with a catch in her voice. "But for Lord Stafford's gallantry, my knight would have been your half-brother's victim!"

"As soon as I am more suitably attired and have taken a small collation with my lady — and not before — " Richard spoke as lightly as he could — but

Anne heard the underlying heaviness in his voice " — we shall speak further of the matter. Then, and only then, shall I go to my mother."

* * *

Two hours later, Anne was seated companionably with Richard in her solar. The fire was bright, the chamber was warm and sumptuously furnished, and Anne was secretly hoping against hope that Richard after he had visited his mother, would pass the night with her. Perchance, she thought to herself — just as she had done so many times before — tonight will be *the* night . . .

"My lord — " she said suddenly, as if she had been mulling the matter over and now must speak or for ever hold her peace " — 'tis whispered about the court that this time your half-brother has gone too far — that, though he be the king's own kinsman, the law must take its course."

"This time, you say?" asked Richard, taking her hand in his.

"Many recall the murder of the

Carmelite friar, my lord," Anne reminded he who needed no reminding. "Needless to say, I have heard from Sir Meles himself how it was that day outside York — and how Lord Stafford died in protecting him."

"Sir Meles, I understand, had previously slain my half-brother's favourite squire," said Richard. "He claims to have done so in defence of Your Grace's honour."

"As was the case, my lord," said Anne defensively, her cheeks flushing. "As was indeed the case."

"Sir Meles has spoken to you of that also?"

"In general terms only, my lord. But I had my steward question one of the Stafford archers and there can be no doubt as to the veracity of Sir Meles's statement. He is a loyal and gallant knight — one whom, as Your Grace well knows, I hold in high regard."

"Such loyalty, my lady, can sometimes cause misunderstanding and jealousy in other courtiers," observed Richard. "They talk, not always guardedly — and thus false rumour and calumniation are spread."

"Sir Meles's knightly devotion to myself, my lord, is beyond reproach."

Richard nodded. That was indeed a fact. He knew it — they both knew it. Never for one moment did he doubt Anne's faithfulness to himself. Never did he have doubt of her love for him — whatsoever the nature of that love. He trusted her implicitly and, in his own way, loved her devotedly. Tales of ardent knights and love-lorn swains lay solely in the imagination of the teller, he told himself. The love he shared with Anne, stemmed from a desire to give each to the other the best opportunity of being at their best.

"John will stand trial," he said quietly. "Have no doubt of it, sweeting. The matter shall be fully investigated. I promise you."

"And the penalty, my lord, if he be judged guilty?" Anne could not resist the question.

"I refuse to consider such a possibility at this stage," Richard replied firmly. "Such would be to pre-judge the case."

"I posed the question, my lord — " Anne said quietly " — because the princess your mother will do likewise. I sought to warn you — that you might before you see her be furnished with an answer!"

"I know. I know," Richard said, fondly kissing her hand. "I shall have an answer ready when I see my mother, as will be very shortly. When I return, I shall speak with my advisers on the matter — and, I doubt not, on a myriad other matters of state!"

"In the morning, my lord," Anne pleaded. "I beg you leave such affairs till the morrow."

He looked weary, she thought. The campaign had been arduous for one unused to soldiering — but he had made no complaint of that. In the months he had been away, he had matured, she noticed — he looked older and there was a quiet strength about him that had not been there before. Perchance . . .

Richard smiled boyishly. "The morrow, 'tis said, never comes. I overheard Froissart saying as much only this afternoon, when someone was questioning him about the campaign. *It was said every day among us, we shall fight on the morrow,* he said, *the which day came never!"*

"Froissart or not, my lord, you need rest," Anne said with smiling tenderness. "Retire early and take your rest ere you burden yourself further. Your ministers can surely wait — only the princess your mother, I fear, cannot be set aside!"

He gazed thoughtfully at her and she flushed a little, wondering what he was thinking. Could it be that . . . ?

"Later, when I have spoken with my mother and my chief ministers, I shall indeed retire — to your chamber, if it please you, my lady."

Anne smiled, her cheeks dimpling in the way that fascinated her lord. She knew a tingling in her belly, an urge to lie with him, to feel his hands on her body . . .

"I shall welcome you most gladly, my lord," she said modestly lowering her gaze. "I rejoice in your safe return from the war. Be at peace, I pray you — your brother's present danger is, I dare say, but a passing shadow!"

15

RICHARD greeted his mother warmly. No one watching them together, could have doubted that they shared a deep affection.

After a separation of several months, Richard was struck by his mother's frailty. She who had been thrice married — lastly to Richard's father, the legendary Black Prince whom she had accompanied on a number of foreign campaigns — had been deeply affected by the brutal assault she had suffered during the Peasants' Revolt. She had never fully recovered her spirits and Richard was concerned as to the effect his half-brother's trial and possible execution would have on her.

Joan, Princess of Wales, asked Richard of himself and of the campaign — but she seemed abstracted, he noticed. Her gaze was restless and uneasy — as if her mind were overburdened with thoughts and fancies, each of them vying for dominance.

He seated himself beside her and they talked for a few minutes of ordinary family matters — of her grandchildren, of her continual prayers that he too would give her a grandchild, of her palace at Kennington and its peaceful meadows. Her hands, like her eyes, were restless and she absently twisted the jewelled rings on her fingers. Noting this, Richard took one of her hands in his and spoke gently to her.

"Pray tell me, *maman*, what ails you," he said, addressing her as he had since early childhood.

The tenderness in his voice, the touch of his hand, awakened memories — and opened the floodgates.

"You know, do you not?" she asked falteringly. "About John, I mean — you know that they have arrested him."

"It had to be, *maman*," Richard replied regretfully. "A nobleman was killed — whether by accident or design has yet to be established. The law, as we both know, must take its course."

"John was ever hot-tempered, as you are aware, my son. He loved Alain de Glanville — as a brother, he always said. Surely then, his slaying his squire's murderer was but an act of justice."

"John did not slay his squire's murderer," Richard pointed out. "He slew Lord Stafford who stood in the way of his slaying his squire's murderer."

"Lord Stafford stood in the way, you say? How very foolish of him! John's slaying him then must have been an accident."

"Maybe. Maybe," said Richard. "*Maman*, John is at present being held in an apartment in the Tower."

"Not in a dungeon?" Joan shuddered. "Tell me, if you can, that my son is not in a dungeon. I cannot bear to think . . . "

"Be assured that he is well accommodated and is provided with all his creature comforts," Richard told her. "Only his freedom is at present denied him."

"At present, you say? Then he is held but for a brief space." Joan's relief was plain. "He must remain a prisoner until his trial. After that, all will be well — that is your meaning, is it not?"

"After that, *maman*, is dependent upon

the verdict," Richard pointed out, wishing he could say differently. "Should John be judged guilty — "

"Judged guilty!" exclaimed Joan in dismay. "Nay, my lord king, you are surely forgetting of whom you are speaking — "

"We must wait and see," Richard firmly interposed. "There is no point in our discussing the matter further at this stage."

"But there can surely be no question of John being punished — that is to say, apart from his present imprisonment," persisted Joan.

Richard watched her, held as always by the still-beautiful face, the stately form. She had remained all that day in her chamber in *déshabillé*, refusing to see anyone save him and her servants. Her hair though threaded with silver, was still of an overriding fairness and flowed freely down her back just as he recalled it in childhood. But her eyes were swollen with much weeping and the hand in his still trembled a little.

"*Maman* — " he said with as much firmness as he could muster " — I refuse to speak further on the subject. We must wait for the verdict."

"Richard, my son, you never could conceal your thoughts from your *maman* — and certainly not when your heart were touched. Just then I heard the doubt in your voice, the anguish . . . " And with that, Joan fell into a fit of weeping.

"This is a fine homecoming!" Richard exclaimed ironically, seeking to change the subject. "Here is your youngest son, home fit and well from the wars — and there sit you weeping and gnashing your teeth as if your heart were broken!"

"Gnashing my teeth?" demanded Joan with a flash of her old fire. Her teeth, pearly-white and all present and correct, were remarkable in a woman of fifty-seven. "Richard, fair son, your *maman* has more respect for her teeth than to gnash them!"

Relieved to see that her mood had lightened, Richard stood up.

"I must away, my lady — there is much demanding my attention," he told her, kissing her on both cheeks. "My ministers and advisers wait on all sides to pester me with their questions and demands. I beg you be of good cheer — John's trial will be within a sevennight and, until then, we must bide our time."

"I shall pray unceasingly for his acquittal," Joan told him. "I shall beseech Our Lord to see justice done."

Acquittal? Justice? thought Richard. *Maman* speaks as if the words were synonymous — yet she surely knows in her heart that John is guilty and that his acquittal would be a travesty of justice.

"Pray for him indeed, my lady," he said, as he took his leave of her. "Pray that John Holland's luck will hold!"

16

RICHARD having managed to circumvent his attendants, made his way a few hours later by a little-used back staircase to the Earl of Oxford's opulent apartments in the palace of Westminster.

His visit would be brief. A greeting, an exchange of platitudes between comrades, no more, he told himself — afterwards he would, as arranged, betake himself to the queen's apartments, there to pass the night in connubial bliss.

Connubial bliss? Wedded contractually for a full five years to a charming young woman he held in deep affection, Richard knew a sense of guilt that the marriage was not in fact truly a marriage.

Despite their regard for each other, their intimate caresses and embraces, their joy in each other's company and a shared predilection for finery and ostentation, their marriage remained unconsummated.

He was just not made that way, Richard told himself. He loved Anne as he loved no other female — he enjoyed her companionship and knew that despite his failings she remained completely loyal to himself.

"He *liked* Anne better than anyone else at all. He needed an heir — heirs — and as time went by, the need would become greater, paramount. Questions would be asked, at first veiled and then, as the years passed, tactful, pointed — and then downright blunt.

The king's great-grandsire, his subjects would say to themselves and each other, he was *like that*. Was not Edward the Second married for four years to Isabella of France ere she bore him a child — God preserve us from another such as him! But this one, mark ye, has already passed five years of wedlock.

Yea, Richard knew what would be said, indeed what was already being said — and it troubled him deeply. Something must be done. First and foremost, he must separate himself from Robert de Vere and the latter's outrageously dissolute male friends. He must banish him, all of them, from court ...

Even as he gave life to the thought, his spirits sank. Robby? Send him away? Banish him, maybe for ever? God in Heaven, he thought, why am I thinking thus! With all his faults, Robby was the one he loved — passionately and devotedly he loved him. He believed Anne was aware of it and that she understood — Anne was an angel. She herself loved him, Richard, but whether or not with a woman's love for a man, vital and wholly carnal, or a maternal love as for a child, he had no means of knowing.

His love for Robert de Vere was on a different plane altogether. Their erotic encounters ofttimes left him uneasy, guilt-ridden — afraid for the future, of being found out. With Anne it was different. They were man and wife — they loved each other dearly, each expressing their love in their own way, she giving, he taking, and thus finding peace in each other's arms.

"So the warrior returns!" was de Vere's greeting when a male servant ushered Richard into the living-chamber of his magnificent apartments.

"As you say," said Richard, not sure if he liked the mocking note in the other's voice.

De Vere, Earl of Oxford and now Marquis of Dublin, had planned with his levies to follow the Scottish campaign. Lack of courage was not one of his failings. But the king's uncles and other leading barons, had made plain their opposition to the plan.

"Your Grace looks older," de Vere said flatly.

"I am older," came the cool reply. "The time before my departure seems part of another lifetime!"

"And how did playing at soldiers suit you?" enquired de Vere laconically. "From what I have heard, 'twas more like a game of hide-and-seek than serious warfare."

Richard, affronted but choosing not to show it, ignored the question. As he well knew, de Vere was trying to provoke him and, once having done so, would flatter and fawn on him until he became tractable, at which time de Vere could have his way in all things. It was the customary pattern, one familiar to them both, but on this occasion Richard had other plans. This was to be but a brief visit, a mere exchange of greetings between friends . . .

"It is good to be home," Richard said simply. "My lady is — "

"Home!" exclaimed de Vere amusedly. "By sweet St George! To hear you, Richy, one would imagine that you dwell in a ploughman's cot!"

"There are worse places, my friend — believe me, there are worse places than a ploughman's cot!"

"There speaks the expert!"

"On the campaign, my lord, one took rest and shelter where one could — a ploughman's cottage can seem like a palace to a rain-soaked man on the march!"

"Then — "

"As I was about to say a few moments ago — " pointedly interposed Richard " — my lady is as beauteous and gracious as ever, and my ministers declare on all sides that their sovereign was greatly missed and that his return is most welcome."

"A courtly reminder that they have a myriad papers for Your Grace to sign, I doubt not!" De Vere, who had in fact greatly missed Richard but was unwilling as yet to admit it, was determined not to give any quarter. "And what of brother John?"

"Brother John?" enquired Richard coldly. "I know none in holy orders of that name."

"I beg Your Grace's pardon. I was but making reference to your half-brother."

"Could you by any chance be referring to the Earl of Huntingdon, my lord?"

"Nay, the Duke of Exeter," retorted de Vere, giving John Holland his other title. "*Jesu Maria!* Did not I warn you that my lord would overstep the mark one of these days!"

"Curiously enough — " said Richard slowly, seating himself and indicating royally that de Vere might do likewise — an unnecessary gesture as, had the latter wished to be seated, as they both knew, he would not have waited for permission " — I recall the Duke of Exeter saying as much of a certain comrade of mine. The latter is still at large — but one wonders for how much longer!"

De Vere affected a shudder.

"The Princess of Wales, they say, is quite distraught — " he said, striking a pose " — fearing the worst for her *favourite* son."

This last provocation met with no response. Whatsoever Richard's doubts and uncertainties, he had absolute confidence in the leading ladies in his life; both loved him devotedly, were utterly loyal. In his womenfolk, he told himself, he was blessed beyond his deserving. Jealousy therefore was not one of his weaknesses, and never would be.

"It is as you say, my lord," he replied carelessly. "I must therefore bid you a good night and shall return to my lady mother's apartments, there to console and comfort her in her distress."

"Much ado about nothing!" declared de Vere — the reunion was not going quite as he had planned. "The duke your half-brother will get a rap over the knuckles from the justices — and then the whole affair will blow over."

"You could be right, my lord,"

Richard said laconically, standing up and preparing to make his departure. "None of us is wrong all the time. Either way, I bid you a good night."

De Vere had difficulty in concealing his astonishment — or could it be disbelief?

"But you will return later, my lord, will you not?" he asked. "You will surely not be holding the princess your mother's hand all night!"

"The queen is expecting me," Richard said quietly. "We have been separated these many months past, she and I, and our reunion is a great joy to us both."

"Then . . . " De Vere, seeing Richard's expression, did not put the question — but it was there clearly enough in his tone and manner.

But Richard would not be drawn. Open as was conversation and discussion in general between himself and de Vere, he never spoke of the queen other than in general terms or gave hint of his personal relationship with her. De Vere therefore could only conjecture — and frequently did.

Totally loyal to each other, sharing an unfulfilled relationship whilst still presenting a picture of a devoted couple, Richard and Anne and their marriage were the subject of continuing speculation. Only as time passed and the queen continued to show no signs of producing a child — the much-needed heir — did speculation amongst Richard's subjects turn to alarm.

17

IT was approaching midnight and the end of a long day when Richard, wearing a ruby red velvet robe, made his way to the queen's bedchamber. Of a style which he himself questionably termed plain, the robe was lavishly embroidered with gold thread, and fastened with a single gold brooch set with emeralds and rubies. He had removed most of his rings, wearing only a gold signet ring set with a large emerald, and another of gold with diamonds and rubies.

A minimum of candles was burning in the bedchamber and Richard thought at first that Anne, having assumed he was not coming after all, had settled down for the night.

But the bed was empty and, as his gaze penetrated the dimness, he saw a still figure sitting on the couch in front of the glowing log fire — a figure which in no way announced its presence.

Without speaking, he seated himself beside his queen. He sighed involuntarily — a sigh of happiness, of perfect peace. He was home. Anne epitomized home. With Anne there was calm, warmth, sensuality of a kind — and the joy of two beings who had absolute trust in each other.

He gently took one of her hands and raised it to his lips, still saying nothing but savouring the joy and happiness of his homecoming.

"I have missed you, my lord," Anne said then, breaking the easy silence. "I dreamed of this reunion."

"I dared not dream," Richard said candidly. "The awakening to reality would have been too painful. Soldiering, alas, is not for me! I fear I am as unlike my father and grandfather as could be!"

"And your great-grandfather?" Anne enquired softly, and there was no accusation in the question. "Are you perchance of his ilk?"

Richard looked thoughtful. "The second Edward, my great-grandfather, begot two sons — though many believed the second was not of his begetting."

"Please God you too will beget sons, my very dear lord," Anne said softly, a trifle breathlessly. "You are but in your twenty-first winter and I dare say I shall very shortly with God's help and yours, be with child."

He pressed his lips to the palm of her hand and registered the ripple of pleasure that ran through her body. He kissed her other hand likewise and then the outline of her breasts through the silk fabric of her gown.

She was in his arms then and he sensed the tension in her. He watched her wonderingly, seeing the long flowing hair, the luminosity of her eyes in the candlelight and the full-lipped sensual mouth.

"Your hair looks red-gold in the firelight," he told her wonderingly. "Pale gold by day, it becomes a fiery mane at night!"

"We all of us have a night-time self, my lord," she said quietly. "We all of us have a side we show only to special people — those we love and whose lives we are privileged to share. We all of us have our ways of loving — our ways of being pleasured, of giving pleasure."

He kissed her and, in a gesture that was at once inviting and submissive, she unfastened her bodice and put her arms around his neck.

With that, he took her hand and led her over to the great bed — that which with its royal coat-of-arms, its steps and boxed sides, was the one which, though differently furnished, had belonged to King Edward his grandfather, and on which it was said the latter had begotten on Queen Philippa all but three of his twelve children.

As chivalry demanded, Richard took off his remaining rings and, dropping them carelessly on to a nearby table, climbed naked into the bed.

Anne watched him for a few moments in silence. How beautiful he is! she thought — the warrior has returned, but in truth he looks more like a golden-haired angel. Her body ached for fulfilment; for a lover who would rid her of her maidenhead and make her truly a woman — a wife and a mother.

"Love me, my lord, I pray you," she whispered. "I want you so much — and you have need of a son. God grant that this be the night!"

As Richard kissed her and lovingly stroked her hair, Anne clasped her arms around his neck and drew him closer, returning his kisses and knowing a mounting sense of excitement.

Conscious then of her naked breasts pressing against his chest, Richard had a sudden and almost uncontrollable urge to push her away, to ask her to wait, to wait . . . Quelling the urge, he kissed her lips and her throat, and whispered sweet nothings to her, assuring her of his undying love . . .

But then, as she drew his head down and fed one of her nipples into his mouth, again he knew an urge to push her away, to free himself, to leave her bed and never return . . .

He had a sudden and disconcerting vision of de Vere — of de Vere watching him, laughing at him . . .

Why think I of Robby now? he asked himself angrily. I love Anne more than anyone else in the world — and yet here and like this, I give thought to another. Why do I have a desire to hurt her, punish her for urging me to make love to her! Why cannot she be calm, cool, practical about the matter . . .

Anne gave a small involuntary cry of pain. He was hurting her and she tried half-heartedly to push him away. But it was no use. Either she lacked the will so to do — or his will, differently motivated, was predominant . . . Conscious of mingled pain and pleasure and the animal satisfaction of suckling this beautiful golden-haired man-child — this being she loved as she loved no other — she gave freely of herself.

Richard cared not any longer whether he pleased or offended. He wished only to be free of this charmer. If she loved him, he told himself, she must accept him as he was. Robby de Vere was his lover. He needed no other. Robby knew how to pleasure him — how to bring him to the heights of ecstasy. With Robby there were no strings attached — no duty to one's posterity, no forcing oneself to attempt that which was repugnant . . .

Richard's male egoism was such that, not for one moment did he consider that, since he could clearly not satisfy his lady's needs and his country's needs, she too might take a lover, an eager and able lover. Already there was one waiting in the wings, straining at the leash — one who carried in his veins the king's own Plantagenet blood, and was ready and willing to do his work for him . . .

Her passion mounting, Anne drew him closer, abandoning herself to his embrace . . . But in one sudden movement he drew away from her and threw himself down on the bed beside her.

There would be no child for a while, that much was certain. But there is plenty of time, Anne told herself firmly, trying to stem her tears. I am a virgin still — but some night, God willing . . .

"I do love you," Richard said defensively, breaking the long silence. "I really do love you."

"And I you, my lord," Anne responded — but there was an emptiness in her voice which troubled him. "You are all things to me — lord, master, husband and king."

But not her lover! thought Richard guiltily. All things save her lover.

He drew her into his arms and kissed her gently, almost reverentially. They lay together then, side by side, for a long time without touch or caress.

Anne must have fallen asleep, for she awoke with a start some time later to find Richard's arm protectively encircling her.

"Then you are still here, my lord," she said in surprise. "It must be near daybreak."

"I am still here, sweeting," he replied, kissing her cheek.

"But usually, when we have lain together, you return forthwith to your own apartments," Anne reminded him who needed no reminding.

Aware as she was of the identity of him who drew her lord from her, she was uncertain as to the true nature of their relationship.

Richard was in fact guilt-ridden at the knowledge that he had, albeit unwittingly, allowed thoughts of de Vere to come between them. He smiled ruefully.

"Does it trouble my lady that her lord did not make an early departure?" he asked, watching her expression. "Is that the reason for her surprise?"

"But your friends — "

"Are simply my friends," interposed Richard. "You are my lady and very dear wife."

"Then the Earl of Oxford — "

"Means naught to me," Richard said firmly, and his own words surprised him. For he knew in his heart that however much he might wish otherwise, the statement was untrue — and that very shortly he would go to de Vere and make his peace with him. Yea, he would give up de Vere eventually, but not yet, not that day or the day after . . . "He is but a comrade, a cousin by marriage — one not to be compared with my own, my very own beloved lady!"

18

RICHARD did not in fact visit Robert de Vere the next evening — nor for several evenings after. Affairs of state pressed heavily upon him and the approaching trial of John Holland was seldom out of his thoughts.

On the night following the trial and the feared but not unexpected verdict of guilty, however, he put aside other matters and went to de Vere's apartments. Shocked by the realization that his beloved half-brother's life lay in the palm of his hand, unable as yet to face the fact and give the order for the prisoner's execution, avoiding both his mother and his wife, he looked to de Vere for solace.

De Vere, genuinely concerned for him and his predicament, at once recognized his need. He had guessed that Richard, whilst apparently keeping away from him of late, would come to him that night.

"My liege — " he said dramatically,

falling on his knees before Richard, as the latter was shown into his library " — I would that I could adequately express my grief at the verdict upon the Earl of Huntingdon, your half-brother!"

"What am I to do, Robby?" Richard asked, his brown eyes melancholy and distressed. "He is indeed my half-brother and, despite his faults, I love him dearly. The princess my mother — "

"There is only one thing to be done," put in de Vere, who had little liking for the Princess of Wales who made no secret of her disapproval of himself and his friends — and their influence upon her son. "Appalled as we both are, we must put the matter from our minds this night."

"Put the matter from our minds, you say?" demanded Richard. "Such is easy enough for yourself, I dare say — but for myself, an impossibility!"

"There is only one impossibility, it seems to me — " de Vere told him " — that being to believe in one's own death!"

Richard shuddered ostentatiously. "Speak not of death, I pray you — not tonight of all nights. The day long, I have been contemplating the death of a much-loved half-brother and the effect it would have upon the princess my mother. I fear that John's execution would destroy her also."

"Sorrowful as she would be, and grieve as she undoubtedly would — " de Vere said " — the princess would come to terms with it in time. Females, it seems to me, are more resilient than we choose to believe."

"Females, you say?" asked Richard coldly. "I will have you remember that the lady in question is not 'females' — she is the king's mother!"

"My lord, be at peace, I beg of you," de Vere said in his most winning tone. "Let the matter rest, if only for a few hours."

"Help me, my lord," Richard said then, his eyes bright with tears. "I feel so alone, you see. The decision must be mine, God have pity, mine alone!"

De Vere put an arm protectively around him.

"We shall speak no more of the matter tonight, my lord. I, Robert de Vere, declare it!" he said firmly. "Together we shall speak of many things, but not of that — it is forbidden. Instead, we shall laugh and gossip, as has ever been our wont. But of that which grieves you so deeply, we shall not speak."

"But — "

"But me no buts, sire," interposed de Vere. "Come, be seated — and my servant shall bring us wine!"

"My heart is filled with sorrow, my lord, and — "

"Tonight we shall drown our sorrow in wine and merriment — " again interposed de Vere " — in the coupling of our bodies and the joys of true love and comradeship."

"Hearken to me, Robby." Richard spoke with uncustomary earnestness and de Vere, who believed he could read the king like a book, assumed rightly that the earnestness had something to do with Richard's lady. "I have resolved — "

"Were you, my sweet prince, to solve each and every problem as it arose, there would be no need for a re-solve!"

"Hearken to me, my lord." Richard was a little on his mettle and there was a twinkle in de Vere's eyes as he looked at him. "I have, as I said — "

"Ah, here is Maurice with the wine!" The servant's entry, as far as de Vere was concerned, was well-timed — and as soon as the man had gone, he gave all his attention to the wine. Richard, his sentence half-completed, shrugged expressively and gave in. Always was it thus with him and de Vere — and in truth, whatsoever others might think and say, it was the way he wanted it.

"The wine, my lord, is laced with certain herbs," de Vere was saying. "Certes it will help us to forget for a while our trials and tribulations!"

19

RICHARD called a meeting of the Privy Council on the following morning. The chief matter on the agenda was the verdict of guilty on John Holland and the sentence which, since the prisoner was a blood relative of the king, was the prerogative of the monarch himself.

The mandatory punishment for murder, of which John Holland stood convicted, was death — by hanging if the prisoner were of the commonalty, or by the axe or sword if of the nobility.

The verdict had been unanimous and John Holland himself, confident of his brother's protection, had made no attempt to deny his culpability. The king his brother, he told himself, would not permit his execution — banishment from the realm for life being the possible alternative. What was in the prisoner's opinion more likely, was banishment from the court — until such time as

Richard judged that his subjects had elected to forget the matter. But what then of the Earl of Stafford, he who had been robbed of his only son? Ah well, said John Holland complacently to himself, there is no cause for alarm there. The earl being weighed down by distress at the loss of his son, has become ill, it is said, and is himself close to death!

John Holland's amoral view was not shared by the Privy Council.

"Holland must die!" said Arundel without prevarication. "He has taken the life of a nobleman of high repute and must pay the penalty."

"Leniency would suggest that the king disagrees with the law of the land — " pointed out Edmund of Langley " — and that, where his own relatives are involved, they might do as they please!"

"My lords, I am not advocating that the Earl of Huntingdon go scot-free," Richard said coldly. "Only that the sentence be commuted to banishment or imprisonment for life."

"Banishment?" snorted Norfolk. "Banish the wretch and, as soon as our backs are turned, he'll be slinking back into the country to see who else's son is ripe for slaughter!"

"Banishment? Piers de Gaveston was banished!" remarked Mowbray with relish — and a consummate lack of tact. "Did not do him much good — was assassinated later on Blacklow Hill!"

"There was provocation in this case, my lords," Richard said mildly enough. "In my opinion, quite severe provocation."

"Permit me to remind Your Grace that the jury did not think so." That was John of Gaunt. "They saw the accused, rightly in my opinion, as a villain."

"The Earl of Huntingdon is loyal to the Crown," pointed out Richard. "None more so, my lord."

Sir Simon Burley was the next to speak. Now in his fifty-first year, he had attended the Black Prince in Aquitaine and had later been made guardian and tutor to Richard. Highly regarded as a man of integrity and honour, Burley was criticised by some — notably the royal uncles — for having encouraged the king's appreciation of the arts rather than of warlike pursuits.

Richard looked expectantly at him as

he rose to his feet, believing that here was an ally. Burley, he reasoned, would convince his peers of the unwisdom of destroying the king's half-brother — on the basis that, in casting doubt upon the stability and the morals of the king's family, they cast doubt upon the king himself.

But Richard was in for a disappointment.

"The Earl of Huntingdon is loyal to the Crown, says my liege," Burley said evenly. "All praise to His Grace for his championship of his family! But some of us recall how, several years since, on the eve of the sacking of the Tower of London by rebellious peasants, the said earl together with his brother, Sir Thomas Holland, did contrive to escape from the embattled fortress and take refuge on his estate in the country — leaving the king, his half-brother, a youth of but fourteen summers, unsupported by his close relatives and at the mercy of the mob!"

There was a stunned silence at this and all heads turned to look at the king. The words, delivered in a benign impassive tone, were none the less a damning indictment of John Holland's character.

Richard met the probing gaze of his councillors with apparent calm, but inwardly he was seething with fury.

Never, he told himself, would he forgive Burley for bringing further discredit upon John Holland. His half-brothers had but left the Tower to gather reinforcements elsewhere — as they had afterwards explained. He none the less recalled with a clarity which surprised him — and did Burley no favours — his own sense of shock and betrayal when he had learned of the brothers' departure.

"Let us keep to the point, my lords," he said icily. "The Earl of Huntingdon has been convicted of the murder of Lord Stafford. How then, gentlemen, should the said earl be punished?"

"By death, sire," said John of Gaunt.

"Death by the axe," said Arundel.

"Execution, sire," said Thomas of Woodstock.

"There is no real choice, sire — the fellow must die!" That was Warwick.

There was general agreement on this. Only Burley, Richard noticed, despite his indictment of John Holland, had failed so far to declare his vote.

"And what of you, sir?" he enquired of his former tutor.

Burley appeared to hesitate — but only for a moment.

"Death by beheadal, sire," he said quietly then. "There is, as has been said, no acceptable choice, alas!"

"Unless Your Grace, mindful of the ties of kinship, elects to exercise the royal prerogative of mercy," put in Michael de la Pole, Earl of Suffolk — the king's private secretary and most trusted adviser.

"Such would be most unwise!" roundly declared the irrepressible Arundel. "Unwise to the point of folly."

"Unwise, sir?" enquired Richard with raised eyebrows. "Unwise — and to the point of folly? We pray you remember to whom you are speaking."

"Unwise for the monarchy," persisted Arundel without batting an eyelid. "The sovereign must always be seen as defender of law and order. The eyes of many will be upon Your Grace when your decision is announced."

"He is my brother," Richard said

quietly. "John Holland is my brother."

"With respect, sire — the earl is your half-brother," said Michael de la Pole apologetically. "He is not of royal blood."

"He is my mother's son, my lord."

There was silence at this. All there remembered that it was the Princess of Wales's pleas which had persuaded Richard, against the advice of his ministers, to open the gates of the Tower of London to the rebellious peasants — thus causing a blood-bath and the brutal assassination of the chief ministers of the Crown.

"We naturally feel for the Princess of Wales at this time," said Burley, but he avoided the king's steely gaze. "But Her Grace's judgement in the matter is understandably clouded by ties of blood."

"Quite so," said Arundel with enthusiasm. "Quite so, sir."

"One recalls the siege of the Tower and how the Princess of Wales prevailed upon Your Grace to give the order that the gates be opened to the rebels," tactlessly remarked the treasurer, whose predecessor had been hacked to death by the mob. "Yea, one indeed recalls the siege!"

Their minds were made up. For once, Richard's ministers thought as one, spoke as one. Nothing but John Holland's blood would satisfy them. He had struck down without provocation a member of the nobility — such a crime could not go unavenged.

"My lords, now that I know you are of one mind, there is no more to be said." Richard, clearly displeased, made ready to leave. "I shall give further consideration to the matter and will in three days' time inform Your Lordships of my decision."

20

IF Richard's meeting with the Privy Council had been disturbing, the interview which followed was distressing in the extreme.

His mother was awaiting him. Dressed entirely in black, as if already she was in mourning for her son, Joan Princess of Wales was wearing no jewellery save her wedding ring and a long gold neck-chain with a pendant gold pectoral cross set with pearls. She looked dazed, a little vacant, as if, finding herself caught up in a nightmare, she must keep silent and aloof, looking only to awakening and the end of her torments.

"Have I disturbed you, *maman?*" Richard asked as he entered her solar and kissed her fondly. "You look nigh to slumber."

"I doubt I shall ever slumber again, my son," Joan said wearily. "When next I close my eyes in sleep, 'twill be that long, long sleep from which none awakens!"

"*Maman*, I cannot keep the truth from you," Richard told her as he sat down. "I would that I could spare you the pain of such knowledge — but, alas, it is not possible!"

"Then the Privy Council is without mercy?" Joan asked on a sob. "They would have you destroy your own brother?"

"Yea, that is so," Richard said sadly. "It is even so."

"But you will refuse." It was not a question — but a statement born of the unthinkable. "You, my son, will banish John from court — from the realm even — but that you would give the order for your own brother's execution, is incredible."

"*Maman*, I . . . " The hand he was holding was trembling with agitation and Richard paused, seeking for the right words.

"Nay, you would not be so cruel," Joan continued. "Why, I recall your birth, how your brothers came to see you — and even to this moment, I can picture the joy and wonderment on John's face as he gazed down at you and held your tiny hand."

"*Maman*, I beg you . . ."

"'I shall love and protect him for ever and a day, *maman*,' he told me and his smile, as I recall, was that of an angel. Now he has fallen into misfortune and you, that once-innocent babe —"

"Madam my mother, I have no choice," put in Richard, trying to contain his grief. "John has been lawfully tried and judged guilty. Were I to banish him from the kingdom, as is indeed my prerogative, I myself should be judged — as a weak king who fails to uphold the law. Were I so to do, it would augur ill for the future. Would you see him who is only son to the Black Prince, your lord and husband, dethroned; and another, a more ruthless monarch perchance, put in his place?"

"You exaggerate, my son." Joan's tone was dismissive.

"Would that I did! Rumour assails me on every side. My cousin Henry, son to John of Gaunt, my uncle, covets my throne, it is said — he makes his plans, plotting my downfall."

"Nonsense!" Joan said sharply — recognizing the truth of what he said but unwilling at that time to acknowledge it. "Richard, fair son, your subjects love you, as well you know. Why, they echo the words of the chronicler Froissart, *Tall and fair among men even as another Absalom!* Whensoever you ride through the streets of the City, 'Absalom! Absalom!' goes up the cry."

"Many of my subjects are none the less of the opinion that Edward the Third, my grandfather of happy memory, would better have willed his crown to John of Gaunt and his heirs, than to a boy of ten summers who had spent most of his life in France."

There was a bitterness in Richard's voice which Joan had not heard before. She watched him, confused and disbelieving — concerned only for the son she saw as a victim rather than a criminal. Richard had been misinformed, she told herself. He was exaggerating — he must be exaggerating.

"Have pity, my son," she whispered. "Only have pity for him — for myself!"

"*Maman*, were I to show leniency to my kinsman and thereby be seen as condoning murder, many would turn from me, declaring that I am unfit to rule."

Joan was a little on her mettle. "Richard, my son, there are more reasons than one why some of your subjects would have my lord of Gaunt's heir, Henry of Bolingbroke, as their king! They have taken your lady to their hearts but, after some five years of wedlock, still there is no sign of an heir. Rumour has it that you yet remain much in the company of the Earl of Oxford and his evil associates."

"Evil associates?" asked Richard with the merest hint of a smile. "Dearest *maman*, sweetest *maman*, I do love you — but you do exaggerate just a little! There is naught evil about — "

"Evil I said, and evil I meant," Joan insisted. "Were your time-honoured sire with us still, think you — "

Richard sighed. He had heard it all before.

"If you recall, madam my mother, we were speaking of the Earl of Huntingdon's sentence — " he interposed with unwonted coldness " — not of the Earl of Oxford's associates."

"I wished you to understand that it is your choice of friends, together with your lack of an heir, which has set your subjects' tongues a-wagging — rather than your loyalty to your brother!"

"Maybe. Maybe," Richard said wearily. "But I pray you to understand, *maman*, that I have no choice in regard to John. The crime he committed, God forgive him, merits death!"

"What of the royal prerogative of mercy, my prince?" asked Joan. "Or is mercy no longer seen as a heavenly virtue in this new-thinking land of ours!"

"Were there extenuating circumstances, I would use the royal prerogative," Richard told her. "There is, according to the evidence, none. John apparently had no quarrel with Lord Stafford. He had a grievance against Sir Meles — but Stafford, protecting my lady's knight, stood in his way. Stafford was slain in front of many witnesses — there can be no doubt of John's culpability. He must pay the price, alas, alas!"

Joan, seeing his determination, her last

hope gone, broke into a paroxysm of weeping.

Richard tried to comfort her but she drew away from him.

"Leave me!" she cried. "Leave me. So self-righteous and uncaring are you, that I cannot bear to look upon you. He is your *brother*, Richard — "

"My *half-brother*," corrected Richard unwisely — for it somehow suggested that it was the other half which had committed the crime!

"He is your *brother*," repeated Joan with emphasis, anger for a moment overcoming sorrow. "Your very own brother. Even now, I cannot believe you will see this deed done. Begone, I pray you — return only when you have had a change of heart."

"*Maman*, dearest *maman*, I beg you as I love you to try — "

"Go, I say!" Joan cried bitterly. "I cannot bear to look upon he who has hardened his heart against his brother, looking only for revenge."

"Nay, not revenge — by my faith, not revenge!" Richard said passionately. "Justice, *maman* — justice."

213

But Joan had turned her back on him and the sounds of her weeping followed Richard as, torn between love and duty, he quietly went from the chamber.

21

"ANOTHER day has passed and still the princess my mother refuses to see me." Richard's tone was aggrieved and somehow suggested that the ways of the female sex were beyond his comprehension. "What should I do, my lady? I have not yet given the order for execution but I cannot any longer dally. On the morrow, I must announce my decision."

"You have no choice, my lord," Anne said quietly, concerned for his concern. "I too had a fondness for the earl but — "

"Had, you say?" interposed Richard. "My half-brother is still with us — or so I have reason to believe."

"In using the past tense, my lord, I was not referring to your half-brother himself — but to my fondness for him." Anne was a trifle on her mettle. Her grief and anger at the loss of Lord Stafford, a flamboyant and popular member of her household, far outweighed any sympathy she might have felt for John Holland. "I find it difficult to ignore the fact that it was not Ralph Stafford, but Sir Meles, my knight, whom your half-brother intended to kill that day. I pray Your Grace remember that an unprovoked attack on a member of the queen's household is an attack upon the queen herself!"

Richard was taken aback by her strength of feeling in the matter. Never before had she failed to see his point of view.

"Unprovoked, you say, my lady — " He spoke quietly, reasonably " — but was it in truth unprovoked? If provocation be the keynote, then perchance Sir Meles himself should be indicted, since it was he slew Alain de Glanville."

"My knight was but defending the queen's honour, my lord — " Anne reminded him, " — which was, as Your Grace knows, both his right and his duty. Those who witnessed the happening, speak with one voice."

Richard watched her for a few moments, his expression unfathomable.

"Then you would I should give the

order for my half-brother's execution?" he enquired then.

Anne's hesitation was momentary. "Flying in the face of justice and public fury would, I fear, do Your Grace immeasurable harm."

"The princess my mother, alas — "

"Is in poor health," put in Anne. "I visited her today and did my best to comfort her — but how does one console a mother for the impending execution of her offspring! God grant that, once the deed is done, the princess will accept the fact that you, my lord, had no real choice."

"My lady has sent word to me that she is setting forth today for Wallingford Castle, there to pass the remainder of her life in seclusion," Richard told her. "She expects, indeed wishes as she reiterates, not to see me again — since, as she expresses it, I am bent on the destruction of my half-brother."

Anne heard the anguish in his voice; saw his distressed gaze. He was willing her to side with the lady Joan, to plead for the life of John Holland. Torn between sympathy and expediency, aware of the political outrage that would result from Richard's display of partisanship for the murderer, Anne steeled herself to make reply.

"It is better thus," she said practically. "Her distress is your distress — and makes doubly difficult your final decision. At Wallingford, away from the press of court life, she will in time, please God, come to terms with the situation!"

★ ★ ★

Richard and Anne went together into the courtyard to see his mother and her retinue on their way.

Joan, heavily veiled and wearing unrelieved black, spoke but a few words to Richard in farewell.

"From this moment I shall pray without ceasing for Your Grace's change of heart," she said, and Richard heard tears in her voice. "Two days from now, we shall both know your final decision. If it be against your brother, then, my son, never again in this life will you set eyes on she who bore you both and loves you both. May Our Lord have you in his keeping!"

With that, she nodded to her steward and the order for departure was given. She herself, her frailty increased through sorrow and lack of sleep, was being conveyed in a horse-drawn litter.

Richard and Anne watched her go — though already the curtains of the litter were firmly closed. They watched with heavy hearts, eyes bright with unshed tears, until the sombre cavalcade was out of sight.

"The lady Joan meant not what she said," Anne told Richard, as together they turned their steps towards the palace. "You will see her again, and very shortly I doubt not — as soon as she accepts that you have no real choice."

"Nay, my lady," Richard said brokenly, avoiding her gaze. "*Maman* meant what she said. For one reason or another, I shall not see her again — not in this life!"

"The princess has suffered much personal sorrow during her life," Anne reminded him. "Edmund of Woodstock, Earl of Kent, her father, was himself executed, and both the Black Prince her husband and his elder son died prematurely. She came to terms with those misfortunes — she will do likewise with this."

"Maybe this will be the last straw," Richard said gloomily.

"It will be as I said, my very dear lord," Anne insisted. "You will see!"

Richard slowly shook his head.

★ ★ ★

On the following day, Richard called a further meeting of the Privy Council. He had made his decision — not without much heart-searching and hoping against hope that some miracle would occur which would enable him to change his mind.

John Holland, Earl of Huntingdon and Duke of Exeter, his half-brother, would, he told a hushed meeting, be beheaded five mornings hence, one hour after daybreak.

A total silence greeted Richard's announcement. Many of those present had expected a royal pardon, and had come there fully prepared to make a strong protest. As it was, most knew compassion for him. The hearts of his councillors were touched. He is no longer a mere lad, they said to themselves — he shows himself to be a man full grown, one who makes decisions, difficult decisions, with wisdom and foresight. He has set aside his personal feelings and interests, for the good of the realm. Bravo! Well done!

As Richard left the chamber, his heart was heavy within him. He could think of nothing save the enormity of what he had done. Whatsoever John Holland's faults — and none could deny they were many — in the final analysis it was he, Richard, who held the power of life and death over him. It was he who was sending him to the block . . .

He made his way to the chapel of St Stephen and, ordering his bodyguard to remain outside, entered his private oratory. He knelt at his prie-dieu, not to pray but to regain his composure — come to terms with his own personal sense of guilt. Pictures of John Holland in childhood floated across his mind: of John giving him a pick-a-back, smiling, laughing, singing a rumbustious song, lifting him up to ride in front of him on his charger . . .

Richard heard a soft step behind him. He turned angrily, expecting to see one of his bodyguards bringing him a message or a minister who wished to speak urgently to him . . .

"Anne!" he exclaimed, swallowing the angry words that hovered on his lips. "Wherefore are you here, my lady?"

"I am here, my lord, because I would not let you hear the words from another," came the answer, and Richard saw then that already her eyes were red with weeping. "The words stick in my craw, alas — as did yours not half an hour since."

"*Maman?*" he asked — but of himself rather than Anne. "You have come to tell me that the princess my mother is unwell?"

Anne fought for composure.

"She passed away in her sleep," she said simply then, clasping Richard's hands. "One of the Princess of Wales's attendants, who customarily slept on a pallet in her antechamber, went at daybreak to enquire as to her mistress's needs. The lady Joan was already dead. May she rest in peace!"

Anne doubted Richard had taken in the last five words, for he failed to make the customary response. He was gazing at her in stupefaction, as if testing the accuracy of her statement.

"Nay, it cannot be," he said. "You, my lady, have been misinformed."

"It is true enough," Anne told him quietly. "Think you I would have come to you else? Would I, who love Your Grace with all my heart, torment you with mere rumour!"

"Have they any notion as to the hour that *maman* died?" Richard asked then — the question seeming suddenly to occur to him.

"The physician believes she died at about one hour after midnight, only a few hours after her arrival at Wallingford," came the reply. "That, it appears, is what he told the priest who performed the last rites. My lady's servants were naturally deeply distressed, and it was therefore the priest who sent messengers post-haste with letters for myself and Your Grace.

He asked me to first inform you of the matter."

Richard took the proffered letter and, with sober mien, read it. Then, his face ashen as if only then had he taken in the fact of his mother's death, he turned away from Anne. Clasping one of the chapel's stone pillars, in an access of self-destruction, he twice struck his forehead against the resisting stone.

Anne went to him and put her arms around him.

"Nay, you must not!" she chided — as to a child. "You are King of England — as such, you had no choice. You did your duty, upholding the law of the land."

"You fail to understand!" Richard said, beside himself with grief. Blood was trickling from a gash on his forehead, falling unheeded on to his fine gold-coloured houppelande. "How could you understand!"

"But . . ."

"I sat up alone into the early hours, trying to come to a decision about my half-brother's execution," he said brokenly. "It was one hour past midnight when I finally reached that decision — and resolved to call a meeting of the Privy Council this morning."

"You mean . . . ?" White-faced with shock, Anne tried again. "You are telling me that at the same time as — "

"At the same time," nodded Richard. "At the very instant I decided that my brother must die, she who loved us both so dearly — receiving knowledge of it as clearly as if I myself had spoken of it — breathed her last."

22

RICHARD again called a meeting of the Privy Council.

He looked pale and tired, but none the less in full command of himself as he addressed the members. He spoke decisively, with none of the obvious reluctance with which he had earlier announced John Holland's execution.

"My lords," he said, "the lady Joan, Princess of Wales, departed this life in the early hours of yesterday. May perpetual light shine on her!"

A murmur of surprise ran through the meeting; some councillors appeared distressed, and bowed their heads in sorrow, recalling the beauty and grace of the princess who had been the bride of the legendary Black Prince. Others clasped their hands and murmured the customary prayerful response — *Requiescat in pace*!

But Richard had more to say. He waited until the general hubbub had died down and then he again addressed the assembly.

"My lords, in these circumstances, it would be improper to proceed with the execution of John Earl of Huntingdon, son to the aforementioned princess." A stunned and disapproving silence greeted these words but Richard went doggedly on. "I therefore grant a free pardon to the aforesaid earl, at the same time recommending him to do penance and make full restitution for his crime."

This caused an uproar. The king's resolution has failed him at the eleventh hour! was the overwhelming verdict of his nobles.

The commonalty, when they learned of the matter, for once shared the views of the nobility. A pity, the people said to themselves and each other, such vacillation and bowing to female pressure, is alien to the English constitution and bodes ill for the future of the realm. Had the Black Prince, the king's father, been our ruler, then would it have been a very different story. The Black Prince, like his father the third Edward before him, would have been firm to the point of ruthlessness. Look at Limoges . . . !

But his son, the young king, had failed the first test; had after all refused the first challenging hurdle. Faced with the princess's grief and subsequent demise, his resolution had failed him. Such the reactions. Such the sentiments.

★ ★ ★

The queen's party — that is to say the Bohemians who had accompanied her from her homeland — were for the most part deeply aggrieved at the king's decision to pardon one who had killed a man for protecting the queen's own knight.

But Anne as always, whilst acknowledging to herself that they were right and that Richard should not have pardoned so heinous a crime — not even out of respect for his mother's wishes — kept her own counsel.

She had made it a rule of life to love all that the king loved and saw compliance with his wishes as her first duty. Estimable as was this policy, it prompted some to regard her as weak-willed. On the premise that one cannot please everyone all of the time, Anne might better have used her considerable influence to steer Richard along a less dangerous path.

Anne's determination to support Richard at all times, despite their incomplete and therefore unfruitful marriage, was to lead her to commit an act of injustice against the Countess of Oxford — she who was cousin to Richard and wife of a sort to Robert de Vere.

* * *

In her will, Joan Princess of Wales had ordered that she be buried in the chapel in the church of the Friars Minor at Stamford, Lincolnshire — close by the tomb of her first husband, Sir Thomas Holland.

This signified to some, notably her erring son John, that Joan had best loved and honoured the first of her three husbands.

After the funeral, Richard and his ministers lost no time in urging John

Holland to leave England for a while and embark on an atoning pilgrimage to Syria.

"Leave the country?" had demanded John Holland of his half-brother. "For Syria, you say?"

"The Privy Council suggests — "

"God's life!" interposed John Holland. "Is there no end to this miserable affair! Already it has cost the life of my beloved mother — now, not content with that, you are banishing myself from the realm."

Richard, taken aback by this impertinence, none the less appeared calm. Richard was learning — but slowly.

"You seem to blame myself for our mother's death," he said doggedly. "I did all in my power to save you from the axe — and risked my crown in so doing."

"All that is in the past, little brother," retorted John Holland. "Over. Done with — as far as this nobleman is concerned. Now, just as I am coming to terms with the injustice of it all — "

"Yea, there was injustice," Richard interposed pointedly. "Ralph Stafford's family could vouch for that! As to the question of your departure — "

"Exile."

Richard's gallic shrug suggested a carelessness he was far from feeling.

"Call it what you will, my brother — " he said " — but for your sake and mine let it be *seen* as an act of atonement."

"Who are you to thus lecture me?" furiously demanded John Holland. "You who — "

"I who am the king?" put in Richard quietly — but there was that in his eyes, a red-hot fury, which reminded John Holland disconcertingly of the Black Prince. "Yea, I am indeed the king. As such, it is my misfortune to have before me a wretch who murdered a man, a knight of the royal household, simply because he stood in his way — a man who sees punishment for the crime as injustice and blames his king for the grief that helped to destroy his mother. Yea, I am the king — never again forget it. You will leave my court forthwith and be on your way to exile by the morrow."

"Richard, I — "

"Begone from my sight, John Holland — now, immediately." Richard's voice was stern and brooked no refusal. He was, in those moments, very much the king. "Utter another word and I shall summon my guards and have you thrown into a dungeon — and the key into the depths of the ocean! I wager that John Holland then, if not his misdemeanours, would be forgotten inside a week!"

Seeing Richard's expression, John Holland blanched. This was his half-brother as he had never seen him before. Richard of Bordeaux, the pretty boy-child whom he and his older brother had loved and protected from the moment of his birth, had of a sudden become a stranger.

"May God forgive you," was all he said — before turning abruptly and making for the door.

Richard watched him go, his heart heavy as lead. John Holland had always been part of his life. Now, he had sent him out of his life and into temporary exile. Temporary? Pilgrimages, particularly to the East, were fraught with perils galore and, as both of them well knew, it was more than likely that they would never see each other again.

"Our Lord have you in his keeping!" Richard said under his breath. "May He who knows what is in men's hearts, bless you and keep you, my brother!"

Eight years were to pass before the brothers met again, long years of change and danger — and of great sadness, particularly for the king.

The brothers were indeed reunited and the reunion was to bring each of them a measure of joy, warmth and happiness. But Time is the great separator — it passes ever more quickly, taking part of ourselves — our loyalties, our memories and our individual lives — with it . . .

John Holland returned. But better would it have been for his brother the king, if he had not done so.

Part Three

The Romance of the Rose

23

"WHAT ails you, my friend?" Richard enquired of de Vere when, some time later, he visited the latter's apartments at Sheen Palace where the court then was.

Careful for his reputation and well aware that tongues were wagging in respect of Anne's seeming inability to give him a child, Richard's sojourns with his beloved Robby were comparatively infrequent and planned on Richard's part with the utmost deviousness.

"Alas, Richy, I fear your scorn!" sighed de Vere, waiting until the king was seated before stretching out languidly on the great bed that was the focal point of his luxurious chamber. "You will, I fear, accuse me of perfidy or worse — and who could blame you!"

Richard gazed consideringly at him for a few moments before making reply, taking his time, seeing the handsome features which bore all the essential qualities of male perfection. Despite his antipathy to all sports except hunting, his dislike of the warrior skills requisite for all young noblemen of his time, de Vere was strong, muscular and courageous, and seemingly inexhaustible in his pleasures.

"Blame you, my lord?" Richard asked at length, well accustomed to the other's attempts to mislead him and not knowing therefore whether to laugh or show concern. "For what crime or peccadillo should I blame you?"

"A crime it surely is," sighed de Vere. "A crime against my sovereign — the most heinous, unnatural and perverted of crimes, alas! Even now I can scarce believe myself capable of such treachery!"

"Tell me, my friend," Richard said quietly — almost convinced by then that de Vere was serious. "Pray let me know the worst."

De Vere sighed heavily.

"My liege, I have . . . " He fell silent. "God have pity that I should be thus afflicted — 'tis beyond my wildest nightmares!"

"I command you to tell me all, my lord."

"All?" De Vere shook his head. "To tell you all would take but a few fleeting moments — and yet the knowledge of it fills my every thought. You see, Richy, 'tis like this . . ."

Another pause, and Richard spoke impatiently.

"Get on with it, Robby — or I shall depart this instant!"

"Doubtless you will do that anyway — as soon as you hear," de Vere said unhappily. "Ah well, here goes — brace yourself against the shock!"

"Against the shock?" Richard's smile was scornful.

"Oh, Richy, would you believe it — would anyone believe it!" exclaimed de Vere theatrically. "Robert de Vere, Earl of Oxford and Duke — "

"Get on with it, Robby!"

" — of Ireland, has fallen in love."[1]

"Oh, that!" Richard responded airily.

---

[1] Robert de Vere, ninth Earl of Oxford, was created Marquis of Dublin with regal powers in Ireland in 1385. Raised to the rank of Duke of Dublin, he was created Duke of

"Methought that new squire of yours had been preening himself overmuch of late — it is scarcely news!"

"Oh, but it is, Richy," insisted de Vere. "That is what I am trying to tell you. I have fallen in love, you see — with a lady!"

"Then am I glad," said Richard quietly, concealing his surprise and still not sure if the other were serious. "The lady Philippa is a charming lady — and being my own cousin, is eminently suitable as a mother for your offspring."

"The lady Philippa is my wife, and an excellent lady in her own way," de Vere said dismissively. "Why, we have been man and wife these nine years past."

Now, none of this was news to Richard. Philippa de Coucy was his cousin, being like himself a grandchild of Edward the Third. The offspring of the late king's

---

Ireland in 1386. These new titles were designed to give the favourite precedence over all the other earls. He excercised his powers in Ireland through a deputy, Sir John Stanley.

eldest daughter, Isabella, and Lord de Coucy, she was gifted and beautiful. The sympathies of every woman — and many a man — at court were with the neglected Countess of Oxford. Feeling on the matter ran high.

"Am I to understand that your latest inamorata is of the female gender?" enquired Richard.

"You have it in one, Richy!" de Vere told him — in the manner of one handing a prize to a somewhat backward pupil. "Full marks — bravo! The lady to whom I have given my heart is no other than her they call the landgravine."

"The landgravine is one of the queen's damsels," pointed out Richard, still not sure if de Vere were serious. "A Bohemian, she is reputed to be of humble birth."

"Only by the English who take pride in their scant knowledge of foreign titles," pointed out de Vere dismissively but with some truth. "It would seem that the Empress permitted the landgravine to accompany the queen to England together with her jewels and valuables, as well as her chamber-furniture. Low-born she is not, but devoted to Queen Anne she was and is."

"And now she is devoted to yourself also."

"As to that, my lord, I know not — but I do know that I am deeply enamoured of the lady and wish to make her my wife."

"But you have a wife," pointed out Richard in bewilderment.

"Unconsummated," said de Vere shortly.

"But the lady Philippa de Coucy is my cousin." Richard spoke aggrievedly, as if de Vere's obvious tardiness in the marriage bed were an insult to the Crown. "Have you forgotten that?"

De Vere was apparently not listening. "The landgravine will have none of me as the matter stands. She is a lady of piety and virtue," he said with an uncharacteristic earnestness which he himself, in other circumstances, would have termed tediousness.

And clever and scheming with it! thought Richard but he refrained from saying as much. He made a mental resolve to place these astonishing facts before the lady Anne at the first opportunity. If de Vere is serious in his intentions, and one can never be certain with him, he thought to himself — then his abandoning Philippa de Coucy for a Bohemian landgravine will cause a storm of protest throughout the land. If he be genuinely infatuated with the lady — then a passing romance of happy impermanence it must and shall remain.

"Why, my lord, are you looking at me so disapprovingly?" asked de Vere.

"Perchance because I disapprove," Richard said simply. "I disapprove most strongly. I still cannot believe you are serious."

De Vere got to his feet then and gazed down pleadingly at Richard.

"Richy, you are the king," he said quietly. "My lady is your cousin-german. The marriage, as I told you and as you no doubt surmised, is unconsummated. I need a son."

"Methought — " Richard started to say, but then he paused.

"Everyone thought — but thinking does not make babies, as I've been told!"

"Who would believe you, Robby — that your marriage is unconsummated, I mean?"

"You believe me, my lord, because I have said as much," de Vere told him. "My marriage, being incomplete, could be annulled — and then, hey ho, I would be free to wed the love of my life!"

"The landgravine is a handsome and pleasant lady," conceded Richard — dismayed by the revelations but determined not to show it. "She might even be well-born — who could say! But, either way, the lady is not for you, my friend. I shall speak to the queen and suggest that the landgravine be sent back to her homeland."

"If she goes, my lord — then shall I follow her," de Vere said stubbornly, seating himself on the bed as if he had given up the argument. "Whither she goes, there shall I go also — which would mean methinks that you and I would be parted."

Richard elected to ignore the apparent threat, but his heart none the less smote him.

"Be assured, my lord, that I shall give

thought to the matter," was all he said.

"I do believe you are jealous!" declared de Vere with satisfaction.

"Jealous?" asked Richard — and de Vere saw that his surprise was genuine. "Jealous of a damsel — a comely enough lass, but yet a damsel!"

"Maybe I shall get over it," de Vere said without conviction. He patted the bed invitingly. "Richy, come here and tell me I shall get over it — that a wench is not for me."

Richard's sigh suggested exasperation but, as his gaze met that of his lover, he saw that de Vere's eyes were warm with desire.

"So it was just a game!" he said, annoyed with himself for being taken in. "I have a mind to turn about and leave this chamber never to return."

"You do just that," said the other carelessly. "You are your own master."

Richard, angry at having been deceived, got to his feet and, throwing on the anonymous dark cloak which always accompanied such night-time excursions, he made for the door. One of his squires, trustworthy and loyal, would be awaiting him in the antechamber beyond.

De Vere's sudden attack knocked the breath out of him . . .

He struggled half-heartedly for a few moments but then, as de Vere pulled off his cloak and kissed him full on the lips, Richard's anger abated. In no time at all, he was lying naked on the sumptuous bed, watching his lover in wonderment . . .

De Vere's face was a conflict of fury and desire. His eyes, bright with emotion, were a trifle wild — and his arms, muscular and powerful, were holding the king in a vice-like grip. But then, seeing his captive gazing up at him passive and wondering, he relaxed his hold.

"Richy — " he said, his expression tense. " — I shall always love you best of all — you need not fear a rival."

"Fear a rival!" Richard exclaimed breathlessly — too much so for his own good. Breathlessness gives away feelings, emotions, unnatural yearnings. A picture of Anne floated unbidden into his mind then and he knew, not for the first time, a sense of guilt. "Why would I, any more than yourself, fear a rival!"

"What if I went away, my lord — was forced to go away?" De Vere's voice was tender, caressing — but the implication was none the less there. "Would not you miss me, pine for me?"

"Miss you?" demanded Richard. "Nay, why would I miss you — "

His words ceased abruptly as, with a round oath that suggested fury rather than some more noble emotion, de Vere seized him, flung him face-down and leaned over him . . .

24

SEVEN days later, the news of the Earl of Oxford's infatuation with the landgravine was all about court — and it was towards the end of that seventh day that Anne the queen learned of it.

"Lady Dulcimer?" asked Anne in surprise as in the early evening she entered her withdrawing-chamber to find there one of the younger and more irresponsible of her ladies. "Why, I had expected to see the landgravine."

How is it, thought Dulcimer, that everyone including the queen refers to the lady thus — as if she were some middle-aged matron instead of a flat-chested pale-as-a-lily damsel from Bohemia!

"The landgravine begs Your Grace's indulgence," she replied dutifully. "She is not herself today."

"You mean she is unwell?" asked Anne in surprise. As far as she knew, Agnes Lancecrona had never had a day's illness in her life — she had however seemed more than a little absent-minded of late. "I shall send someone to enquire after her."

If that lass is unwell, it can be for only the one reason, thought Dulcimer — though knowing a certain gentleman as I do, none better, it would be the wonder of wonders!

"The landgravine is upset by the rumours, my lady," she said. "As far as I know, there is naught wrong with her health."

"Upset?" asked Anne in surprise. "You are surely mistaken, Dulcimer. Why, I have known the landgravine since we were children in Prague. Always she is of a serene temperament."

Why does the queen show such concern for that one? Dulcimer wondered. Some say that she, the landgravine, is the bastard of the Emperor, Her Grace's father, and is like a sister to her. But that rumour is as naught compared with the one which was this very morning raising eyebrows all around the court.

"Serene is as serene does, my lady!" she observed daringly. "Dark secrets and dark undertakings are not close kin to serenity!"

Anne gazed thoughtfully at the young woman for a few moments. Dulcimer was wont to let her tongue run away with her and Anne had reason to believe that her morals were questionable. There was the matter of her infatuation with Robert de Vere — rumour having it that it was she who had revealed to de Vere, and thereby to the court, the details of the assault upon the lady Joan, Anne's late mother-in-law. Whatever the facts, Joan had retained the young woman in her service and, after the princess's death, Richard who had seemed concerned for the damsel had asked Anne to take her into her own household.

"Dark undertakings, you say?" frowned Anne, a note of displeasure in her voice. "If you have heard aught to the landgravine's discredit, then I command you to keep it to yourself. Rumour is the life-blood of any court — or so it would seem — and it is unwise to be influenced by it. Indeed, gossip is something I will not tolerate in my household, so be warned, Lady Dulcimer, if you please."

"You will hear soon enough, my lady," the young woman said on a note of defiance — and Anne was surprised to see tears in her eyes. "*His* reputation is such — and indeed I myself know him to be a brutal and cold gentleman — that no good will come of it. They can say what they like, my lady, and can pity the poor duchess all they will — but that devil means to marry the other, come what might!"

Anne sighed. She should reprimand her, refuse to hearken to such nonsense, but her curiosity was getting the better of her. It was plain that this was not just idle gossip.

"The poor duchess?" she heard herself asking. "To whom precisely do you refer?"

"Why, the Duchess of Ireland, my lady!" came the reply. "She is such a lovely lady and deserves better than him."

"Are you by any chance referring to the Duke of Ireland?" enquired Anne, using the title recently conferred on that gentleman by the king. She tried to sound unconcerned but her heart had missed a beat as it always did when her lord's paramour was mentioned. "One must not make judgements, Lady Dulcimer — what passes between husband and wife is not the business of others."

She speaks with feeling, thought Dulcimer. If ever a wife was wronged . . . Why, Robert de Vere's reputation is such and his ill-deeds so many, that 'tis a wonder none has seen fit to put an end to the sodomite's life!

"My lady," she said, "you can whip me or have me put in irons for speaking thus, but I will no longer keep from you that which all the court knows."

Anne, arrested by her earnestness, said nothing but waited for her to continue.

"The court is a-buzz with the tale that the duke plans to annul his marriage to the lady Philippa de Coucy, and take to wife the landgravine."

Anne concealed her astonishment only with difficulty. Then it is as I suspected, she thought, and indeed as Richard implied — de Vere treated Dulcimer badly, taking advantage of her infatuation with him. Now, she seeks revenge. The lass then must be taught a lesson. A wagging tongue is not to be borne in my household.

"You are a wicked young lady," she said — and her voice, though controlled, in no way concealed her anger. "Such a tale could cause great harm to the Duke of Ireland and his duchess. Lady Dulcimer, I will have none of it. Go to your chamber, and remain there until I have decided what shall be done with you."

Dulcimer started to weep.

"Send me not away, my lady," she pleaded. "That which I have told you is God's own truth, as Your Grace will discover very shortly."

"I will hear no more," Anne said firmly. "You will learn of my decision anon."

Dulcimer fell on her knees.

"Have me held in a dungeon or thrown to wolves — " she said dramatically " — but send me not away, Your Grace, I beg you!"

"Leave me," commanded Anne, herself near to tears at the implications of the tale, and ringing her bell to summon another of her ladies. "Ah, Lady Twyford

— pray escort the lady Dulcimer to her chamber. She is relieved of her duties until further notice."

As the surprised Lady Twyford escorted the now distraught young woman from the queen's withdrawing-chamber, one of the king's gentlemen paused courteously outside the doorway to let them pass. Then with a word to a servant, he briskly entered the queen's presence to announce that the king was on his way to her apartments.

* * *

Troubled by the stormy scene with Dulcimer, the king's visit following hot on its heels, suggested to Anne that something really was amiss. Rarely did Richard visit her apartments so early in the evening.

Richard was grim-faced and seemingly preoccupied when he entered her withdrawing-chamber. He curtly dismissed her attendants and indicated that she herself be seated prior to his revealing the purpose of his visit.

"My lady, there is gossip within the

court," he said then, much as had Dulcimer not half an hour earlier. "Methought we should speak of it together, in order that we might be seen to be of one mind if or when the storm breaks."

"Pray speak on, my lord," Anne said quietly, registering his hesitation and realizing that, if there were truth in Dulcimer's tale, then the knowledge must have come as a shock to him also.

"The Duke of Ireland," Richard said formally, "is seeking an annulment of his marriage."

"Is that so, my lord?" Anne asked calmly.

Despite his concern, Richard registered her apparent lack of surprise and wondered at it.

"The said duke wishes to take to wife a certain lady — " he continued " — one well-known to Your Grace, she being of your household."

"The landgravine?" asked Anne in a low voice, her face paling.

"You have heard?" asked Richard and the possibility seemed to please him — as if it relieved him of an onerous duty. "The lady confided in you, perchance?"

"Nay, my lord, if there be truth in this, then am I as surprised as yourself." Anne spoke firmly, recognizing that more than affairs of state and the gossip and disapproval of the court were involved here. My lord would be an injured party, she thought, were his paramour to have designs on another! "I heard gossip, no more — and discounted it. Indeed, just prior to your arrival, I was sending the lady Dulcimer packing for repeating gossip!"

"The matter of the duke's marriage is true enough," Richard said heavily. "He regards the lady with such ardour, it seems, that he is desirous of making her his bride."

"But that cannot be!" Anne said forthrightly. "Philippa de Coucy, Duchess of Ireland, is your cousin-german, being the daughter of the late king's daughter, Isabella, and the lord de Coucy, Earl of Bedford. She is of royal blood. Why, the situation would be impossible, my lord — it just cannot be!"

"Cannot, my lady, is a word alien

to the duke's vocabulary, alas!" Richard observed.

"I doubt the duke is serious in his intention," Anne said practically, having suddenly reached that conclusion. "The gentleman delights in fomenting rumour and scandal, it seems to me — I dare say that even at this moment, he is enjoying the stir he has caused."

"He had already spoken of the matter to me, my lady — ere the storm broke! I, too, did not at that time believe him to be serious."

"I doubt the Privy Council would permit such a situation, my lord — " said Anne " — even if non-consummation of the marriage could be proven."

"It would be for the religious courts to decide the rights and wrongs of the matter," Richard pointed out. "But whatsoever their decision and that of the Privy Council — to say naught of my own — one thing is certain. My royal uncles would assuredly not accept such a situation, the lady being their kindred no less than mine — and my subjects would, I doubt not, be scandalized."

"And if the duke persists in the

matter, what then, my lord?" Anne asked curiously. "What of Agnes Lancecrona herself? She has not spoken to me of the matter."

"If the duke proceeds without the consent of parliament and the courts, he could be stripped of his titles and privileges," Richard told her. "I confess that such a possibility appals me."

"And Your Grace believes that the duke would so proceed?" asked Anne curiously, still puzzled as to why the landgravine had kept silent about the matter.

"It could well be," replied Richard unhappily. "I know it and it distresses me deeply. I hold the duke in high regard, as you are aware, my lady. The imagining of the disgrace and public opprobrium which awaits him if he follows such a course, fills me with dismay. Robert de Vere is my friend and dearest companion. He is — "

"I know, my lord," firmly put in Anne, hurt but trying not to show it. "The duke's loyalty to Your Grace is unquestionable. Could not you persuade him of his folly?"

"I fear not. The lady in question has stolen the duke's heart . . . " The words *from myself*, though omitted, were none the less there by implication. "I did not at first take him seriously."

"And now, my lord?"

"Now, I am in no doubt that he means to marry the lady, come what might and despite all the complications!"

"What of your uncles, my lord?" Anne asked uneasily. "Are they aware of the situation as yet?"

"I know not for certain," came the answer. "But they are calling on me on the morrow — perchance to speak of the matter."

25

THE royal uncles, though frequently spoken of collectively, were in fact rarely seen together. Only at times of crisis, notably family and therefore royal crises, did they act together, supporting each other and presenting by any standards a formidable force.

John of Gaunt, Duke of Lancaster, titular king of Castile and Leon, was at this time in his forty-eighth year. He had been twice married — his first wife Blanche, mother of his heir Henry of Bolingbroke, having died young of plague. His second wife, Constance of Castile, being in poor health and preferring the Castilian climate, he had taken a mistress, Catharine Swynford, a lady of comparatively humble origin who had already borne him two sons.

Edmund of Langley, Duke of York, was a year younger and was married to Isabel of Castile, sister of John of Gaunt's second wife.

Thomas of Woodstock, Duke of Gloucester, seventh and youngest son of Edward the Third and Philippa of Hainault, was then in his thirty-third year and was married to Lady Eleanor de Bohun who had borne him two children.

All three of this gallant brotherhood of princes were champions in the field, as well as warriors of repute who had seen service in France, Spain and Scotland. Every morning, when not engaged in actual warfare, wearing plate-armour, they took violent exercise in the tilt-yard for hours at a time.

All were learned, elegant and chivalrous — Thomas being the artistic one. Patron of John Gower, the poet, who had lived for a time in his household, Thomas possessed an extensive library, and had composed and drawn up in book form comprehensive plans for the overall defence of the realm.[1]

The Plantagenets, descendants of the

---

[1] *L'Ordonnance d'Angleterre pour le Camp à l'outrance, ou gaige de bataille*

Angevins of western France, were by tradition leaders of men and lovers of women. All the sons of Edward the Third were formed in the same chivalric mould. Amongst themselves, they argued, disagreed, quarrelled and played the sides against the middle from time to time — but in the final analysis, no matter what, they were devoted and utterly loyal each to the other.

These lines by an Anglo-Saxon rhyming chronicler, though written for Lionel of Antwerp, Duke of Clarence — Edward the Third's third son, who had been killed in Italy some years earlier — aptly describe all the brothers.

> 'In all the world there was no prince him like.
> Of high stature and of all seemliness,
> Above all men within the whole kingrike
> By the shoulders might be seen, doubtless.
> In hall was he maid-like for gentleness,
> In other places famed for rhetoric,
> But in the field a lion Marmorike.'

The three brothers were seated with Richard now around a large table in the king's withdrawing chamber. The atmosphere was stormy, to put it mildly, and Richard no longer had any doubt as to whether or not his uncles had got wind of the latest court scandal.

"The fellow must be banished," said Edmund of Langley. "There are no two ways about it. If the Duke of Ireland carries out his — er — boast, and seeks to annul his marriage with our beloved and long-suffering niece, then he must be banished!"

Now this was far removed from Richard's own solution to the problem. Despite de Vere's faults, Richard loved him dearly. He was of the opinion that, whilst de Vere genuinely believed himself in love with the landgravine, given time, he would come to see it as a mere passing infatuation. Given time? Ah, but there lay the difficulty! For some unfathomable reason, de Vere was already going out of his way to make public his infatuation, along with his intentions, to anyone who would listen — thereby riding roughshod over the feelings, principles and sensibilities of practically everyone in the land.

"Banished, my lord?" enquired Richard in apparent surprise. "Why would we banish him? Since the forces of law, of both church and state, apparently have no grievance against the duke — why should I, his monarch and cousin by marriage, take such a step?"

Thomas of Woodstock affected a sigh. "Sire, your partisanship — for want of a stronger word — for Robert de Vere, has long given scandal both at home and abroad. This is Your Grace's opportunity to amend the matter. Let it be seen clearly and unmistakably that you hold no brief for such as him — that the creature is anathema to you no less than to your subjects."

"And — " added Edmund of Langley for good measure " — if by some miracle, it could be announced at the same time that your consort is with child, Your Grace's subjects, I dare say, would not find it hard to forget your past — er — indiscretions."

Accustomed as he was to his uncles' plain-speaking, Richard nevertheless had difficulty this time in hiding his chagrin.

"The Duke of Ireland is my closest comrade," he said unwisely. "His personal arrangements have no bearing on our friendship and his loyalty. As to the matter of the queen, there is — "

"To which queen is Your Grace referring?" enquired Thomas of Woodstock poker-faced.

"There is, as I was about to say, my lords, plenty of time," Richard continued coolly. "My lady, I doubt not, will with God's grace bear me a child in her own good time."

"With God's grace indeed, sire — " agreed John of Gaunt sombrely, breaking his silence " — and a little help from the king's grace!"

"We have been wed but six years," said Richard — as if it were six days. "Man proposes and God disposes, remember!"

"And Robert de Vere reigns supreme!" sighed Thomas of Woodstock. "Be warned, nephew — remember your great-grandfather!"

Richard was white-faced with fury. He was only too well aware of how Edward the Second had jeopardized his crown and his posterity for love of two men, Piers de Gaveston and Hugh le Despencer. His own case was different, he told himself. He was happily married — to Anne whom he loved and respected and would one day make the mother of his child.

"Threaten me not, my lord," he said angrily. "You go too far!"

"And presumably Your Grace does not go far enough — " was the retort of his youngest uncle " — in respect of begetting an heir!"

"How dare you, sir!" exclaimed Richard furiously. "Retract those words or — "

"Gentlemen! Gentlemen!" interposed John of Gaunt. "This is no time for recriminations. The subject under discussion is the Duke of Ireland — not the secrets of the royal bedchamber."

"The ways of God and nature are inscrutable — 'tis not for us to question them!" remarked Edmund of Langley — but whether this was a reproof to his younger brother or an attempt to pour oil on troubled waters, was not clear. "Have patience, nephew!"

Richard, taking this as support, smiled

appreciatively at the speaker.

"My lady is of virile stock, my lord," he said cheerfully. "She will not fail me!"

John of Gaunt watched him for a few moments in silence, his expression inscrutable.

"Then, sir, see to it that you do not fail her — " he said plainly then " — and your subjects!"

26

RECALLING later the meeting with his uncles and dismayed by the realization that his shortcomings had apparently become common knowledge, a subject for public debate, Richard resolved to visit Anne that same evening. He would inform her of the facts, discuss with her the meeting with his royal kinsmen; and seek to ascertain whether or not he could count on her support in the matter of de Vere, and the latter's determination to divorce his wife and marry the landgravine.

"My lady, should the matter turn out as my uncles predict and I dare say hope, 'twill be a sorry day for your lord," he said as he seated himself companionably beside her in her solar. "They see the matter as a heaven-sent opportunity for separating me from my valiant and estimable comrade."

Now, Anne herself would not have described de Vere in such terms. However, her loyalty to Richard was such that, whatever her private opinions, doubts and fears, she would outwardly give him her full support. Had she borne him a son, she might well have viewed this particular matter differently, as the heir to the throne's accession could well be jeopardized were his father declared unfit to rule. As it was, having been denied the means of conceiving the child for which she yearned, Anne's hopes and ambitions lay solely in Richard himself.

"Has Your Grace reason to believe that the duke's marriage is unconsummated?" she asked plainly, registering as she did so his sudden tension. He seemed to be wrestling with the question — or maybe with his conscience.

"I cannot lie to you, my lady," he said then. "I have heard the duke say as much."

It was Anne's turn to wrestle with her conscience. The duchess, Philippa de Coucy, was well-known to her, she being Richard's cousin. Elegant, gifted and virtuous, she was a popular and much-loved member of the royal family and of the court. Public opinion saw her as a victim of Robert de Vere's perverted sexual appetites — a view shared by Anne. She sighed now, her loyalties divided, her loyalty to her lord at odds with her conscience.

"My lord, if you desire it of me — " she started in a low voice, as if hoping and praying that he would fail to hear what she said " — Agnes Lancecrona, her they call the landgravine, being my compatriot and kinswoman, I will undertake to write forthwith in my own hand to His Holiness the Pope. I shall beseech him to sanction the annulment on grounds of non-consummation of the Duke of Ireland's marriage — and to authorize the marriage of the aforesaid duke with Agnes Lancecrona."

"You would do as much for me?" Richard asked, touched by her devotion. "You would put your name to such a petition, knowing as you do of my own infidelity in certain quarters?"

"Yea, my lord, if it be to your benefit and happiness," Anne replied readily enough — it having just occurred to her that with Robert de Vere committed to a marriage with a young woman on whom, for the time being at least, he apparently doted, Richard might then turn to her for solace and physical fulfilment. Inexperienced, she was inclined to equate the one kind of physical union with the other. "To please and accommodate you at all times, to be your solace and confidante, has ever been my sole care."

"Many would oppose such a solution," Richard pointed out. "My princely uncles would look askance at such a proposal."

"Your uncles are not the king," Anne replied, with a confidence she was far from feeling. "Even they, I doubt not, would see merit in my supporting in all things my lord and sovereign."

"My lady, I thank you for your goodness to me," Richard said — and there was a hint of guilt in his voice. "Your devotion and kindness is, alas, beyond my deserving! How could I, who am so unworthy, ever repay you!"

"One day you will," Anne said wistfully — thereby acknowledging his debt. "One day, my dear lord, you will take me in your arms and give me the child that both of us desire and need — your son and heir, please God!"

"Tonight — "

"Nay, not tonight, my lord," Anne interposed — though she was in fact mistaken in what she assumed he had been about to say. "Tonight we both have much on our minds. I have a letter to write to Pope Urban, if you recall — and you, I dare say, will wish to inform certain persons of a possible solution to the Duke of Ireland's predicament."

"Hearken to me, my lady — much as I love you — "

But like a ship in full sail, Anne went on regardless. Uncertain at first as to the wisdom of the exercise, telling herself now that such a solution could well solve more problems than one, she forged ahead with all speed.

"I doubt not that the Holy Father will hearken sympathetically to my petition," she told Richard confidently. "Am not I daughter to the Emperor Charles the Fourth — am not I known throughout Christendom as a dutiful wife!"

Anne's refusal of what she had mistakenly taken to be Richard's tentative approach to lovemaking, was quite deliberate. On Robert de Vere's wedding night, when the bedding ceremony was over and he lay with the lady, the landgravine, who was apparently the love of his life — then would she, Anne of Bohemia, offer solace to her lord and king.

★ ★ ★

Thus it came about. After a considerable delay at Avignon — where the papal court then was — and a deal of discussion between the papal envoy and the parties concerned, the marriage betwixt the Duke of Ireland and the lady Philippa de Coucy was annulled on the grounds of non-completion.

Two days later, with indecent haste as the English people saw it, the king's erstwhile lover, the dissolute and pleasure-loving Robert de Vere, wedded and bedded the landgravine Agnes Lancecrona.

Anne believed she had found an acceptable answer to the liaison between her lord and his lover. She imagined that, by separating Richard from his paramour and trying to bring good out of evil, she had achieved a happy solution for all concerned — not least herself and her unborn children. She was, alas, in one respect soon to discover her naïvety!

27

THE king did indeed visit the queen's chamber on the night following his paramour's second wedding — and she, receiving notice of his intention and recalling her earlier resolution, made ready to welcome him with open arms.

Now that Robert de Vere had taken to wife the landgravine, a lady with whom he was seemingly besotted, she must ensure, she told herself, that Richard overcame his infatuation with that nobleman and became at last truly her husband . . .

But it is not easy for a woman long denied the physical attentions of her husband, to greet with spontaneous joy and ardour one who comes to her bed grim-visaged, heart-sick and clad in unrelieved black.

"Anne," he said woefully, standing beside the bed, "what am I to do! It was needful I should speak with you — to whom else could I turn in my extremity?"

Anne's smile was loving — if a trifle forced. It was now or never, she told herself. If she could not console him with her body now, wean him from his lover and unnatural practices — then she never would. She spoke lightly.

"You appear, my lord, as one about to sing the dirge!" she said. "Yet here am I, your loving and still-virgin bride, ready and eager to take you in my arms and console you in any way I can!"

"I confess I can think of naught else — " said Richard gloomily.

"Then, my sweet lord . . . "

" — save he who has deserted me for another. I think of them together, sharing the same bed . . . "

Anne, humiliated by the unconscious rebuff, was determined not to show it.

"Sharing the same bed, you say!" she exclaimed cheerfully. "After all the trouble the duke has courted by changing one wife for another, one could hardly expect them to lie in separate beds!"

"It is no matter for levity, my lady!" Richard said aggrievedly — and without a glimmer of a smile.

"Might one suggest, my lord, that we

both try to put the Duke of Ireland and his fads and fancies from our minds!"

Anne was a little on her mettle. Her former resolution was becoming a trifle tarnished. "There is naught to be gained by — "

"Might one enquire, madam, as to whether oneself is in the category of a fad — or a fancy!" Richard asked coldly. "If you, my lady, are intent upon taunting me about my lost lover, instead of helping me come to terms with my sorrow — "

"Taunting you, my lord?" Anne interposed in astonishment. "I wish only to love you, to welcome you to my bed — to hold you in my arms and have you know me carnally."

"You understand not how it is with me!" There was sorrow rather than accusation in Richard's voice.

Anne drew back the coverlets to reveal her nakedness and took his hands in hers. Her voice when she spoke was warm and loving.

"Understanding has naught to do with the case," she said softly. "Lie here beside me and let me caress you — nature I doubt not will do the rest!"

Climbing lithely in beside her, he removed his robe and drew her into his arms. He kissed her forehead, her lips, her throat and caressed her body tenderly. But his kisses lacked ardour . . .

"God have pity, I cannot help but think of *them*!" he said of a sudden, his eyes bright with emotion. "That Robby could choose — "

"Hush, my lord! Think, I pray you, of the child we wish to make — the infant, the little prince who would secure your crown and bring us both such joy!"

Richard drew away and looked down at her with an expression she could not read. Could it be chagrin, sorrow?

"You understand not how it is with me," he said again, "How could you understand — since I myself know not why it should be so! You in your inexperience, my lady, have not recognized the truth. An infant prince, you say — I fear that can never be."

"Tell me," she said softly, though a great fear filled her being. "Tell me, pray, your meaning. Is it myself — am I in some way unpleasing to you?"

"Foolish one!" he chided, kissing her fondly. "How could you ask such a question — why, you surely know I love you with all my heart!"

"Methought it was so," Anne said, close to tears now. "And yet you refuse to make love to me — all these years you have shied from completing our union. Could it be that you wish to annul your marriage as your lover has done, and take another to wife?"

"Nay, nay!" he cried, and she saw that he was weeping. "O grief of heart that I should have caused you to think such a thing! I love you, my very dear, with all my soul — never have doubt of it."

"Then why, my lord — "

"You must believe me," Richard persisted. "You must surely believe that I love you dearly. Why, you are as you have ever been — my one true friend."

"Friends are not necessarily lovers, my lord," Anne said on a small note of reproof — which, no sooner said, she regretted. "My lord, I — "

"Have I shown you aught but consideration and a deep regard — " Richard asked " — save in the one matter!"

"Then . . . ?" Anne gazed at him in bewilderment.

"I cannot," he told her, his voice constricted with emotion. "I know not why — but, heaven help me, I cannot! 'Tis through no fault or failing of yours — or indeed of Robby de Vere. I am simply unable to perform in the way necessary for the begetting of offspring."

She stared at him blankly for a few moments. His amber-brown eyes, reflecting the candlelight, shone with emotion — with woe and mute appeal.

She answered the appeal. The tragedy was hers as well as his — but, as she firmly told herself, a tragedy shared is a tragedy halved! They loved each other dearly — there was no doubting that. This then was a tragedy they must share — would share.

She drew him into her arms.

"I had no idea," she said on a sob, as she held him close, loving and comforting him — as if indeed he were her child rather than her lord and husband. "I knew not how it was with you."

"And now that you know?" he asked quietly — and his forlorn expression touched her heart. "Can you still love me — share your life with me?"

"I love you, my sweet lord," she answered, her tears mingling with his. She tried to ignore the small voice within her which told her that there are many different ways of loving; many kinds of love. "I love you, just as I have always loved you."

★ ★ ★

When the facts regarding Anne's letter of appeal to the Pope eventually reached the ears of her lord's subjects, there was widespread disapproval and criticism of her. Her popularity diminished almost overnight.

What manner of person was it, asked the Privy Council, who being aware of the unsavoury reputation of the husband, wrote in her own hand to the Holy Father, beseeching him to annul the marriage of the wife — because the aforementioned husband wished it!

Maybe the queen had her own axe to grind! said the king's subjects. Was not the landgravine her dearest friend — a woman of property from her native Bohemia? Were they not frequently seen in each other's company? The landgravine was unusually tall for a female and had the figure of a boy — and what was more, prior to meeting the Duke of Ireland, she had received no offers of marriage despite her being like the queen in her twenty-fourth year. Was it like to like? they asked themselves and each other. After all, the queen had borne no children and any woman who knew her onions and had the right equipment, could get a child out of a man with whom she shared a bed!

Thus the talk — thus the sentiments.

The storm of public indignation fell not only upon Richard and Anne — but also upon members of their households.

Sir Simon Burley, the king's former tutor and guardian, one of the most accomplished and hitherto highly regarded men of his time, was the first to feel the weight of public opprobrium. Burley, declared the royal uncles, the Privy Council and the commonalty — speaking for once with a single voice — should have overridden the king's wishes in regard to the Duke of Ireland's marriage. He should furthermore have ensured, they said, that the queen — for whom Burley was said to have a great admiration — kept aloof from a matter which was in plain language none of her business.

Well, yea, a scapegoat there had to be! Burley just happened to be in the wrong place at the right time. He who had frequently taken the king to task for consorting with sycophants and homosexuals, was to be held culpable for his royal master's sins and omissions.

Burley, shocked and distressed at the rapid turn of events, was arrested and — together with other members of the royal household, de Vere among them — sent for trial on ten charges.

28

PARLIAMENT assembled on the third of February at Westminster Hall, where Burley and others similarly charged were to be judged by their peers.

Richard, magnificently apparelled, was seated on his throne, the prelates on his right hand and the lay magistrates on his left. The chancellor was behind the king; the five accusers — Gloucester, Arundel, Warwick, Derby and Nottingham — in front. These noblemen, each wearing a golden surcote, were almost as gorgeously apparelled as their monarch.

The first and most important charge was read out: it contained the essence of all the charges and applied to each of the prisoners.

"The accused," it was claimed, "seeing the youth of the king, accroached to themselves royal power, and induced the king to follow their courses."

Of the individual charges, de Vere was

arraigned for treason in connection with a report much prevalent at that time.

"You are accused, my lord, of inciting the King's Grace to act contrary to the interests of the nation." This created a stir and all eyes turned to de Vere, to see his reaction — but worse was to come. "Under pretence of a pilgrimage to Canterbury, the king would cross the sea and deliver up Calais to the King of France — "

Such an uproar greeted these words that it was some time before the speaker could continue.

"The King of France — " he went on at length " — in consideration of that cession, would engage to supply the King's Grace with an army to subdue his rebellious subjects and establish an arbitrary government upon the ruins of the English constitution."

Pandemonium broke out in the Hall as the speaker, having delivered his *coup-de-grâce*, bowed and sat down. Richard turned pale — and anger seeming to be directed against him rather than the accused, the hands of his knightly bodyguards went to their sword-hilts.

Only de Vere himself appeared unconcerned — he stood calm and unmoved like a man apart. He said nothing, contemptuously refusing even to deny the charges.

★ ★ ★

Five weeks later, when the trial was resumed — de Vere having in the meantime escaped from custody — fifteen articles of impeachment were presented against four of the king's chamber knights: Burley, Salisbury, Berners and Beauchamp. These gentlemen were accused of having taken advantage of the king's youth to set him against his appointed advisers, and the three last-named of having been in the employ of the aforementioned traitors.

Burley, now fifty-three years of age, a man of hitherto unblemished character, who had been appointed guardian to the young Richard by Edward the Black Prince, his father, had long feared that he would be held culpable for his sovereign's failings. Further to the other charges, he was accused of encouraging the king to keep company with Robert de Vere, Duke of Ireland, of giving bribes to the Bohemians and — something which in his worst nightmares he could not have envisaged — making illicit use of the Great Seal.

There was much public sympathy for Burley who, unlike de Vere, had chosen to stay and answer the charges. He elected to defend himself with his body, this winning him much sympathy in parliament — with the result that, though pronounced guilty on two of the charges, his fate was not decided until after a six-week adjournment.

Anne meanwhile, knowing Burley's worth and appalled by the threat hanging over him, went on her knees to two of the king's uncles, Thomas of Woodstock and Edmund of Langley. They, assuming that she was behaving thus at their nephew's behest, were none the less uneasy in the face of such an appeal.

"Dear lady — " said Edmund of Langley " — praiseworthy as is your appeal on the gentleman's behalf, we cannot, alas, grant your request. Those who have long influenced and encouraged the king in his unwise associations, however innocent their motives, must pay the price of their foolishness."

Anne, recognizing then that her mission had failed, could not restrain her tears. This was too much for Thomas of Woodstock who had long harboured a warm regard for her.

"Lady — " he said gently, taking her hand to assist her to rise " — you should not kneel to us. You are queen of England and our quarrel is not with Your Grace."

"My lord, I know Sir Simon Burley to be innocent of the charges made against him," Anne said, weeping. "He is a kind and God-fearing gentleman. I therefore beseech you not to take his life."

"The law must take its course, my lady," Thomas of Woodstock told her, asking himself not for the first time why she herself had not long since seen how matters were going in regard to Richard and his dangerous choice of friends. "Luxury and effeminacy prevail throughout the court, and timidity and dispute in the cabinet. Such a state of affairs cannot, must not, be allowed to continue. In Burley's case, it could be that there must be a scapegoat!"

As, having exchanged glances with his brother, Thomas of Woodstock escorted Anne to her apartments, two of her attendants following, he knew a great sadness for her — and for himself. Why, he thought, with such a one as she, is Richard not content? Ever since the day of our first meeting at Canterbury, I have known a deep yearning for her . . .

★ ★ ★

Of those charged and found guilty, only Burley, Beauchamp and Berners were present when the court sat again on the fifth of May — the others having followed de Vere's example and escaped in the interim.

Gloucester, Arundel and Warwick refused to be moved by the many pleas for mercy from the assembly. Their resolve was hardened by the news, received only that morning, that Robert de Vere, having escaped to Chester, had raised a body of troops and was planning to march on London.

"Imprisonment, my lords," pleaded one member when votes were taken on the fate of the prisoners. "Surely a spell of imprisonment would bring the gentlemen to their senses!"

Others supported this and the three lords conferred. Thomas of Woodstock spoke for them.

"My lords, we have heard the evidence — " he said evenly " — and have hearkened sympathetically to your pleas. The sentences must stand in the case of Beauchamp and Berners. In the case of Burley — he being a Knight of the Garter and having given great service in Aquitaine to the king's own sire — he shall be shown the court's mercy."

There were thunderous cheers at this, but Burley himself had seen the unrelenting expression on the faces of the three judges. He knew he was finished. All the years of sacrificing his own life to keep his young monarch on the right path — of cajoling, advising, speaking his mind — had been set at naught. Once de Vere had engrossed the affections of the king, he had governed him with absolute authority. He himself had done his best.

He could have done no more . . .

As the cheering died down and Thomas of Woodstock continued speaking, Burley himself was the only one there who showed no surprise at his words.

"Simon Burley, he being Knight of the Garter and due to his exemplary service to His Grace's father and the high esteem in which the prince held him — " he said " — shall have his sentence commuted."

Deafening cheers greeted this statement, but Thomas of Woodstock raised a hand for silence. He had more to say.

"In lieu of hanging, the punishment prescribed — " he said soberly " — the sentence shall be commuted to beheadal."

* * *

The execution by hanging of John Salisbury, condemned as a traitor for allegedly conducting negotiations for a treaty with France, marked the last of the executions.

The royal uncles had won the day. Burley and the others had been made to pay the price for their monarch's sins — and the fury of parliament and people was now satiated.

When parliament re-opened for the next session, those who had formerly been closest to the Crown having departed — whether by the hand of the executioner or to a convenient if temporary hiding-place — the assembly, already primed by the royal uncles, laid down ground rules for those directly in the king's service.

Anne was to find herself personally affected by the new order of things. The Bohemians who had accompanied her from Prague and who made up her household were, with the exception of Sir Meles, her knight, to be dismissed and sent back to their homeland.

As if by way of celebrating this radical and unlooked-for new order, on the last day of May, Richard, with Anne at his side, entertained the parliament at Kennington Palace — his mother's former manor.

The royal couple, as extravagantly attired and bejewelled as ever — the male of the species having the brighter plumage — greeted their guests graciously, and as if nothing were amiss. As if Anne had not just bade farewell to her entourage, to all those familiar faces who had set forth with her years ago from Bohemia — and as if Richard had not been separated from his favourites, his chamber knights and his courtiers, and Burley who had in reality been more of a father to him than had Edward the Black Prince.

Three days later, Richard and Anne, in full regalia, attended a thanksgiving service at Westminster Abbey. After High Mass, which was attended by every noble and high dignitary in the land, the Lords and Commons renewed their oaths of allegiance, after which Richard addressed them.

The theatricality of the moment appealed to him — to his love of admiration, his pleasure at being the cynosure of so many pairs of eyes. Was not he a second Absalom? If only Robby de Vere could have been there . . .

The words came easily to him — in truth, they meant little but they were apparently what the congregation gathered before him wished to hear.

"I, Richard, lord and sovereign of this realm — " he started — and his hearers saw, or fancied they saw, the holy light of truth and dedication in his gold-brown eyes " — do hereby swear before God, his Church and saints and all the company of Heaven, and my loyal subjects here present, to be henceforth a good and dutiful king and lord!"

"*Deo gratias*," responded the congregation in one joyful voice.

29

SHEEN PALACE was Anne's favourite royal residence. Built by Edward the First, it was charmingly situated on hill-slopes between woodland and the River Thames. Not over-large, it had a character all its own. Richard, seeing Anne's fondness for the palace, had three years earlier added a new wing. Refurnished and refurbished entirely to Anne's taste, Sheen had become a real home.

Following the recent and traumatic events at Westminster, Richard and Anne had moved with the court to Sheen, there to try to come to terms with their sorrows and recover their equilibrium.

On the second evening after their arrival, seated beside the log fire in her chamber in that part of the building known as the Queen's House, bereft of her Bohemian friends and servants, some of whom had been part of her life since earliest childhood, Anne was none the less cheered by the certainty that Richard would be with her shortly.

After the trials and tribulations of recent months, and the utter misery of it all, she had looked to Richard for companionship and solace. Kindred spirits, since he was mourning the loss of his lover and she the loss of her compatriots, each derived comfort from the presence of the other.

Anne gazed happily around the magnificent chamber. Furnished in greens, blues and gold, the four walls were hung with magnificent tapestries: known as The Four Seasons, these depicted the everyday life of the fourteenth century in spring, summer, autumn and winter. The double oaken doors were padded to keep out the cold — it was a chamber for lovers, Richard had once said, one where none could be overheard. Anne had laughed at the time, but even to herself the laugh had sounded a little hollow . . .

A low door of carved oak was set into the outer wall and was mostly kept locked and bolted, Anne herself retaining the silver key. It gave access by way of a short flight of outside steps to a small rose garden, sheltered and overlooking the moat. Richard and Anne were wont to sit there on summer evenings, hands linked and at ease. It was their own special place, protected by the moat and accessible only from Anne's chamber door.

But where was her lord now? she asked herself. It was well past ten o'clock and her customary bedtime — and here was a servant, come to damp down the fire for the night.

Anne, surprised and concerned at Richard's nonappearance, none the less spoke lightly to the woman.

"My lord the king?" she enquired. "Is he at present in the King's House?"

"Nay, my lady," came the reply. The young woman seemed uneasy, avoiding Anne's questioning gaze and busying herself with tidying the hearth. "It seems not."

"Then I doubt not His Grace is in the chapel." Anne's tone suggested that the matter was of small concern. "He will surely be here anon."

"The king rode out an hour since, my

lady — to an unknown destination, I was told," the servant said, still without meeting Anne's gaze. "With a small retinue, 'twas said — only two of His Grace's knights riding with him."

"I see," Anne managed to say. "Thank you, Alice. 'Tis a fine evening — doubtless my lord, after the rigours of the day, wished to take the air."

"As you say, my lady," agreed the other. "As Your Grace says — after the rigours of the day!"

★ ★ ★

Anne passed a restless and dream-ridden night.

She had at first lain awake, still half-expecting that Richard would come to her — but then, as the night wore away, expectancy turned to disappointment, and disappointment to resentment and anxiety.

Why, she wondered, had her lord ridden out in apparent haste without personally informing her of his intention — or sending a messenger? Always hitherto it had been his wont to tell her when he expected to be away all night. Had some harm befallen him? What or who had summoned him away in such haste that it had apparently overshadowed all else? she asked herself then. The answer, the unpalatable answer, was there in her mind — but she refused to give heed. Nay, she thought, it cannot be — *he has fled to France* . . .

The child came to her again that night; the little lost boy-child with the dark-brown curls and the brilliantly blue tear-filled eyes.

She awoke — or so she imagined — to find the tiny hands clawing the side of the bed, trying to reach her . . .

"Wait," she cried, "and I will help you. Why, my pretty one, are you in such a hurry!"

But even as she reached out for the child, feeling his baby-warm breath on her cheek, he slipped from view — only to reappear a moment later on the opposite side of the bed.

"Wait!" she cried again. "See, I am holding out my arms to you — *maman* wants you so much! Why, my precious, are you always just out of reach? Come to me, come . . ."

But even as she grasped the tiny hands, feeling the baby-soft flesh, the child, its hands stretching out to her, was pulled away as if by an invisible force.

Anne awoke to her own sobbing and, distressed and more than a little fearful, not understanding, she remained awake, truly awake, for a long time.

What did it mean? she wondered. Was it her yearning for a child that prompted the dream? Was the visitation caused by frustration; by the emptiness of her arms, her heart, her womb? One day, she thought with a mixture of hope and defiance, I shall reach the child and hold it close. One day it will be part of me. One day . . .

30

THOMAS OF WOODSTOCK, Duke of Gloucester, was not a happy man. Far from it. A warrior by nature as well as by training, he found it galling that the king had no inclination for warfare. What in Thomas's opinion was even worse, was that Richard should be wasting his time, wealth and possessions on time-serving courtiers who flattered and fawned, and generally encouraged his extravagant tastes and pastimes.

Whilst Richard was consorting with dissolute companions, the princes of the blood — notably Thomas himself and his brothers, John of Gaunt and Edmund of Langley — with their highly-trained private armies, were cooling their heels and being denied the stimulus of military action against their hereditary foes.

Several years had now passed since the peasants' revolt and the royal marriage which had followed it. During those years, Richard had accomplished little in real terms — there had been no campaign against the French and what had amounted to little more than a military exercise against the Scots.

Despite the general shake-up which had followed the firm action of what had since become known as the Merciless Parliament, all was not well with the royal household. The sycophants still lounged like gaudy butterflies about the court — though their numbers had thinned a little of late.

Worst of all, Richard had no heir.

★ ★ ★

On the morning after Richard's sudden and inexplicable departure from the palace of Sheen, Anne was returning from the chapel after Mass, her ladies following, when a party of fast-riding horsemen entered the courtyard.

Surprised, half-expecting to see Richard himself, Anne turned and at once recognized the leading rider as Thomas of Woodstock. Horses and riders looked weary and travel-stained, as from much hard riding but Thomas, seeing Anne, at once dismounted and strode towards her.

After greeting her formally he drew her aside, out of earshot of her ladies. He asked her of Richard and his whereabouts.

"He rode out last night, my lord," she told him, unable to keep a tremor from her voice. "He left no word as to his destination."

"Then it is as I feared," said Thomas grimly. "My lady, it is necessary that I speak with you alone. Time is of the essence, and there is much to be done. I must needs be on my way again by midnight."

"Alone, you say, my lord?" asked Anne with an expression that the duke could not fathom. "I am alone now — or as near so as makes no difference!"

"Pray hearken to me, my lady," said Thomas sternly. "What I have to say is of the utmost importance. It concerns the king and is for your ears only. I would prefer, for Richard's sake, that we be not seen in conference together. Alone, my lady, and discreetly, if you please."

"Then, my lord, be so good as to be

at my chamber door — the private one that leads to the rose-garden — at the hour of nine this evening. I myself shall admit you — none else will know."

"Then, my lady, I shall bid you adieu," came the misleadingly light-hearted response — and, so saying, Thomas of Woodstock bowed and went his way.

* * *

Anne, seated by the fire in her chamber that evening as the hour of nine approached, was half-heartedly reading a book to while away the time till her visitor's arrival. Her already discarded sewing lay to one side, and the book, a favourite of Richard's, failed to hold her attention. Her thoughts were on the forthcoming visit and the news her visitor had to impart to her.

She suspected that he had news of Richard, and feared that something was very much amiss. Had her lord been taken ill — or taken prisoner? Never before had he failed to inform her of his movements.

She was formally attired in a deep blue cotehardie with a white border, over an undergown of apple green.

She had loosed her hair from its binding — a concession to the lateness of the hour — and it hung like a golden mane down her back. She had dismissed her ladies for the night, having no further need of them — only Lady Twyford remaining on call in the ante-chamber.

A light tap on the garden door made her jump guiltily — though she could not have said why. Taking the silver key, she unlocked the door and stood back that her visitor might enter.

As Thomas of Woodstock came through the low doorway, ducking his head as he did so, and into the queen's chamber, Anne was reminded of three things. Firstly, though he was the king's uncle, never had they been alone together before, not truly alone; secondly, that he was unusually handsome; and thirdly, of how on that journey from Canterbury to London when she had first come to England as a bride, she had fallen a little in love with him . . .

Tall and well-made, having the physique

and hard muscles of a warrior, Thomas of Woodstock had the piercing blue eyes of the Plantagenets and bore a strong likeness to Edward the Third, his royal sire, and to John of Gaunt.

Wearing a capacious dark cloak ready for journeying, he had apparently left his leather riding-boots outside the door. Removing his cloak, he dropped it on to a nearby chair and was seen to be wearing a short dark-blue cotehardie with a jewelled waist-belt, bagpipe sleeves and dark-blue hose.

Anne graciously bade him be seated, but he merely nodded and remained standing. Clearly he had much on his mind.

"The king is with the Duke of Ireland," he told Anne practically. "The duke was believed to have left England but he must have contrived to send a message to the king — by what means I know not, my lady. A secret meeting was arranged. Should the duke be captured, needless to say he will not live to tell the tale. But no time must be lost, and tonight I and my men are going in search of him."

"And what of the king?" Anne asked quietly.

"My brothers and I fear that the king might attempt eventually to accompany the duke to France and there seek the assistance of the French king," came the disturbing reply. "This must be prevented at any cost and I intend, therefore, to intercept my nephew and bring him back, if necessary by force, before irreparable harm is done."

"Irreparable harm, my lord?" asked Anne nervously.

Thomas, not wishing to distress her further, hesitated before replying.

"Madam," he said then, "when neither the king's ministers nor senior members of his household have knowledge of a sovereign's whereabouts, that sovereign is statutorily deposed — perchance only temporarily."

"If that be the case, then the king must have been taken and held prisoner against his will," Anne said white-faced. "He would not voluntarily jeopardize his sovereignty."

Thomas said nothing to that. He had no wish to disagree with her and thus increase her agitation — at the same time he could not agree.

"Time will give us the truth of that," he said instead.

"You believe he is still in England?" Anne asked tremulously.

"Intelligence tells us it is so," Thomas said soberly. "To find the king then is, amongst others, my mission. You will understand, I doubt not, the reason for secrecy and haste. I shall depart with my men at midnight and journey under cover of darkness to a destination which shall be nameless."

"My lord was deeply grieved at the prospect of the Duke of Ireland sharing the same fate as Sir Simon Burley," Anne said, as if by way of an excuse. "He loves the duke like a brother."

Thomas looked at her in surprise. Does not she know? he asked himself. Does not she realize that the prancing popinjay is her lord's lover? Her concern is all for Richard, it seems — for his happiness. God in heaven, is it possible!

"My lady, weep not for de Vere and his ilk — weep for yourself who have been so woefully neglected these many years. Weep for England, if you will — but weep not for the de Veres of this world!"

"But I love my lord," Anne said defensively. "I love him dearly."

"And I dare say that in his own way, my kingly nephew loves you — but a king needs sons, my lady, heirs to secure his dynasty."

Anne was a trifle on her mettle. Is my lord of Woodstock blaming myself, she wondered, for the king's lack of an heir? Or is he perchance blaming de Vere? My lord of Woodstock, it would seem, is over-ready to cast aspersions!

"I am aware of that, sir," she said coldly. "How could I not be aware of it? Think you I do not weep because I have not borne my lord a child!"

How entrancing she is! Thomas said to himself. I thought so at our first meeting at Canterbury — and think so now. I fell in love with her then and, God have pity, I love her still!

He changed the subject. He would speak of the rest presently. He picked up the book she had been reading and, seeing its title, smiled.

"*Le Roman de la Rose!*" he said. "That is surely a book for lovers."

"'Tis a poem, my lord, and most circumspect!" Anne told him, seeing his expression and puzzled by it.

"How much have you read, my lady?"

"Not much as yet, my lord."

"*Le Roman de la Rose* was written by two poets," he told her. "The first part, by Guillaume de Lorris, is a formal exposition of the courtly code."

"And the second part, my lord?"

"The second part was written by Jean de Meung, and takes over just as the lover is advancing to pluck the rose."

"Indeed, my lord?" Anne asked, innocently. "And what of Jean de Meung's contribution to the poem?"

"Certes, dear lady, de Meung's work is a very different matter — and could by no manner of means be termed courtly!"

"What mean you, my lord?"

"The second part, taking over as the lover advances to pluck the rose, tells by what mischievous and varied ways the rose may be plucked."

Anne blushed — and he thought, how

adorable she is! Again I must change the subject.

"Perchance the king, rather than yourself, my lady, might benefit from reading *Le Roman de la Rose*," he said poker-faced. "He might find it helpful!"

"But my lord ofttimes reads it," she said. "The book is his — I merely borrow it."

"I have just written a book[1] — my second, in fact."

"I would that I might read it, my lord!"

"Unless, my lady, you are thinking of becoming a latter-day Boadicea, I doubt it would bring you much joy!"

"Perchance, after all, I should persevere with Jean de Meung!" Anne said with a smile.

"My lady, I must not detain you any longer," Thomas told her then, making to don his cloak. "But pray answer me one more question ere I depart."

"Speak on, my lord."

---

[1] *A History of the Laws of Battle*

"Are you happy, truly happy, here in England?"

"Happy, my lord?" She looked surprised, as if she had not before given thought to the matter. "Why, yea . . . "

"Your happiness means much to me," he told her, seeing her hesitation. "Was not it I who welcomed you first on your arrival in England. You stole my heart then, my lady, and have it still!"

There was a momentary silence. It lay like a challenge between them — a challenge to be accepted or rejected. Chivalry permitted no other course.

"I know, my lord," Anne said then, and he heard the tell-tale tremor in her voice. "I know — you were so kind and patient with me, a stranger."

"Kind? It is easy to be kind to those we love." His tone was rueful but his blue gaze was unwavering. "Anne, this I shall say to you and for ever after hold my peace. I have watched and wondered these many years past . . ."

What occurred next was so unexpected, so uncontrived by both parties, that Anne was afterwards to ask herself how it had happened. Maybe it was the sense of isolation in that opulent chamber, the soporific warmth of the log fire — or maybe for Anne it was simply his maleness and the brilliance of his gaze . . .

Whatever it was, she found herself in his arms. She made no real attempt to resist him, only a word or two . . .

"Nay," she protested but softly — so softly that he only just caught the word.

"My lady — " he said, his voice warm and low " — say but the word and I shall turn and go, never to trouble you again."

She shook her head.

"Nay, my lord," she said, "leave me not, I pray you. Love me a little, if you will. A moment since you spoke of *Le Roman de la Rose* — I fear that this rose has much to learn!"

He glanced significantly towards the bed and she nodded.

"Yea, my lord," she said quietly. "What better place to teach me of love?"

He unfastened the complicated ribbons and tapes which secured her gown and, as the gown slithered to the floor, she turned away from him and removed the rest of her clothes — whilst he did likewise.

Climbing into the bed, she lay back on the pillows, shy of a sudden — and a little fearful.

How handsome he is! she thought. So big and strong — his hands are warrior's hands, powerful but well-kept.

"Anne — " he said tenderly, leaning over her " — I love you now as I loved you at our first meeting — methinks I have always loved you."

"Then pray teach *me* of love . . ."

He kissed her lips slowly, tenderly and without passion — and ran the palms of his hands over her body, gently, persuasively, moulding her shoulders, breasts, thighs.

Sighing, she said nothing, — but lay there, letting him stroke and caress her. Such blissful fondling . . .

He caressed her thighs and belly and she spread her legs, quite unprepared for what happened next . . . His fingers, exploring her secret places, were suddenly stilled.

"*Jesu Christe!*" he exclaimed.

He sat back on his haunches and

looked down at her without speaking for a few moments.

"God forgive me, I had no idea — " he said quietly then " — no idea at all!"

"No idea, my lord — that I am a virgin?" she asked softly — so very softly. "Nay, 'tis not something one calls to the high hills — not something of which one is particularly proud!"

He leaned over her then and kissed her lips, stroking her face and murmuring endearments to her.

"Anne, forgive me — and tell me, I pray you, what you would have me do."

"You love me, you say?"

"Sweeting, I love you with all my heart and soul."

"Then take me, my lord — take me here and now, sparing me not. Take my maidenhead and make a woman of me!"

He kissed her again. "I shall be gentle as an angel," he assured her.

"Nay, nay — be not too gentle. Only take me, make me into a woman — let me feel, know, suffer pain . . . Take me, use my body as a pillow and make me into a woman . . ."

He needed no further bidding. His passion roused to fever point by her words and the discovery that she was *virgo intacta*, he caressed and coaxed until they became one . . .

She gave a small cry then and he placed his fingers gently over her mouth. She bit one of his fingers and drew blood.

"*Touché!*" he said with the briefest of smiles, having other things on his mind.

She moaned a little, tossing her head from side to side as if after all she wished to elude him — until, her body lost in his powerful embrace, he rode her triumphantly as a warrior his steed . . .

★ ★ ★

Anne must have fallen asleep then, for she awoke some time later to find her lover leaning on one elbow and looking down at her.

"Are you all right, sweeting?" he asked concernedly.

Anne smiled. "I am all right, my lord," she replied.

"Believe me, my lady, I had no idea. All these years — "

She placed a finger to his lips.

"Speak not of it, my lord," she said. "The deed is done. Anne of Bohemia is a woman now and perchance some day, who knows, she will bear the King of England a child!"

"Mean you what I think you mean?" asked Thomas of Woodstock — and Anne smiled at the conflicting expressions that crossed his face.

"It would be a Plantagenet child, would it not?" she asked innocently. "A Plantagenet child for a Plantagenet king."

"I doubt Your Grace will find herself to be with child this time," observed her lover. "The first time — well, I expect you know the old rhyme."

"Maybe you have forgotten, my lord, that I was not born in England. In my homeland, we have our own customs and rhymes — not all of them polite, it must be said!"

"Oh, this is polite enough — but prophetic, one might say! It goes like this:

'The first is for joy,
The second a boy,
The third for a lass
The fourth . . . '

Nay, I'll not tell you the rest, or my retinue will be waiting out there till kingdom come!"

"But —"

"I must away, dear heart. In a little over an hour, my men-at-arms will be mounting up ready for departure — we must be well on our way by dawn." Thomas paused, debating whether or not to put her fully in the picture. "Robert de Vere is reportedly marching on London with royal troops — I plan to intercept them."

"With a handful of men-at-arms, my lord?" asked Anne, as if it were this that concerned her most.

"Nay, not exactly." Thomas smiled. "Young Henry of Bolingbroke is awaiting me *en route* — with the duke his father's Lancastrian troops and mine from Gloucester."

"Then it is civil war," Anne said fearfully. "Alas that —"

"A skirmish, no more!" cheerfully interposed her lover, kissing her. "Be not troubled, dearing!"

"You will be weary, my lord," Anne pointed out. "All day, I am told, you have been about the king's business."

"Weary?" he asked, looking at her in surprise — as if, Anne thought, she had uttered an improper word. But then he smiled broadly.

"Bayard is well accustomed to his master falling asleep in the saddle," he told her. "Indeed, he welcomes it — it makes him feel important, as indeed he is!"

"Bayard?"

"My stallion — named after his grandsire, the king my father's favourite horse," Thomas explained. "Every warrior worth his salt must and does master the art of sleeping thus — otherwise it could well be the enemy which catches us napping!"

Anne put long slender arms around his neck and drew him to her.

"Make us a child, my lord, I pray you," she said softly.

"Make us a child and I swear, by God

and all his saints, that I shall love you for evermore!"

Thomas of Woodstock looked down at her — smiling, teasing her a little. But his eyes were shining with love and joy.

"As my lady commands . . . " he said.

Part Four

The Leave-taking

31

THE royal troops led by Robert de Vere, formerly Earl of Oxford and Duke of Ireland, were confronted at Radcot Bridge, near Oxford, by the private armies of Thomas of Woodstock and John of Gaunt — the latter headed by his eldest son, Henry of Bolingbroke.[1] In the ensuing battle, the royal troops were defeated, de Vere managing to escape during the mêlée . . .

Having a price on his head and already judicially under sentence of death, de Vere knew that he could expect no mercy from his opponents if he were captured. With a few loyal comrades, he went into hiding, having first contrived to send a message to Richard.

★ ★ ★

---
[1] The future King Henry the Fourth

Richard dismounted and, with a pat for Lionheart, his favourite stallion, ordering his escort to wait, he strode alone from the clearing. Taking a path through the trees, following the scrawled instructions on the roughly-drawn map he was holding, he arrived a few minutes later at his destination.

"Robby!" he exclaimed as he entered the ramshackle stone building in the heart of the forest. "Robby, my dear friend!"

"So Your Grace received my message," said de Vere, embracing him warmly. "I have been lent this place by a friend — a profligate friend, as Lancaster would say! None knows I am here, save he and a couple of trusty squires."

"Rumour has it that you have escaped to France," Richard told him, registering the fact that de Vere looked tired, older, and that his appearance was more than a little unkempt.

"I have, in theory," came the reply. "By the morrow, God willing, I should be there in fact."

"Only for a time, Robby — only for a time!" Richard assured him.

"To tell the truth, my lord, I cannot get there fast enough — to hell with this God-forsaken land!"

"It will all blow over, Robby — already the signs are there."

"The signs, you say? Why, 'tis your princely uncles who have been hounding me — and still are, I doubt not. Thomas of Woodstock is determined to get me this time — and has already boasted, I understand, that if captured, I shall not live to stand trial!"

"Again," said Richard quietly.

"Again — what mean you, my lord?"

"You were sent for trial and charged, if you recall," Richard pointed out. "Had you not escaped — "

"I would now be dead as mutton — you know it, Richy, and I know it also!" de Vere said cheerfully. "And speaking of mutton, I trust you brought your dinner with you."

"My dinner?" frowned Richard. "What in God's name do you mean?"

"Well, you see, Richy my friend, food is a wee bit scarce in these parts, and — "

"*Par Dieu!*" interposed Richard. "Are

things truly as bad as that? I had no idea. I — "

"I doubt I shall return — to England, I mean," put in de Vere soberly — as if, after all, exile mattered to him. "When there is a price on one's head, 'tis astonishing how valuable one becomes to oneself!"

"Is your lady here with you?" enquired Richard who, having laid the blame for de Vere's change of heart solely on the landgravine, preferred on the whole to ignore her existence. "Had she been still in the queen's service, she would by now have been packed off to Bohemia with the rest of them."

If Richard refrained from adding *and good riddance*, the words were none the less there in his tone!

"My lady?" asked de Vere with a frown. "Oh, you must be referring to Agnes Lancecrona, the landgravine. In truth, she is not my lady — nor ever was!"

"What mean you?" asked Richard in surprise.

"Come, Richy, be seated here beside me," said de Vere, patting the ramshackle bed. "The furniture is hardly de Verian but 'tis a mite better than taking one's rest on a rush-strewn floor — or plain honest-to-God bracken. I am something of an expert, you see — I have of late tried them all!"

Richard looked curiously around the dilapidated stone building — as much to gain time as anything else. Events had moved so swiftly of late, that it was difficult to keep up with them. He had been told that de Vere had fled to France, that he was now an uxorious husband and had taken his bride with him — but here he was, still in England, speaking dismissively of his new lady.

"I fail to understand," he said, stretching out on the bed beside de Vere.

"So do I, Richy," said de Vere laconically. "So do I, my friend. Methought I knew myself — but it seems I was mistaken. I and Agnes Lancecrona are not in fact man and wife — when it came to it, you understand, neither of us was much use to the other. Birds of a feather, I suppose!"

"What in Christ's name do you mean?"

demanded Richard. "Or is this just another of your jests!"

"I am not jesting, my lord." De Vere looked suddenly serious and Richard saw with some concern the ravages of the past weeks — of being a hunted man, one dispossessed of everything, not least his freedom and hereditary titles. "After all the troubles the lady has caused me — the annulment of my former marriage, parliamentary displeasure, your princely uncles howling for my blood, and my impending exile — think you I find the matter entertaining? As soon as it is feasible, I shall seek an annulment of my marriage to the landgravine."

"Birds of a feather was your saying, my lord," frowned Richard. "What meant you?"

De Vere sighed, but this time Richard was convinced that his story was genuine — that the second marriage which had been the start of all the trials and tribulations that had afflicted him, was after all a dreadful mistake.

"'Twas her very boyishness, her lack of femininity, which appealed to me, I suppose — " de Vere told him, speaking slowly, collecting his thoughts — and Richard took his hand and held it consolingly, " — though I recognized it not then. Unusually tall for a female is Agnes Lancecrona, with the figure of a youth and an apology for a bosom — well, you know how I dislike such appendages!"

Richard, who held rather different views in this respect, had the grace to blush.

"Well, Richy, to cut a long story short — and ignoring a very tedious night — Agnes Lancecrona is no more inclined for the opposite sex than am I myself." De Vere laughed then, despite himself. "Methought a boyish-looking creature with child-bearing propensities, would be both interesting and practical — you, Richy, are not the only one in need of an heir! I now suspect that Agnes Lancecrona consented to the marriage, solely to gain an influential husband and — having in mind some gossip she had overheard — to avoid the likelihood of being packed off to Bohemia with the rest. As it is, I am the one being packed-off, whilst she remains in the lap of luxury here!"

"Robby, must you go?" asked Richard — as if only the last part of the revelation concerned him. "Could not you flee to the North and lie low in some Northumbrian village for a while — till the hue and cry dies down?"

"Richy, my liege, I should die of boredom!" exclaimed de Vere. "Nay, I shall be well enough in France for a while. I have friends in Louvain and I dare say I shall find myself a nice little niche at the French court."

"I would I could go with you, my lord," Richard said wistfully. "In fact, I myself when I leave here am not returning to Sheen. I shall retire for a while to Bristol Castle — remaining there until such time as this whole matter is resolved and the fate of my servants decided. Sheen is too near to Westminster for comfort at the present time — heaven alone knows who the Privy Council will next be sending for trial!"

"What of the queen, my lord? Is she accompanying you to Bristol?"

"I shall send for her — and there we shall lodge until I deem it safe for us to return to the capital. The royal troops which scattered at Radcot Bridge are, I am told, mustering at Bristol ready for my arrival."

"Then you believe that you yourself are in danger?" asked de Vere, with unwonted seriousness. "You believe that Your Grace might be held culpable for the sins and omissions of your servants?"

"It could be so," Richard said sombrely.

"Come with me, sire — to France," de Vere urged him. "Come with me and be damned to them!"

"And what then of the queen?" asked Richard — as if she were his one concern. "Would I leave my beloved lady to the mercy of those ruffians at Westminster! Why, they will likely be sending Her Grace for trial next — after Burley, God rest him, aught is possible!"

"Sire, the queen is safe enough," pointed out de Vere, feeling as always a stab of jealousy at Richard's playing the uxorious husband. "The princes your uncles will see to it that no harm befalls the queen — they hold Her Grace in high esteem."

"As they should. As they should."

"As they should indeed, my lord," agreed de Vere whole-heartedly. "And it has to be admitted that Thomas of Woodstock's regard for the queen is wholly commendable."

Richard shot him a thoughtful look. Why does Robby speak thus, he asked himself — as if he is trying to tell me something? But there — it is, as ever, naught but one of his little games!

"Then the time has come to say farewell, my friend," he said, trying to keep the emotion from his voice. "We must for a time go our separate ways."

"Your Grace to Bristol and myself to France," said de Vere with seeming cheerfulness. "A true parting of the ways!"

"Life at Bristol will be dull in the extreme," Richard said with a sigh. "Believe me, I shall return to Sheen at the first opportunity."

"Bristol is the second city in England," pointed out de Vere in a how-lucky-you-are tone of voice. "King Stephen was held prisoner there in the twelfth century."

"If Bristol be the second city, then — by

sweet St George — it does not say much for the others!" remarked Richard with a grin. "And as to the other piece of information, one can only exclaim, 'Poor King Stephen!'"

"I shall return, Richy," de Vere said, with an earnestness that belied his earlier words. "I swear that, by hook or by crook, Robert de Vere, former Earl of Oxford and Duke of Ireland, will return!"

"But if — "

De Vere laughed. "By my faith, my lord, you are a picture of woe, whilst I — deserted by my troops at Witney, stripped of my titles, and living like a gypsy in a barn not far from London — set my sights on the future! Look at you — is this the picture I must take with me!"

"But what if you should not return?" Richard asked quietly. "What if we should never meet again?"

"As is likely," came the nonchalant reply.

Richard paled. "But only a moment ago, you — "

"That was, as you say, a moment ago," agreed de Vere. "Now I give thought to it, there are some mighty handsome gentlemen at the French court. When it comes to it, I might not wish to return."

"Stay here, I beg of you — "

"Here, my lord?" asked de Vere in a horrified tone, gazing around the half-derelict building. "In this hell-hole!"

"It is but a temporary refuge," Richard reminded him. "Stay here — keep your head down for a while. Somehow I should find a means of having you with me, Robby — life without you would be intolerable. There must be a way."

"It could cost Your Grace his crown," de Vere reminded him.

Richard shrugged, not trusting himself to speak.

"Hearken to me, Richy," de Vere said, putting an arm around the other's shoulders. Then, speaking in the cadences that pleased the king, his voice that of a lover, he said earnestly, "I shall return some day, somehow — I, Robert de Vere, swear it. I was but jesting a moment ago, making pretence of not caring if we met not again. But I swear before God and all the company of Heaven, that one day you, my very dear lord, will look again upon the face of your lover."

"Oh, Robby, how empty my life will be without you!" Richard said woefully.

"There will still be jousts and masques, finery and dressing-up," de Vere pointed out, knowing Richard's weakness for such display. "Still you will parade through the streets to the cheers of your subjects — and though it breaks my heart to remind you, my sweet lord, there are other lovers!"

"None as beautiful as you, Robby — as heart-warming as you."

De Vere nodded complacently. "True, my liege. But handsome enough, I dare say."

"None is as entertaining as yourself."

De Vere, never one to hide his light under a bushel, nodded at this also.

"I cannot deny that you are right, my lord," he said gravely. "But might one venture a word of advice?"

"Advice?" Richard sounded vexed. "Advice as to my choice of friends, mean you?"

"Look to your crown, Richy, when I am gone. Do your duty by that wench you married — get a child on her!"

"But — "

De Vere placed a firm hand over Richard's mouth.

"Nay, ask me not how — I must leave something to God!" he said with an affected sigh. "Get a child on the queen — and you will delight your subjects and secure your crown at one and the same time."

"You know that I cannot," Richard said reproachfully. "You, of all people — "

"You show much fondness for your lady," put in de Vere. "That is surely a good start."

"I love her — in a brotherly kind of way," Richard told him. "I take pleasure in my lady's company and ofttimes at night we lie together — but only in friendship, platonic friendship. I cannot, you understand — "

"There is no such word as 'cannot', my lord — or so my erstwhile tutor insisted!"

"Could *you*?"

"Naturally I could not. I respected my lady de Coucy and took pride in her beauty and grace — but the idea of physical union was anathema to me."

"And what of your landgravine?" Richard asked curiously. "Were not you attracted to her in the first place?"

"Her very boyishness, her flat chest and hips appealed to me initially," came the answer. "Indeed, without the padding she tucked into the bodice of her gowns, she was, would you believe it, as flat as two pancakes with cherries on!"

Richard laughed. "Well then . . ."

"Nature, in her case, had made a mistake — as I discovered to my cost." De Vere smiled ruefully. "She, unlike myself, liked buxom females. Oh, Richy — dear Richy — what a funny old world it is! We lay together, Agnes Lancecrona and I, that first night, like two adolescents unsure as to what anything was for — and she having no curiosity to find out!"

"And the next night, my lord?" Richard asked soberly enough. Why is it, he thought, that whenever de Vere speaks of such matters, I know an almost irresistible urge to laugh!

"There was no second night," de Vere admitted with a sigh — though whether of relief or disappointment was not clear.

"I did not go to her chamber — no point in asking for trouble, I told myself — and neither of us ever referred to the matter again. Oh, we were civil enough when we met — or were unable to avoid each other — but that was the end of it."

"You too, Robby, are in need of an heir?" Richard pointed out. "Eventually, I doubt not, your earldom, if not your dukedom, will be restored to you — it will be my especial care."

De Vere shrugged. "I have a nephew, Aubrey de Vere who, I doubt not, would play the role of Earl of Oxford better than I."

"Then this is farewell," Richard said with a sigh.

"Yea, my lord — for the time being. I shall leave under cover of darkness just before prime. All has been made ready."

"Prime is two or three hours away!"

"My squires will call me in two hours' time, my lord. You had best be away before then."

"Two hours?" There was joy as well as sorrow in Richard's voice. "So short a time in which to say farewell."

"Two hours in which to take our pleasure," said de Vere firmly. "Two hours to remember!"

As they lay together on the dilapidated bed, both were conscious of the poignancy of the moment. Richard was distressed by thoughts of separation, by the emptiness of parting — but de Vere's distress, though he kept it to himself, was the keener.

Even as he caressed his willing young monarch and held him close in his arms; as passion grew to a frenzy of desire — de Vere knew that this was the last time they would be together thus . . .

What he knew, had nothing to do with Philippa de Coucy or her successor — nothing to do with the queen or Richard's need of an heir. It had everything to do with time and fate; with premonition and a sixth sense.

Robert de Vere knew without a doubt that he would never again look upon Richard of England. He knew also, and with no less certainty, that Richard, whom he loved as he loved no other, would one day look upon him . . .

32

RICHARD remained at Bristol Castle for only three weeks.

He had sent word to Anne, asking her to join him — but she had prevaricated, having other things on her mind. At the end of three weeks, boredom was getting the better of him and, on receiving word from parliament that his automatic dethronement had been revoked and that his presence was required at Westminster, he at once made ready to leave.

In truth, the Privy Council having received proof that Robert de Vere was now living in exile in France, much of the feeling against Richard had evaporated.

He had been given a salutary lesson, his ministers told themselves and each other. He had voluntarily betaken himself to Bristol, there to contemplate his sins and omissions. Henceforth, he would mind his P's and Q's, be more amenable to their wishes . . .

In the event, the Privy Council discovered its mistake. In less time than it takes to say *houppelande, cotehardie, red velvet mantle lined with ermine, blue and gold dalmatic, gold shoes and jewelled necklace*, Richard of Bordeaux was back in the swing of things — or so it seemed to the king's ministers.

He resumed his former indolent, pleasure-loving way of life as if none of it — executions, imprisonments, banishments and the rest — had really touched him. He divided his time for the most part between the palaces of Westminster and Sheen — Anne having remained all the while at the latter.

The lavish displays of former years, expenditure on entertainments and outlandish modes of dress, had in no way diminished.

Much of Richard's extravagance arose from his generosity to others — to Anne, to his favourites and notably to his subjects. His open-handedness, his joy in giving, whilst endearing him to his people, brought further condemnation from his ministers. The latter, alarmed at the fast-emptying state coffers and the king's total indifference to the situation, sought desperately for a means of controlling his expenditure.

★ ★ ★

Matters came to a head when, not long after Robert de Vere's departure, an outbreak of plague afflicted the country.

Plague had first visited England some forty-five years earlier, during the previous reign. Originating in China, it had unwittingly been conveyed by Genoese traders to a number of Mediterranean towns, whence during the year 1347 it had entered and decimated all the major ports of Southern Europe.

Despite every precaution, the pestilence had crossed to England in the year following, entering the country by way of Melcombe Regis, a small coastal town in Dorset, and wiping out all its inhabitants. Moving on through Wiltshire and Hampshire, it had reached London at the beginning of November, where it rampaged through the narrow City streets, bringing the capital to a halt and destroying in a matter of weeks half its population. It had remained in London until the following Whit Sunday when it abruptly departed, laying a trail towards Norwich and thence to Yorkshire.

Having wrought death and destruction throughout the land, on a scale seen neither before nor since, the pestilence left England and unleashed its fury on Scotland. In the space of one year, the population of England had halved.

Following that first outbreak in England, the plague — of the bubonic type and called the Black Death because of the nature of its symptoms — remained endemic in the soil, returning three times in a generation at first and then, prior to the outbreak in Richard the Second's reign, only once each decade.

Richard moved the court from Westminster to Sheen which, with its clear air and leafy surroundings, was believed to be relatively safe from the contagion. Since the pestilence was at that time thought to be air-borne, rather than endemic in the soil, the palace of Sheen, standing amidst green trees and having a sparkling river running by, was seen as a refuge.

"My lady, the air is surely as pure and free from contagion here as anywhere on God's earth," Richard said on the afternoon of their arrival. "I believe Sheen to be truly a haven."

"A haven indeed," agreed Anne, as they strolled in the beautiful gardens that looked towards the river. "A blessed haven — and our one real home, my lord."

Now, Anne was in need of a haven — as well as a home. After some twelve years of marriage, she believed herself to be with child. She had spoken to none of this, not even to Richard — least of all to Richard. Because Richard would know, if none else did, that she could not be with child — not with *his* child.

Thus Anne needed a haven — one in which to dream and plan and look to the future — the future of herself and her child. Were she to reveal her secret to Richard — how would he react? she asked herself more than once. Richard needed an heir — oh, how greatly he needed an heir! But since he himself could not provide the necessary heir and was aware that he could not, how would he react to someone else's having provided an heir for him!

Anne suspected that Thomas of Woodstock knew her secret — even though on those rare occasions when he was at court, apart from observance of the courtesies, she had not spoken with him alone since that one magical night. Sometimes she gave thought to that night and, when she did so, her pulses quickened and she knew, not a sense of guilt but a sense of joy. Thomas of Woodstock was enamoured of her and she, if the truth be told, of him. But he had a wife and children; whilst she, Anne, had Richard, and Thomas's child — or so she believed — and with them she must and would be content. But how and what to tell Richard, that was the problem. Was it too late, even now, to . . .

Nay, the idea was abhorrent to her — as much so now as it was by nature to Richard himself. Her body was a cradle for her child — nothing must disturb the child, Anne told herself, make it feel unwanted, threatened . . . It was too late for Richard, much too late. She was clear about that — but what then was she to do?

She had a deep regard for Thomas of Woodstock, a fierce hunger. The flames of love which had burned in them both that night, had left a great yearning ... Yet still, in a different way, she loved Richard, her lord and king.

But Anne's love, her feelings and desires, were as nothing compared with her love for her unborn child. Her feelings for her husband and her lover could, if necessary, be hidden away for ever in the secret recesses of her mind — but her child could be hidden away for only a few more weeks ...

Yea, Anne needed a haven — in which to think, to yearn, to prepare, to make a decision — the right decision. Please God, she prayed each night on her knees, let me think clearly, act wisely — do what is best for my innocent babe!

Anne was on the whole content — in her shared and secret love, in the possible fruit of that love, and in her role as her lord's queen and comforter. There at Sheen she was content. The child could not remain in her womb for ever and it was at Sheen that he, her little prince — she was certain it would be a prince — would first see the light of day . . .

Richard was looking at her — curiously, Anne thought.

"Of what is my lady thinking?" he asked lightly. "She looks to be lost in thought — in a dream of a seventh heaven!"

"I was thinking, my lord, how fortunate I am," she told him, trying to collect her thoughts. "I look at those poor people who gather each morning at the palace gates, and give thanks that Your Grace and I have been spared the pestilence!"

The side effects of an outbreak of plague were only a degree less devastating than the contagion itself. A murrain had in this instance destroyed great numbers of livestock — five thousand sheep having died in a single pasture. Farmers, concerned for their livelihood, had little time and sympathy therefore for homeless and starving peasants.

Plague having a predilection for attacking the strong rather than the weak, bereaved and homeless women with a brood of children, as well as the old and the infirm, were a commonplace amongst the beggars. Driven from their dwellings, seeking charity where they might, they were a pitiful and all too common sight.

Richard and Anne were as one in their concern for these unfortunates. At all the royal palaces, people gathered in groups outside the gates, pleading for sustenance.

Richard, prevailed upon by Anne, himself a master of the grand gesture, had given orders that none should be turned away empty-handed from the gates of the royal residences. Each was to be given bread and a mug of ale — and meat when possible. Meat, bread and ale formed the staple diet of the peasantry but the former, due to the slaughtering of disease-ridden herds, was in short supply.

At Sheen, Richard and Anne regularly went together to the gates, where they helped with the distribution of the victuals. Anne, kind-hearted and distressed by the plight of these people, could on such occasions scarcely hold back her tears.

On the morning in question, her

troubled gaze fell on a woman with a baby at her breast and two small children beside her. She watched uneasily as the mother, given a hunk of bread, divided it in two, before dipping the pieces into a mug of ale and giving a piece to each of the children.

"She has taken none herself," Anne said in an undertone to Richard. "Look there, my lord — how, without sustenance, will she suckle her child?"

"She will down the ale, I dare say, and refill the mug with water from the brook for her children," Richard answered practically.

"She is thin as a scarecrow and so pale and wan," Anne said unhappily. "She looks to have been on the road for days."

"Many have, poor souls!" said Richard who, not having an affinity with the woman as had Anne, was inclined to view the beggars collectively.

"Could not we take her in, my lord?" persisted Anne. "Offer her and her children shelter."

"Into the palace, mean you, sweeting?"

"There is room enough," said Anne

defensively — displaying a talent for understatement.

Richard shook his head. Out of deference to the feelings of his subjects, wishing for once to underplay his love of rich apparel, he was wearing a plain black all-enveloping dark mantle, devoid of jewellery or decoration of any kind — and a black felt hat. But his golden hair, shining and close-curled under the hat, enhanced by the many gold and jewelled rings he was wearing on fingers and thumbs, created a dramatic and riveting effect which was far from that intended.

"It is better that we do what we can for the many, instead of singling out a few," Richard said practically. "Many will die, I fear — food is short everywhere. There is just not enough to go round. I have already given orders that the large barn on the edge of the forest be cleared and made over as a shelter."

Before he recognized her intention, Anne had gone up to the gates to speak to the woman.

"Pray tell me your name — " Anne said to her " — and whence you come."

"Rhoda, me lady — that's me name," the woman replied nervously, taken aback by Anne's arrival and modestly covering her breast. "We've come from nigh the Moat Lake."[1]

"And your husband?"

"My man was took by the pestilence, me lady — 'im first and then two of me little ones."

She began to weep and her nursling, robbed of its sustenance, started to wail. Anne, at a loss how to assist her, impulsively drew off one of her rings — gold set with an amethyst.

"Pray take this, Rhoda," she said gently. "Use it to buy food and shelter for a while — till you can find a more permanent abode."

The woman looked uneasy. "Nay, nay, me lady — 'tis good of ye but 'twould be no use."

"The stone is an amethyst — " Anne told her " — but the ring, being gold, should fetch a fair price."

The woman shook her head and the

---

[1] Mortlake

children gazed up at the stranger, fascinated by the richness of her garments — a mantle trimmed and lined with white fur, and dainty shoes such as none of them had seen before, they themselves being barefoot.

"My lady, 'tis no use," the woman said again. "You don't understand — how could you! I'd not be able to keep the ring, you see — someone would take it off me in a trice and maybe slit me throat into the bargain! Then where would me little-uns be? Besides, I doubt even gold'll buy food — seeing as there's no food to be 'ad!"

"She is right," Richard said quietly — standing now at Anne's elbow, concerned for her safety. "God have mercy, she is right!"

"My lord, I must help her," Anne told him in a low voice — registering that the king's knights had moved closer, hands on sword-hilts, ready for action. Before Richard could stop her, she turned again to the woman. "Be here again on the morrow, if you will — we shall meanwhile seek for a means of assisting you."

The woman made to reply but an official outside the gates spoke brusquely to her.

"Be on your way!" he ordered. "You have received your bounty — there are many other mouths to feed!"

Anne was about to remonstrate when Richard gently but firmly took her hand.

"Desist, my lady," he said in a low voice which brooked no refusal. "Others are looking, watching — you could do the woman a disservice by a display of partisanship!"

"Alas, my lord, I fear greatly for her and her little ones!" Anne said tearfully as he led her away. "If only — "

"Already my ministers complain of what they term 'the king's extravagance'," he said ruefully, as they made their way back to the palace. "God knows I feel for these people — as my subjects, they are my responsibility."

"Your ministers complain, you say, my lord — of what now do they complain?"

"The king's extravagance nothing can repress, they say, raising their hands in despair." Richard sighed and Anne realized that the plight of those outside the gates had touched him also. "To hear them talk, one would imagine that the entire revenues of the nation were being squandered on fripperies and entertainments."

Anne looked at him. His extravagance in dress, public tournaments and the refurbishment of the various royal palaces, in gifts to his favourites — and to herself — was a byword.

"By my faith, 'tis not my personal expenditure alone that drains the treasury!" he assured her, guessing what she was thinking. "Every single day since the pestilence once more blighted this land, six thousand persons have been given food and drink at the gates of the royal palaces — by my direct order!"

"So many, my lord?" Anne asked in surprise.

Richard nodded. "Most are indigent peasants — victims of the pestilence and its attendant ills. And the outbreak, though slowing down, is by no means over yet — every day, fresh cases are reported in outlying districts, two today from near the Moat Lake."

The Moat Lake, situated between the

river and the palace moat, supplied water to the latter.

"Six thousand is a goodly number," Anne said, "but could not we, by denying ourselves, assist an even greater number?"

"I doubt it would help," Richard told her with truth. "As I have indicated, the root cause of the problem is lack of food, rather than lack of money — did not that woman with the children who so excited your sympathy, say as much!"

"She still has the ring, my lord," Anne said with a triumphant smile. "She was on the point of returning it, when that great ruffian pulled her away!"

"And I dare say that same great ruffian is at this very moment flaunting on his person a rather handsome gold and amethyst ring!"

Anne's face fell. "Please God, nay — I wished to give her something, to let her know of our concern, my lord!"

Richard patted her hand lovingly. "You are too tender-hearted for your own good, my lady — and I love you for it. One of these days, when my head is turned, I doubt not you will be pawning the crown jewels to buy gold rings for all my subjects!"

Despite his assurances and a genuine concern for his subjects, Richard prided himself on the fact that he was said to surpass in magnificence all the sovereigns of Europe. His treasury was as always at a low ebb, but the revenues that went to assist the victims of the pestilence and the consequent famine, were only part of the story. Still he employed no fewer than three hundred servants in his kitchens; while Anne, in spite of the departure of her Bohemian entourage, employed a like number in her household.

Richard and Anne were alike in their love of finery and ostentation. Their concern for Richard's indigent subjects was genuine enough — but neither had any real understanding of the overall situation and its possible remedies. Richard, lightly dismissing his ministers' well-justified complaints, cheerfully left them to devise a means of raising money from other sources to fund his and his consort's boundless extravagance.

33

ANNE looked for the woman, Rhoda, when on the following morning she accompanied Richard to the palace gates. The crowd outside was larger than ever, many looking hollow-eyed and exhausted from hunger and privation.

Anne sought in vain at first for the woman who, perhaps because she had looked about her own age, had caught her attention. She saw her then at the back of the crowd and motioned to one of the guards to bring her to her. Some in the crowd glared balefully at the woman, before grudgingly making way for her. Rhoda looked nervous and in worse case than on the previous day.

As she drew closer, Anne saw that she was weeping and that an ugly bruise was showing above the bodice of her ragged gown — a bruise that had not been there the previous day.

The guard opened one of the iron

gates just enough to give passage to the woman and her infant. Those around her grumbled and swore, and tried to elbow her aside, but the guard drew her inside the gate which was then promptly locked and barred.

Anne had meanwhile prevailed upon Richard to go less splendidly attired to these daily encounters; at which they, as a token of their concern for Richard's subjects, assisted in dispensing bread and ale — and on this occasion soup — to the unfortunates. Her suggestion had not met with any enthusiasm.

"To show oneself to one's subjects less than well dressed, would be to dishonour them," Richard had said.

"Neither honour nor dishonour means aught to a starving child, my lord," Anne had told him.

"Would you have me appear in sackcloth and ashes, my lady?" had demanded Richard. "It is through no fault of their sovereign that my subjects are in such bad case."

"Your Grace must do as he will," Anne had said. "As for myself, I shall don my plainest gown."

She was pleased, if a trifle taken aback, to see that in the event Richard was wearing a plain dark tunic and darned hose — these apparently having been borrowed from one of the lower servants.

Anne herself, attired in a plain but immaculate blue gown and a serviceable woollen mantle, wore the customary veil but no jewellery other than her wedding ring.

"I should like you and your children to come and stay in my household, Rhoda," she told the woman, drawing her aside from the hurly-burly of feeding and watering a large crowd of hungry people. "My servant here will take you to the palace and give you refreshment and a change of clothing. Later, when you are rested, we shall speak further."

"Thank you, my lady," the woman said, trying to hold back her tears. "I can sew a straight seam and do embroidery and all, should Your Grace be wanting summat o' that sort. But there's me babby — he'll 'ave to be with me till he's weaned."

"He will indeed," agreed Anne — a

new idea leaping into her mind. In six or seven months' time, she told herself, she would have need of a wet-nurse — and who better than Rhoda? "I see you left your other children at home today."

"I ain't got no home, me lady," Rhoda told her. "So many died there, you see, that the cottage was put to the torch by him as owned it. Just one small outhouse escaped his attention and me and the young 'uns sleeps there of a night."

"So you have left the children there today," Anne said lightly. "I shall send someone with you to collect them later."

"I dunno about that, me lady." Rhoda looked worried — as if talk of the children was not to her liking. "We'll just 'ave to wait and see!"

Wait and see! Anne thought in surprise. Wait for what, I wonder? But she dismissed the matter from her mind — at the time.

* * *

Anne, interviewing Rhoda later, learned that her husband had been a tenant farmer and that she herself was a skilful needlewoman. The farm, it appeared, had supported a number of serfs and female servants — all of whom, together with Rhoda's husband and children, had within the previous two weeks succumbed to the pestilence. In less than forty-eight hours, Rhoda had found herself widowed, homeless and destitute and with three children to support. The other children, the two who had been with her on the previous day, belonged not to herself, but to her sister, a widow, who had lived and worked on the farm.

"Just after me sister was taken — she was the last, you see, me lady — " Rhoda explained " — I heard shouts and guessed as the villagers were a-coming to set light to the cottage. There was no time to be lost and I bundled up everything I could, telling my nieces to do the same, poor mites! Then I grabbed up me babby and we left by the back door just as the first brand was thrown."

"You may bring your nieces here until a suitable home can be found for them," Anne told her, "I shall see to the matter myself, so you need have no fears for their welfare."

"Thank you, me lady — 'tis kind of ye but I can't say about my nieces. You see . . ." Rhoda paused and then, without explanation, changed the subject. "This I do know, me lady — I couldn't 'ave gone on much longer like we was, without proper food or anything. I saved a crust or two for me nieces and left them this morning in an outhouse — but I doubt they'll touch the food."

"I expect they are pining for their mother," Anne said sympathetically. "Once they are here, all will be well, I am sure."

"Yea, me lady," Rhoda said politely, but she failed to meet Anne's gaze — and again Anne was puzzled. "I expect you be right."

"Now, Rhoda, I shall ring for my housekeeper and she will take you to where a servant will be waiting with the horses. You will leave your baby here meanwhile. On your return, my housekeeper will make arrangements for your nieces, whilst you come back here that we might discuss your duties."

"Yea, me lady." Rhoda looked ill-at-ease. "I'm truly grateful but you see — "

"One thing at a time, Rhoda — one thing at a time." Anne's enthusiasm was wearing a little thin, and she needed time in which to give thought to certain rather personal problems of her own. "Your infant will be taken good care of in your absence. Go now, and bring back your charges."

"Yea, me lady — of course, me lady," Rhoda said hastily, registering the new impatience in the queen's voice. "You are very kind."

* * *

"You see, madam, methought at first that the children were not there, so silent it was in the outhouse."

The manservant who had accompanied Rhoda on the ride to the burnt-out farm near the Moat Lake, where she had lived with her husband, spoke apologetically — as if he felt in some way to blame for what he was about to reveal.

"Pray continue," Anne said quietly, seeing his hesitation. "Were the children no longer there?"

"Oh, they were there right enough — in

a manner of speaking."

"Are you telling me, sirrah, that some ill has befallen them?"

The man had returned sooner than expected and without Rhoda. He had at once requested and been granted an interview with his royal mistress.

Anne had straight away noticed his agitation and assumed at first that Rhoda had met with an accident. Brigands abounded now in the area and few set forth on a long journey without an armed escort. But the servant had been armed and the farm had been little more than a mile away.

"'Twas the stench that hit me first, madam," he said then. "It told its own story — the plague carries an odour that, once in the nostrils, is never forgotten."

"The plague?" Anne paled at the dread word. "You are telling me that Rhoda's nieces, those little ones not above two and three summers, have taken the pestilence?"

"Aye, madam, they'd taken it right enough — or maybe 'twas it had taken them! According to what Rhoda told me, they were poorly yesterday — but she saw no signs of plague. They must have been taken bad in the night and died around daybreak!"

"God have mercy!" cried Anne, at once recognizing the implications. "What of the corpses, sirrah — they must needs be laid in the earth right away."

"Rhoda was too stricken to do aught but wring her hands and weep," came the reply. "I did what had to be done and then, telling her to bide there, I returned with all speed to enquire as to Your Grace's will in the matter."

"The poor soul! I must at once send someone to bring her back."

"My lady, Rhoda left the outhouse as she says before daybreak this morning," the manservant reminded her. "That being so, it must already have been plain as a pikestaff that her nieces had taken the pestilence. I suspect they were already dead — or close as makes no difference!"

"How did you dispose of the corpses?" asked Anne.

"I dug a deep hole close by the Moat Lake and buried the little ones there — and with them everything else in the outhouse," came the answer. "I shovelled on quick-lime and filled in the grave — and then, leaving Rhoda to say prayers for the little ones' souls, I rode back here to the palace."

Anne said nothing for a few moments, the full implications of the matter having only just dawned on her. She had, after all, other things on her mind than two unknown children . . .

"You fear that Rhoda, too, might have taken the contagion," she said. "Is that why you left her at the outhouse?"

"That is but part of it, madam," came the reply. "Assuming that the children died on the day following the onset of the contagion, Rhoda and her infant are likely to have taken it also — they slept in the outhouse this past week and could well have been affected by the pestilential air."

"Poor Rhoda," sighed Anne. "She and her infant must remain at the outhouse until we can be sure. I would have you, sirrah, if you be willing, return to the farm with blankets and clean straw, and victuals sufficient for two or three weeks."

"I be willing enough, madam — " came the reply " — but my meaning was more than that. If Rhoda and her little one have taken the contagion — as God forbid — what then of Your Grace?"

"No further deaths from the pestilence have been reported for a seven-night," Anne told him. "Methinks therefore that the children probably died of some other malady."

"As you say, my lady," said the steward. "If it be your will that the infant be returned to its mother, one of the maidservants could accompany me, carrying the child, when I set forth with the victuals."

Anne nodded. She had no right to keep the infant from its mother. Indeed, in the circumstances, she had no wish to do so. There were other mothers to be considered; other infants. There were infants as yet unborn . . .

Her face was unnaturally pale, giving away more to the other than she realized.

"Yea," she said, "take the nursling to its mother, keeping your distance, sirrah. Summon Rhoda from the outhouse and, placing the child in a blanket on the ground with the victuals, quickly make your departure."

"Then, my lady, you too suspect that — "

"Nay, not the plague," interposed Anne vehemently. "Go now, sirrah, if you will and attend to the matter."

The man had almost reached the door when Anne addressed him again.

"One thing more, Grimes," she said carelessly. "To spare the king needless anxiety, we must keep this whole sorry matter from him for the time being."

"You have my word on it, madam," said he to Anne — but to himself he said, my lady is more concerned than she pretends, God keep her! "When it comes to the plague, the least said the better — unless it be to Almighty God!"

34

IT was Thomas of Woodstock, Duke of Gloucester, who seven days later broke the news to Richard.

The king had given a magnificent banquet at Sheen to celebrate what was assumed to be the departure of the latest outbreak of the plague — not that Richard needed an excuse for hospitality on such a scale or that it was in any way rare. No borrowed mantles or unringed hands here, no plain felt hats — this was a sparkling ostentatious affair, attended by the court and practically everyone who was anyone in the land.

The evening with its masques and other entertainments, was nearly over. Anne, who had more things than one on her mind, had retired, the other ladies following as protocol required. The more circumspect noblemen had betaken themselves to the North Gallery, a chamber of much elegance, smaller than the Great Hall and distinguished by its panelling which, on one side, slid open to reveal windows that overlooked the Great Hall. The latter had been taken over by Richard and his foppish friends who, posturing and jesting, could be watched from above by anyone who was interested.

It was with some surprise that, close to midnight, Richard caught sight of Thomas of Woodstock coming purposefully towards him. His associates, following the direction of his gaze, gaped at the duke, and more than one quip was uttered in a stage-whisper, seemingly unheard by the newcomer:

"Daniel cometh into the lion's den!"

"Behold Gloucester of the wooden stock!"

"Who is for stock-taking!"

The duke, with his handsome looks and warrior's physique, magnificently arrayed in deference to the occasion, put in the shade every other male there — a fact not lost on Richard who registered it with a mixture of chagrin and family pride.

"I would speak with Your Grace alone," said Thomas impassively.

"Naughty! Naughty!" exclaimed one of

Richard's confidants, in an aside that was ostensibly meant to be *sotto voce* but was in fact *molto voce*. "Uncle Tom wishes to speak alone with naughty Richy!"

"Richy must say nay to naughty nunky!" added another who was plainly in his cups.

"Then naughty nunky would tell his brothers and they would — " The next word, though spoken under the breath, was made plain by the gesture that went with it, " — naughty Richy!"

"My lord — " Richard said coldly to Thomas of Woodstock " — might not the matter wait till morning?"

"It might indeed — " said the duke, seeming impervious to the ribald comments around him. "Then again — it might not."

Now, Richard knew Thomas of Woodstock well — none better. Despite his frequent resentment of him and his brothers — of their criticism and above all their having played a major role in the removal of members of his household — he had a healthy respect for him. Richard also had a sense of lineage — of the blood ties which were the common heritage of them all.

"Nunky is waiting, Richy..."

Richard rounded on the speaker.

"Be silent, sirrah!" he said sharply. "You go too far."

"I am waiting, my lord," said Thomas coolly. "I suggest we betake ourselves to Your Grace's library."

* * *

Richard was uneasy. He knew that Thomas had good reason for interrupting the merry-making — it was not in the latter's nature to indulge in speculation or idle gossip.

"I shall not beat about the bush, my lord," the duke said, as the library doors closed on a departing servant. "I am, alas, the bearer of ill-tidings! Pray let us be seated."

Richard, saying nothing, seated himself beside the great fireplace which, holding a burning tree-trunk, gave off light as well as heat and would in fact burn for several days. He looked at the other, as if to read his mind and it was a full minute before either of them spoke.

"You have news of Robert de Vere, have you not?" Richard asked at length. "He has been captured perchance and brought back in chains to England."

"Hearken to me, my lord," said Thomas quietly. "I know not how one might break such news gently — so here it is. Robert de Vere, lately Earl of Oxford and Duke of Ireland, is dead, God rest his soul!"

"Dead?" asked Richard — as if the word were new to him. But then he shook his head. "Nay, that cannot be — he swore to return some day."

"He died honourably, nephew — killed at Louvain during a boar-hunt," said Thomas. "It seems he was thrown from his horse by an overhanging tree-branch into the path of a charging boar. His head pierced by the creature's tusk, he died soon after."

Richard said nothing. He sat there, pale as ashes, his eyes on his kinsman. Was this some dreadful nightmare? he wondered. Had my lord of Woodstock come to taunt him, wound him with such a tale? He, Richard, had after all long been aware of his disapproval of his association with Robby . . .

"Is it true, my lord?" he asked brokenly. "You are not — ?"

"My lord king, disapprove though I might, and indeed did, of your relationship with de Vere, I none the less accept that your regard for him was deep and genuine." Thomas of Woodstock's voice was cool, perfectly controlled — but there was a warmth in his blue gaze that Richard had not seen for a long time. "I therefore tender my condolences and assure Your Grace that I shall act in the matter in accordance with your wishes."

"I thank you, my lord," Richard said, seeking to regain his composure. "How did you come by the knowledge?"

"Charles of France, cognizant of the matter, had his ambassador inform myself of de Vere's death," came the reply. "De Vere having been declared an outlaw in England and having a price on his head, it was, as Your Grace will appreciate, a delicate matter."

"And . . . ?" Richard could not find the words.

"The obsequies have taken place — "

Thomas said, as if reading the other's mind " — the deceased being given Christian burial by Charles's command, and his remains interred in the church at Louvain."

"I shall set forth for France immediately — "

"Nay, my lord — " Thomas's tone was uncompromising " — that would be unwise. De Vere was by any standards an outlaw — one who escaped justice in England and took refuge in France. I beg you have patience."

"Patience?" asked Richard, his distress plain. "How will patience help the case? Would patience bring him back, make him less of an outlaw, less of an exile — would it make me love him less?"

Thomas of Woodstock's sigh was almost imperceptible. Richard's extravagant language in respect of his lover, never failed to irritate him — to offend his sense of propriety.

"Time heals all things, Richard," he said quietly — overriding his own reactions out of a desire to help the distraught young man before him. "Have faith, I beg you — and when the moment is right, when sufficient time has elapsed, we will arrange to have de Vere's remains brought home to England."

It was the word *home* that affected Richard. His royal kinsman could well have said brought *back* to England. But home is an emotive word, a companionable word, warm and intimate — even a fireside word. Richard of England put his head in his hands and wept.

"O grief of heart!" he cried. "O grief of heart!"

"Richard — " said Thomas of Woodstock " — do you wish me to leave?"

Richard shook his head.

What a child he is! thought the duke. In his twenty-seventh year, still he is a youth at heart — a lonely, sensitive, immature youth who, God help him, was not endowed with the right qualities for kingship! He would better have been born a lass . . .

"Is there aught I can do, nephew?" he enquired solemnly. "Are there any you would have me inform?"

Again Richard shook his head.

"Richard, fair nephew, I pray you tell me how I might serve you."

For several minutes there was silence in that great book-lined chamber, only the occasional crackling and spitting of the burning log breaking the silence. Richard seemed lost in his own thoughts, his own grief — and Thomas sat there, concerned for him but at a loss how to help him . . .

Presently Richard looked up. His smile was slight, fragile — but was none the less a smile.

"I thank you, sir," he said huskily. "I thank you for telling me — it cannot have been easy. I shall follow your advice in respect of my lord de Vere's remains — I shall indeed await the appropriate time. Our Lord have you in his keeping, *mon oncle*!"

35

ANNE learned of Robert de Vere's death from Richard himself. He had seemed strangely composed, as if the void it had left in his life had not as then really touched him.

Anne herself had never liked de Vere — oh, he was courteous enough, quite charming in fact! Richard would have permitted no less. She had the curious feeling that de Vere did not see her as a person, a flesh-and-blood person — but as an inanimate object which had somehow found itself wedded to the King of England. Was it jealousy, she had asked herself — uncertainty as to her true role in his paramour's life? Whatever the answer, Anne had long since given up speculating about the matter.

She grieved only for Richard himself. She had latterly been under no illusion as to the nature of his association with de Vere. Since Richard, whatever his physical predilections, publicly praised and supported her at all times, and in his own way loved her, Anne accepted the situation — on the basis that what could not be cured, must be endured!

Anne, like Thomas of Woodstock before her, had tendered her condolences. She had embraced Richard lovingly and murmured what seemed to be the right words. But that had been an end of it — at least for the time being. Richard had gone his way, departing for a day's hunting in the forest — and Anne had set about her own duties and self-imposed tasks. She, after all, had other things on her mind. The days were passing, turning into weeks, and the weeks into months . . . Soon she must tell Richard — but what to say, that was the question! The child was hers — the secret was hers. It was more than two months since her joyous encounter with Thomas of Woodstock. In a few more days . . .

★ ★ ★

Anne had almost managed to put the matter of Rhoda from her mind. The lass was well cared for, or as much so as was possible in the circumstances. A serving-woman who, having herself taken and survived the plague in childhood, had been given the task of visiting Rhoda, had reported that all was well with mother and child.

More than a week passed without news of Rhoda. But then, one afternoon, the serving-woman, sombre-faced, was admitted to the queen's solar.

Anne realized at once that something was wrong. The woman looked weary to the point of exhaustion. With a nod, Anne dismissed her ladies.

"Tell me what has happened," she said anxiously, as the door closed. "You look to be the bearer of ill-tidings."

"Aye, I am that, my lady," came the reply. "Rhoda took ill two days ago, not long after my last report to Your Grace — and within the day, the babe too was taken poorly."

"You are saying that both Rhoda and the child have taken the pestilence?" asked Anne with a frown. "Why, two weeks have passed since the last case was reported and the outbreak was believed to be over."

"That's as maybe — but plague it was, Gawd help us! Rhoda died this morning, out of her mind with pain and fear for her infant — the infant dying an hour later!"

"May they rest in peace!" Anne said, crossing herself and trying to contain her tears. "Who would have thought it — why, Rhoda looked so bonny after she had taken food and rested, and the infant was a sight for sore eyes!"

"That's the pestilence for ye, me lady!" commented the woman. "It takes the strongest and healthiest — and cocks a snook at the others!"

"Men must be sent at once to the Moat Lake to dig a pit and bury the bodies," Anne said, making to ring her bell. "I — "

"'Tis done, my lady," the woman told her. "I couldn't leave her and the little one there in that place — crawling with rats, it was! I've never seen so many outside of the City in my life. So I took a spade and dug a deep hole. I did it a bit at a time — me being not as young as I was — and I wrapped 'em in a blanket and buried them together, the babe on its ma's breast."

"No wonder you look weary unto death!" remarked Anne. "You must take a good long rest — but first, pray remove those soiled garments and have one of the gardeners burn them."

"Arsenic is what's needed!" remarked the woman as she made to leave. "Arsenic for them there rats — I've seen before, that where the plague strikes heaviest, there's always rats galore."

"Then I shall have one of the wardens go there and place arsenic all around the area," Anne promised. "But it is commonly held that plague comes not from the ground, but from the air — borne on the wind."

"That's as maybe, my lady," said the woman. "They can talk daft as they like — but it don't rid us of plague! Get rid of the rats, I say — and the plague won't call!"

★ ★ ★

Anne sat for a long time, alone and sorrowful, after the serving-woman had departed.

She had taken a liking to Rhoda and her cherubic infant — and had promised herself that, when the time came, Rhoda would be appointed wet-nurse to her own child. She had lain awake the previous night, making plans, looking forward — and always in those plans was Rhoda and her baby, the child by that time just beginning to find its feet.

She fell into a fit of weeping . . .

Thus she was when Richard, unannounced, came into her solar. Taking in the scene before him, he straight away went to comfort her — falling on his knees before her and taking her hands in his.

"Anne, dear heart, what ails you?" he asked in concern. "Has it to do with the woman you wished to help? Rhoda methinks was the name."

"Rhoda is dead, my lord, and her child with her — the plague took them, you see!"

Richard nodded. "I was informed — news of the pestilence travels as speedily as its subject methinks!"

"Alas, my lord, I tried to keep it from you!" Anne sobbed. "I know I am being foolish — people have died of the contagion in their thousands these past months. But, you see, I had taken a liking to Rhoda and had made such plans for her!"

"Plans?" asked Richard in surprise. "What plans were they, sweeting?"

Anne bit her lip. She had said too much.

"Rhoda was good and kind," she said, evading the question. "I knew it. I sensed it. I wish, oh how I wish . . ."

"Wishing cannot bring back the dead, alas, nor heal our aching hearts!" Richard said with feeling — thoughts of his lost lover never far from his mind. "But always there is the future — with its promise that the good things of life will not fail."

"Oh, Richard, I do love you! Did you think thus when he whom you loved was taken?"

He looked stricken for a moment and Anne wished the question unasked.

"Not at first," he admitted then. "Not at first. But at such times of grief and bereavement, one hears, if one listens, the voice of God. With the voice comes peace and acceptance — the certainty that all that comes from God shall yet return to him."

Anne watched him, tears in her eyes.

"You have never spoken like that before," she said quietly.

"Nay," Richard said, his eyes shining with emotion. "Methinks it is harder for most of us to bare our soul than our body — yet one's soul cannot be compromised or debauched!"

"You really and truly believe that all which comes from God returns to him?"

"I do — most certainly I do." He took her in his arms and kissed her tenderly. He thought he had never loved her as much as in those moments — but this was not the time for love-making.

"You believe that Rhoda and her nursling are now with God?" Anne was asking.

"I doubt it not, sweeting."

"And him you loved?"

"Him I *love*," Richard corrected, and she heard the catch in his voice. "I doubt it not. We give them back to God who gavest them to us."

Silence lay between them for a few moments — a happy easy silence. They were together. They were friends, good friends. They were young still, each in their twenty-seventh year. Their lives lay ahead of them . . .

So they reasoned. So they believed.

But one of them in the not far distant future was to recall that conversation, that sharing of sorrows — that baring of souls.

All that comes from God shall yet return to him . . . But, please God, not too soon!

36

WITH the arrival of the month of June that year, the weather changed dramatically. Following the dull skies and rain-soaked earth of May, the first day of June dawned bright and fair. A perfect spring day it was, that first of June, giving promise of a glorious summer.

But for Richard of Bordeaux, King of England, it was a false promise — one which ever after at that time of year brought him remembrance and heart-ache. The English climate, with its sudden swings from rain to sunshine, drought to flood, hailstones to heatwave, is ofttimes linked ever after in the minds of the receptive, with the events of that particular day. Thus it was with Richard.

He was seated at his writing table one morning, signing some papers and wishing the task done, when his private secretary, his expression sombre, entered the chamber.

"One of the queen's ladies has just informed me, sire, that Her Grace is a little unwell this morning," he said.

"Unwell?" asked Richard in surprise. Anne was rarely unwell — indeed he would have been hard put to it to recall the last time. "I shall pay her a visit very shortly."

"The queen, I am told, is presently asleep, sire."

Richard put down his quill.

"Then shall I go forthwith!" he declared with a contrariness his servants knew all too well. "There is no time like the present!"

Anne appeared to be asleep when, unannounced, he entered her chamber — but she stirred as he reached her bedside as if sensing his presence. He observed a rash on her face and neck. Now, Anne's milk-and-roses complexion was a byword, the most remarkable and enviable feature of one who was perhaps comely rather than beautiful.

"You have a small rash — " Richard told her cheerfully when she awoke " — which will give heart, I dare say, to other ladies about the court!"

"Pray hand me that small looking-glass, my lord," Anne said.

She scrutinized her face consideringly and Richard registered her alarm.

"What you need is a good rest," he said with a smile. "You have not spared yourself these past weeks in organizing food and shelter for the homeless and orphaned."

"That is so, my lord, but you see — " Anne paused and seemed to be debating the wisdom of giving utterance to her next words " — I have something to tell you — something I must tell you. The child, you see — I must tell you of the child . . ."

"The child is dead, alas!" Richard told her quietly. "You must try and put it from your mind."

"Dead? Nay, nay, you understand not — you are mistaken!"

"You are a little unwell — you must dwell only on happy things."

"But the child is a happy — "

"Hush! Hush!" Richard lightly interposed, leaning over to kiss her — and registering, as he did so, that the rash looked brighter than it had just a few minutes ago. Something nagged at the back of his mind, demanding attention, but he pushed it aside. "Sleep. Rest — think only of good things, beautiful things. I shall return anon."

"Oh, Richard, I do love you," she said softly, turning away from him as if already sleep were claiming her. "I do so love you . . . "

Richard turned and left the chamber, ignoring the enquiring glances of the queen's ladies and speaking to none. His heart was heavy. Fear clutched at his throat, at his mind, at his vitals. He was being foolish, he told himself — allowing the sight of a mildly fevered woman to affect him. But the rash? What of the rash? he asked himself.

He wished, oh how he wished, that Robby de Vere were there! He would have spoken to him of his misgivings and Robby would doubtless have laughed at him, teasing him and telling him he was behaving like a silly wench. Robby could always bring him cheer, lull his fears, make him laugh . . . Laugh? Why, it was surely many moons since he had laughed like that — and he doubted he would ever laugh again.

37

THE royal family, when not entertaining, customarily dined at midday and supped in the early evening. Richard, having dined alone on that first day of June, was expected to attend a meeting of his chief ministers of state at the council chamber within Sheen Palace. Later, when the meeting was over, he would go again to see Anne — the latter being his overall priority.

Never renowned for his application to the more tedious and on-going affairs of state, he listened on this occasion with only half an ear to the debates — asking himself not for the first time why such discussions went round and round in circles. They look so grave, so solemn, he thought to himself — even in regard to the most trivial of matters, they somehow give the impression that their lives depend on it.

"Gentlemen — " he interposed, during a diatribe about the low state of the treasury — a sore point with Richard. His interpolation was prompted solely by the need to prevent himself falling asleep, " — pray let us be brief. I have an important engagement following this meeting and would first see these matters agreed."

"With respect, sire, affairs of state should not be hurried," said Arundel weightily. "Decisions made in haste, are wont to be regretted at leisure."

There was a small polite laugh at this witticism.

"In that case, my lords, I suggest that we leave the matter in abeyance," said Richard. "The treasury, I promise you, will still be at a low ebb a week hence!"

Richard himself having called the meeting in the first place, this suggestion did not meet with much enthusiasm.

"The state of the treasury, sire, is of the utmost importance," said Warwick. "Money, after all, does not grow on trees!"

"Then, my lord, I suggest that we are planting the wrong trees!" Richard said — to laughter. "Now, if we might — "

"With respect, sire — " interposed another minister " — flippancy will not help the case! Without money, how should we finance the proposed war with France?"

This was too much for Richard.

"I put it to Your Lordships that we should abandon all thoughts of war, at least for the forseeable future," he said.

There were cries of "Shame! Shame!" to this, but Richard went doggedly on.

"In that case, gentlemen, whether or not money grows on trees, is of small consequence. Indeed, it could be that in France, money does grow on trees — though not in Bordeaux, I assure you! — thus giving our foes a natural advantage!"

There was uproar at this point. Richard's antipathy to war and warlike pursuits, was well known — but such blatant opposition as this was intolerable.

Unabashed by the stir he had created, Richard meanwhile looked around the chamber. His ministers, as he had expected, were of one mind in their opposition to their sovereign's proposal.

"I can give Your Lordships but fifteen

minutes more," Richard said, making himself heard above the hubbub only with difficulty. "Then the meeting shall be closed."

"Fifteen minutes, sire?" demanded Arundel. "Why, such a limitation is preposterous. There are a number of other matters demanding our attention — fifteen minutes would be insufficient."

"Fifteen minutes is insufficient, you say, my lord?" Richard spoke cheerfully — pleased that they had fallen into the trap. "Useless, would you say?"

"I would indeed, sire," agreed Arundel vociferously. "Utterly useless."

Richard rose abruptly.

"This meeting, my lords, is now closed," he said coolly. "I have but fifteen minutes available and that, as our honest and plain-speaking friend tells us, would be utterly useless. I therefore bid you a good day, gentlemen."

★ ★ ★

Richard left the meeting and retired at once to his own apartments, called the King's House. Almost immediately one of the queen's ladies was shown in.

Her expression was grave.

"Your Grace — " she said with unwonted hesitancy " — I know not how to say this — but the queen, we fear, has taken a turn for the worse."

"Her fever has increased?" asked Richard.

"It has indeed, my lord."

"I shall go to my lady forthwith."

"With respect, sire — is that wise?"

Richard frowned. "I fail to understand your meaning. Are you perchance suggesting that it might be unwise to visit Her Grace?" he enquired coldly.

"In the circumstances, my lord, it might be so."

"Then there is something — " Richard said, not to her — but to himself " — something else!"

"Sire, I have to tell you — " the woman said still with that same hesitancy " — though she herself forbade it."

"Who forbade what, *par Dieu*!" demanded Richard. "Have the goodness to explain your meaning, madam."

"The queen, sire — she forbade me to tell Your Grace." The woman was close to tears. "But the matter can be hidden no longer, I fear. The physician is with Her Grace now — but we none of us have any doubt that the queen has taken the plague!"

"God have mercy!" exlaimed Richard. Why, he thought, they must all have taken leave of their senses! Such is impossible — totally impossible. Would not I, who have seen the ravages of the contagion all too frequently of late, have recognized the symptoms! "Can this be true? Nay, I cannot believe it. Why, only this morning I . . ."

Richard fell silent, overwhelmed by the enormity of the other's disclosure.

"We, the queen's ladies, suspected even then, my lord," the attendant admitted. "Indeed, ever since the woman, Rhoda, came here with her infant, we have all of us been on our guard. And now — now there can be no doubt, alas!"

"But the queen looked not ill — not seriously ill," remarked Richard on a note of puzzlement — as if there must be another explanation but it had temporarily eluded him. "I myself shall speak with the physician."

"Please God the physician can allay our fears!" said the lady-in-waiting with more fervency than hope. "As Your Grace is doubtless aware, plague strikes swiftly — it does not drag its heels! This morning the queen was poorly — but no more than that. I none the less saw the rash — "

"As did I myself, God help me!" put in Richard.

" — the tell-tale rash. Yet still I was not convinced — or so I told myself then." The woman sighed. "Alas, the tangled web of self-deception!"

38

"**M**Y lord of Woodstock awaits Your Grace in the ante-chamber," one of the queen's ladies told Richard. "He desires speech with you."

Richard, seeing that Anne was now sleeping peacefully, went at once to the ante-chamber. He had sent messengers to inform his royal uncles of Anne's illness but John of Gaunt and Edmund of Langley were each at that time in their own domain and more than a hundred miles away. He knew that they could not reach Sheen in time — and that Thomas of Woodstock, though nearer than his brothers, would have a two-day journey. His surprise then was great when he set eyes on the duke.

Thomas of Woodstock, travel-stained from much hard riding, was still wearing his great-cloak. He had made the journey without the customary escort, every ten miles changing horses at hostelries along the way to maintain speed. Appalled by the news of Anne's illness, one thought was uppermost in his mind — to reach Sheen in time. He had wished for no company save his own . . .

Now, as he set eyes on Richard, he did not beat about the bush.

"How is she?" he asked, placing a firm hand on Richard's shoulder. "When I received Your Grace's message, I set forth at once and have ridden throughout the night. How is the queen?"

"Sick unto death, I fear," Richard told him, unable to conceal his distress. "I remained at her bedside all night, watching her grow weaker with every passing hour."

"She could recover."

"Few do so."

"You see before you one who did, my lord," said Thomas of Woodstock. "I took the pestilence in early youth. Like the bee, it stings but the once!"

"I dare not hope — " Richard told him brokenly " — whilst yet I cannot accept!"

Despite his own personal anguish, Thomas of Woodstock knew genuine sympathy for Richard. He had previously resolved that when Richard learned that Anne was with child, he would falsely confess that he had forced his attentions on her. Thus would Anne's honour remain unsullied. The penalty for ravishment was death, as he was well aware — but many a chivalric knight had gone to his death to protect his lady's honour. In such circumstances he, Thomas of Woodstock, could and would do no less. Now, unless Anne miscarried her child, as was possible in the present unforeseen circumstances...

"Sire," he said firmly, "you should look to your health and sovereignty. I myself, as I said, took the pestilence. As your closest kinsman here present therefore, I will, if you wish it, myself maintain a vigil."

Richard was surprised by the emotion in his voice. Thomas of Woodstock had ever seemed to him the most ruthless of his uncles — and he had long been aware of his disapproval of himself. But he was gazing at him at that moment with warmth and compassion — was that shining warrior who had come to him now, was supporting him now . . .

"I shall stay, my lord," Richard replied. "Until the end I shall stay. Why would I do else? My lady is my only true friend — without her, Richard of England would be as naught."

"There is yet hope, my lord."

"Maybe there is, sir," Richard conceded — whilst knowing in his heart there was none. "Maybe there is — else what a waste of one so dearly loved!"

Dearly loved she is indeed! thought Thomas of Woodstock. But 'tis a waste, not of one life, but of two — heaven help both Richard and myself! Yea, he knew that Anne was with child. He had seen the signs — the bloom on the cheek, the look in the eyes. Yea, he knew . . .

"I shall return anon," he said with a calm he was far from feeling. "And then, if you wish it so, I shall keep the vigil with you."

Richard nodded, too full for words.

With a pat on the shoulder for his distressed kinsman, Thomas of Woodstock turned abruptly and took his leave.

*　*　*

Richard was appalled by the havoc wrought in Anne in the space of a few hours. Returning to her bedside, he thought at first that she was either asleep or comatose, for she made no attempt to speak as he looked down enquiringly at her.

The rosy rash suffused her face now, her breathing was laboured and she was plainly in some pain.

"Look not so sorrowful, my lord," she said lovingly then, her words coming with difficulty. "I shall recover — in a day or so, I shall be good as new."

He nodded and took her hand, unable to express himself for emotion. He kissed her hand, its feverishness seeming to sear his lips.

But the effort of speaking had been too much, it seemed. Anne sneezed several times in succession, violent spasms which left her breathless and scarcely able to see — and then, to Richard's further alarm, she vomited and spat blood . . .

She lay speechless upon her pillows as her attendants, women allotted the task as having themselves had and survived the plague, came to her assistance.

"My lord," Anne whispered then. "Stay not here, I beseech you! The contagion, you see — you should not stay!"

"I shall remain here until you are better," Richard told her with a brave attempt at a smile. "Whither would I go, except to my own beloved queen!"

"The child," she whispered. "If only . . ."

"All will be well," Richard said gently, not understanding. Why, he wondered, does she speak now of our not having had a child? "Just rest and conserve your strength. I shall remain here beside you until you have fallen asleep."

She slept for several hours, exhausted by fever, her attendants watchful, waiting unobtrusively in the background.

Every precaution had been taken against the spread of the contagion. Anne's attendants each had a posy of sweet-smelling herbs attached to the waist of her gown to ward off infection; other herbs being burnt continually on the logs in the hearth.

The physician, when attending the

patient, wore over his head the customary bird-like covering, perfumed inside with medicinal herbs. He handed out lozenges — these containing, as he said, rare medicaments — to be sucked slowly in the mouth; instructing at the same time that rose water be used frequently to bathe the brow and hands of those in attendance upon the stricken queen. There was little else he could do.

Of the medicaments Richard would have none, brushing them aside impatiently when offered them. Outwardly composed, it seemed to him that his heart was made of lead.

To please Anne whose favourite colour it was, he was wearing a cotehardie of kingfisher-blue; together with a jewelled waist-belt and parti-coloured long-pointed hose — one leg kingfisher-blue, the other white and displaying a gold jewelled garter. He looked a picture of elegance: he felt a picture of woe.

He greeted the return of Thomas of Woodstock with untold relief. Having removed the evidence of many hours of hard riding, the latter looked elegant and relaxed in a houppelande of dark-red and gold. He seated himself on the further side of the bed.

Anne, lost in a feverish haze in which she flitted in and out of consciousness, was in the main unaware of what was going on around herself. She dreamed many dreams, some good, some bad — all were divorced from reality, save the one. She spanned many years in those fevered hours — she crossed stormy seas, sat by the bedside of a dying emperor, bade a tearful farewell to her beautiful mother, was tossed to and fro on a storm-ridden ship and was met at journey's end by a handsome prince. The prince's face though, seemed to change from one to another, confusing her . . .

The child weaved in and out of her dreams — the little lost boy-child with the tear-filled eyes and the tiny imploring hands . . .

A bout of coughing awoke her. Her vision was hazy at first but then, as it cleared, she found she was in bed in her own sumptuous chamber at Sheen — but she was not alone. Others were in the chamber, most in the background, but for some reason she could not fathom the gaze of all seemed to be directed at herself.

She caught sight then of the child, the child of her dreams. He was close by her bed, watching her . . . But this time she was awake, truly awake, or perchance . . . It *was* the child, she was certain, for he had dark-brown hair, and eyes of such a brilliant blue as held the gaze of the beholder. But this time the visitant looked older. This time he was neither infant nor toddler — in fact he was not a child at all. This time, he was a man full-grown. He looked sorrowful, just as the little one had, and his eyes as he met her gaze, were just as the child's had been, shadowed with an emotion she could not fathom . . .

She tried to move, to take his hand, to ask him if *he* knew who the child was, what it had been asking of her, and why it looked like him and had always been just out of her reach . . . But it was no use. She was too weary to move, to ask . . .

"The child — " she whispered.

Richard bowed his head, believing he knew what she meant — and too full for words, the tears overflowed . . .

Thomas of Woodstock, seeing Richard's distress and guessing Anne's true meaning, took her outstretched hand in his.

"Be at peace, my lady," he said, kissing her hand oh so gently. "All of us are in God's hands."

She gave a little smile at that, as if she had taken his meaning and very soon after, fell into a peaceful sleep.

The next two hours passed slowly and without incident. Those in the queen's chamber — the king, the duke, the queen's attendants and serving-women — suffered the burden of any such all-night vigil: the frustration of inactivity combining with the uneasy hope that the night would never end.

A further bout of coughing awoke Anne and brought forth a veritable fountain of blood, prompting her attendants to hasten to her aid with bowls and warm herb-scented cloths. It was seen then that her glands were beginning to swell and that the hard black buboes which had given *The Black Death* its name, were forming in her armpits and groin.

Richard, a little out of his depth,

looked enquiringly at his uncle. The duke hesitated and then, very slowly shook his head. The infection had entered the lungs and bloodstream. The new symptoms, as he well knew, were the presagers of death.

Thomas of Woodstock, keeping a tight rein on his emotions, was none the less reminded of how, as a youth of fifteen summers, he had stood with his father, King Edward the Third, at the bedside of his dying mother.[1] His brothers and sisters, incredibly all of that large brood of sons and daughters, had been for one reason or another out of England at the time, unaware of Queen Philippa's approaching death. He, the youngest of the family, had been the only one there. He had seen his father's grief, whilst trying unsuccessfully to stifle his own.

But his father had understood. He recalled with a cruel clarity those moments when, immediately after his mother's death, weeping and with his father's arm held protectively about his

---

[1] see *The Whyte Swan* by Philippa Wiat

shoulders, the two of them had walked slowly from the queen's chamber . . .

Twenty-four years had passed since that day and now it was all happening again. Another queen was on her deathbed — the one loved no less than the other, though in a different kind of way. Again he was the only one there; the only one present to comfort a sorrowing king, a sorrowing kinsman — when he himself was stricken beyond belief. But on this occasion he was no youth. He was a man, a warrior in his thirty-ninth year and, no matter the provocation, he would hide his grief, must hide his grief . . .

With a quiet word to Richard, he turned and went to the ante-chamber to summon the priests.

The priests, their faces solemn as they entered the queen's chamber, retired with soft tread to the background where, in a darkened recess, the queen having already received the last rites, they began to recite the prayers for the dying.

Anne rallied a little before the end. She tried to speak but no words came. Seeing this, careless of the contagion, Richard gently stroked her face and kissed her forehead.

She rambled, muttering and murmuring and Richard lovingly took her hands in his. But then she fell silent and, despite the banked-up herb-strewn fire, a curious chill pervaded the chamber.

The night passed slowly until, two hours after midnight on the third day of June, Anne of Bohemia, Queen of England, ceased to breathe . . .

Richard, still holding her hand, was the first to register her passing.

"May God who has called you, bid you welcome!" he said quietly, as he closed her eyes — registering as he did so Thomas of Woodstock's sudden tension. "May a choir of angels welcome you!"

He crossed her hands on her breast and kissed her tenderly on the lips. Stepping back, his tears falling unheeded, he bowed his head whilst the priests intoned the prayers for the dead.

As the prayers came to an end and the priests went noiselessly from the chamber, Richard nodded for the attendants to do likewise.

Thomas of Woodstock, holding in leash

his emotions, went then to Anne — in an apparently formal farewell. He too kissed the smooth still-warm forehead, before placing the palm of his right hand over her crossed hands.

Mindful of his unborn child, in a voice that was all but inaudible, he said, "Lord, grant them eternal rest, and let perpetual light shine on them!"

He had loved Anne from the moment he had first set eyes on her at Canterbury; he would love Anne — and mourn her and their child — until the day of his death . . .

He turned away and, with a few words of sympathy to Richard, he too made to leave the chamber. He who had on her arrival in England, escorted Anne of Bohemia on her first journey, had seen her depart on her last journey . . . He had kept the vigil. He had kept faith.

He fancied he felt a hand on his shoulder, a strong consoling hand . . .

This has happened before, he thought, long ago — some twenty-four years ago. Then we shared our grief, my lord father and I — our sense of loss. Yet still those loved ones are there in our darkest moments, unseen but seeing, aware of our anguish, our need of solace — bringing us comfort, reaching out to us in our extremity.

He went through to the ante-chamber, and those gathered there, silent and watchful, noted that the duke's features, composed and unmarked by grief, bore a rare but riveting spirituality.

He appeared oblivious of those around him and none ventured to address him as he passed on into the king's presence-chamber beyond, where it was incumbent upon him to make a formal announcement of the queen's death to the state dignitaries.

* * *

As the doors closed after the departing Thomas of Woodstock, Richard was conscious then of the stillness, the total silence in the chamber — even the fire, stifled perhaps by the sweet-smelling herbs, appeared to have given up the ghost. He, Richard, was alone — alone with his departed lady. The stillness seemed tangible but at the same time unreal; the corpse before him was recognizable yet without form. Aloneness overwhelmed him, pervading every part of his body, as he knelt by the great bed.

"Anne — " he said brokenly " — why did you leave me thus? Why, now, when life has much to offer us! God knows I deserved you not — yet Richard of England will be a sorry fellow without you!"

He stood in silence for a few moments — as if he half expected an answer.

He bowed his head, seeking to compose himself, before following the others into the ante-chamber.

39

HE watched it burn.
Standing there in the fire-lit darkness, with a mixture of feelings of which grief and desolation were foremost, he watched the flames leaping upward into the night sky.

Anne's funeral had taken place at Westminster on the previous day, Monday the third of August — exactly two months after her decease. Her plague-ridden body had been placed in a double-lead coffin almost immediately after her death — but the funeral had been postponed until Richard was satisfied that his detailed instructions had been carried out and that the obsequies, down to the smallest detail, would be in accordance with his wishes.

The horse-drawn bier had been carried by way of hamlets, villages and highways, from Sheen to Westminster. The cortège had been accompanied, at the king's command, by all the English nobility, male and female, riding horseback. All were clothed in unrelieved black and, again by the king's command, wore black hoods.

Flambeaus and torches had been sent from Flanders — and were in such dazzling abundance that it was generally agreed by the onlookers that nothing like it had been seen before . . .

Now that, too, was in the past. The late queen had been interred with all honours and the mourners and onlookers who had lined the streets *en route* to the abbey had gone their separate ways. The pomp and ceremony were over and Richard, King of England, was alone with his grief.

He had returned to Sheen only that afternoon. Shortly after his arrival, he had insisted on visiting the chamber where Anne had died. Clothing, bedding, tapestries and furnishings — all movables, were gone. Following Anne's demise, the chamber had been stripped and its contents reduced to ashes outside in the gardens. The room had then been fumigated and sealed off — to remain thus for three weeks.

Richard, though naturally aware of the customary procedures following death from plague, was none the less deeply distressed. The beautiful chamber in which he and Anne had passed so many happy hours and which she herself had so lovingly planned and furnished, was now an empty shell.

Ashen-faced, he had turned and fled from the scene — in the manner of one chased by a phantom. On reaching the gardens, his gaze alighting then on the great pile of ashes, he had changed course and climbed the hill until he reached the edge of the woods.

It seemed to Richard in those moments that every trace, every memory, of his beloved and honoured queen, had been removed from the face of the earth.

Looking back thence to the panorama of palace, river and gardens spread out before him, he was of a sudden oppressed with such grief and desolation as could scarcely be borne.

Dusk was approaching and a golden sunset was lighting the western sky. But the beauty of nature accorded ill with his spirits — and perchance it was that same fiery sunset which gave him the idea.

He was alone. Utterly alone. Utterly bereft. Self-sufficiency was not his forte. Twenty-seven years of age, he had lost his father and his only brother — both of whom should have been king before him. He had lost his mother, his lover — and now his beloved wife. All had died prematurely.

It was as if they had never been; as if long ago, he had had a dream, and the dream had been peopled by names — unreal but well-loved names as in a child's story-book. The Black Prince, his larger-than-life father; the Princess Joan, his beautiful and gracious mother; Prince Edward, his quiet and studious brother; and Robert de Vere, his lover in whose company none could be sad. Now . . .

He knew they were plotting to seize his throne. John of Gaunt, it was said, had ambitions for his eldest son, Henry of Bolingbroke. Well, he, Richard, would see about that when the time came . . .

"Burn it!" he ordered his chamberlain. "Level the accursed place to the ground."

His chamberlain gaped in astonishment. "Sire, the royal bedchamber has been dismantled as was requisite — "

"Sheen Palace shall be levelled to the ground — and at once." Richard's voice was stern and brooked no argument. "Not one stick or stone shall remain — to remind me, to taunt me ... "

His chamberlain looked curiously at him. Still he could not believe that the king was serious. He looked serious enough but ... Burn the palace, the beautiful palace — why, it was the late queen's favourite residence!

"But the servants — " he ventured.

"Shall be paid off or transferred where possible to Windsor or Westminster — I care not the where or the why! Sheen Palace, the scene of my beloved lady's demise, shall be razed from the face of the earth!"

"Forgive me, sire, but would the queen have wished it so?" asked the chamberlain boldly. "It was, I understand, Her Grace's best-loved palace."

"And it took her life — it repaid her love by destroying her!" Richard's eyes were cold with anger. "Nay, Sheen shall be no more. The deed must be done forthwith. At the second hour after midnight, the time when my lady departed this life, Sheen shall do likewise."

And so it was done. Despite the pleas and remonstrances of the king's ministers and advisers, the palace was put to the torch.

Richard stood and watched, alone in the midst of many — a solitary figure against the fire-lit sky.

"Farewell to joy — " he murmured on a sob " — to youth and happiness."

The king had six years more to live. God be thanked that none of us — royal lovers, uncles and princes, chroniclers and authors, and particularly monarchs called Richard of Bordeaux — knows what lies ahead!

Author's Note

Robert de Vere, ninth Earl of Oxford and Duke of Ireland, was killed during a boar-hunt at Louvain *circa* 1394. Three years later, his body was brought back to England by the sorrowing King Richard, for burial among the earl's ancestors in Essex.

The king gave orders that the coffin be opened, whereupon he was said to have gazed long and fervently upon the face of the embalmed corpse, fondling the jewel-laden hands and weeping profusely. The coffin was subsequently re-interred with great solemnity at Earl's Colne.

P.W.

Bibliography

Age of Chivalry: (1963) Arthur Bryant
Battles in Britain: volume I (1975) William Seymour
Chivalry: (1975) Michael Foss
Chronicles of Froissart: translated by John Bourchier, Lord Berners
Dictionary of National Biography
English Costume: (1952) Doreen Yarwood
English Social History: (1944) G. M. Trevelyan
Froissart's Chronicles: translated by John Joliffe
Lives of the Queens of England: volume I (1840) Agnes Strickland
Medieval Britain: (1973) Denis Richards and Arnold D. Ellis
Medieval England: edited A. L. Poole
New Complete and Authentic History of England: compiled (circa 1790) by Alexander Hogg

Outlaws of Medieval England: M. Keen
Oxford History of England, The Fourteenth Century: (1959) May McKisack
Short History of the English People: (1874) John Richard Green

Other titles in the Ulverscroft Large Print Series:

TO FIGHT THE WILD
Rod Ansell and Rachel Percy

Lost in uncharted Australian bush, Rod Ansell survived by hunting and trapping wild animals, improvising shelter and using all the bushman's skills he knew.

COROMANDEL
Pat Barr

India in the 1830s is a hot, uncomfortable place, where the East India Company still rules. Amelia and her new husband find themselves caught up in the animosities which seethe between the old order and the new.

THE SMALL PARTY
Lillian Beckwith

A frightening journey to safety begins for Ruth and her small party as their island is caught up in the dangers of armed insurrection.

THE WILDERNESS WALK
Sheila Bishop

Stifling unpleasant memories of a misbegotten romance in Cleave with Lord Francis Aubrey, Lavinia goes on holiday there with her sister. The two women are thrust into a romantic intrigue involving none other than Lord Francis.

THE RELUCTANT GUEST
Rosalind Brett

Ann Calvert went to spend a month on a South African farm with Theo Borland and his sister. They both proved to be different from her first idea of them, and there was Storr Peterson — the most disturbing man she had ever met.

ONE ENCHANTED SUMMER
Anne Tedlock Brooks

A tale of mystery and romance and a girl who found both during one enchanted summer.

CLOUD OVER MALVERTON
Nancy Buckingham

Dulcie soon realises that something is seriously wrong at Malverton, and when violence strikes she is horrified to find herself under suspicion of murder.

AFTER THOUGHTS
Max Bygraves

The Cockney entertainer tells stories of his East End childhood, of his RAF days, and his post-war showbusiness successes and friendships with fellow comedians.

MOONLIGHT AND MARCH ROSES
D. Y. Cameron

Lynn's search to trace a missing girl takes her to Spain, where she meets Clive Hendon. While untangling the situation, she untangles her emotions and decides on her own future.

NURSE ALICE IN LOVE
Theresa Charles

Accepting the post of nurse to little Fernie Sherrod, Alice Everton could not guess at the romance, suspense and danger which lay ahead at the Sherrod's isolated estate.

POIROT INVESTIGATES
Agatha Christie

Two things bind these eleven stories together — the brilliance and uncanny skill of the diminutive Belgian detective, and the stupidity of his Watson-like partner, Captain Hastings.

LET LOOSE THE TIGERS
Josephine Cox

Queenie promised to find the long-lost son of the frail, elderly murderess, Hannah Jason. But her enquiries threatened to unlock the cage where crucial secrets had long been held captive.

DATE DUE

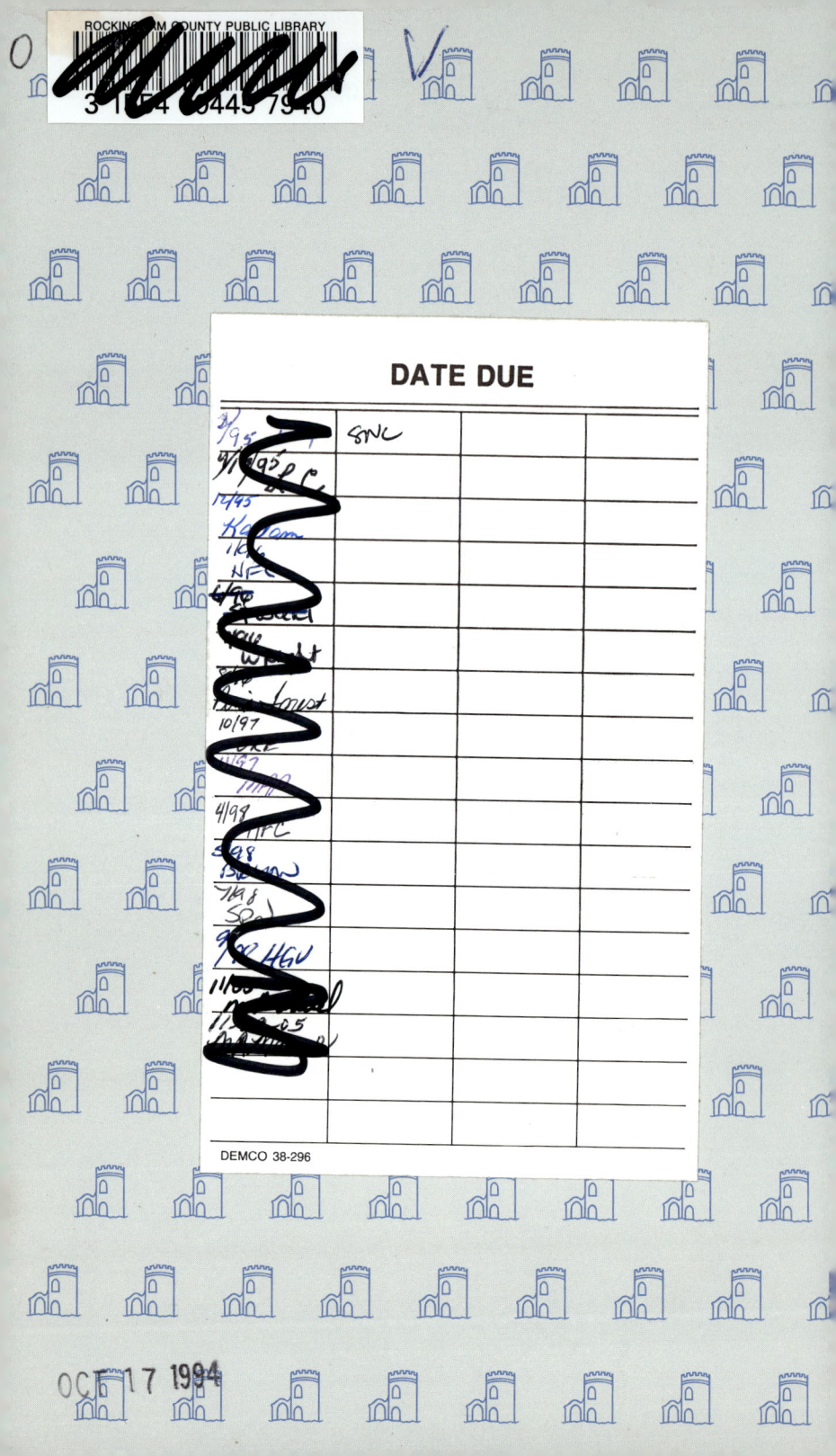

OCT 17 1994

DEMCO 38-296